Trust Me

By Shawn Settle

Illustrated By Amanda Bonner

Special thanks to my friend, Carrie Burke, who has read many revisions and been my support along the way.

www.shawnsettle.com

ISBN-10: 15-3749-855-X
ISBN-13: 978-1-5374-9855-3

Table of Contents

Errand

Twenty-two-year old Matty McKinley hung up his cell phone and slid it into the front right pocket of his jeans. He ran a hand through his light brown hair as he thought about the unexpected twist his day was now taking. How was he going to pull off the task which now lay before him? Matty looked at the walls to the hallway; the light yellow color had always been warm and comforting. He took in a deep breath in an attempt to ease his now racing mind. It brought a little relief. Matty now focused on the door located a few feet down the hall. On the other side were his three business partners focused on a project they were fine tuning and hoping to complete that day; a project he was deeply engrossed in when his phone rang. What would he say to explain his sudden abandonment of them? Whatever it was, he needed to do it fast. Time was now working against him.

Matty quickly headed toward the room, opened the door, and called over to the three gentlemen his age. "Something urgent has come up, I have to go. Call me on my cell and let me know if you get it figured out." Matty glanced at his guitar for a second debating if he should bring it. He decided he'd get it later, putting it into the case and the trunk of his car would take too long.

Lex gave him a surprised look. "Where are you going?"

"I don't have time to talk about it." Matty turned and quickly hurried out the door, into the hallway, and up the stairs that lead out of the basement studio and into the main part of the house which was owned by Lex, and where his other two partners, Paul and

1

Henry, lived.

Lex was right on his heels. "You don't usually have 'urgent engagements'. Is something wrong with April?"

"April's just fine," Matty walked out the front door. "It has nothing to do with her." He opened the driver's side of his car and turned to look at Lex, "I've got to go."

(Lex)

"I'm coming with you," Lex jumped into the passenger seat of Matty's blue Toyota Corolla full of curiosity. Work could wait.

"Do me a favor and punch Long Beach into Google Maps. See if you can tell it to go to the West End." Matty backed the car out of the driveway and started driving down the road.

Lex was puzzled by this request. "You don't have an actual address?"

"No, I'm hoping to get it soon."

"What's going on down in Long Beach?"

Matty glanced over with an uneasy look on his face. "It's complicated... Maybe I should drop you off somewhere. I don't think you'd understand this."

"Try me."

"It's just something you wouldn't expect, and I'm not sure what your reaction's going to be."

"We're best friends. You know you can trust me. If you're in trouble, I can help you."

"I know that," Matty appreciatively replied and then paused

2

before continuing. "How do I explain this without hurting your feelings? ... Your perspective of the world is different from mine, and at the moment, I don't want to listen to your commentaries."

"It other words, you don't want my opinion about what you're doing."

"Exactly."

Lex was too curious to be annoyed. He noticed they were getting on the one-ten to leave Los Angeles and head down the coast. Matty was very focused on the road. He looked worried.

"If I guess it, will you tell me I'm correct?"

"Sure, but you'll never guess this."

Lex thought for a few moments. *Something unexpected for Matty.* "You're putting a hit on someone?"

Matty shot him a surprised glance. "No, don't be ridiculous."

"You borrowed money from a gangster, and he wants to see you."

Matty chuckled. "Not even close."

Lex was glad he was able to lighten Matty's serious mood for a moment. He'd never seen Matty look so tense. "Good, 'cause I'm your loan shark."

"Since when have I ever borrowed money from you?" Matty was serious again.

"Never, but if you needed some, I'd give it to you."

"Thanks, that's nice to know."

They rode in silence again. Matty was staring intently at the road, weaving in and out of traffic.

"Give me a hint. Are we talking about a person or a thing?"

"A person."

"Male or female?"

"Female."

"Do you care about this female?"

"You could say that."

Now Lex was stunned. "Oh my gosh, you're cheating on your wife. Matty, you guys were highschool sweethearts. You just got married earlier this year. You're the happiest couple I've ever seen. I can't believe this."

"Call Charles to come and get you. I'm pulling over to drop you off."

"I'm right?" The realization hit him harder than the initial thought.

"No, you're not right. I can't believe you'd even say that." Matty was pissed.

"Look at the road. You're going to hit someone in this traffic if you're glaring at me." He defensively replied. "You said it was something I wouldn't expect. Don't pull over. You're in a hurry, remember?"

Matty sighed.

Lex thought for a moment and decided to try a different approach to finding out why Matty was so tense and driven.

"So, this woman in Long Beach, she didn't give you an address?"

"No."

"That's strange. Why not?"

"I didn't actually speak to her. I got my information from another person who didn't have the address."

"Then how do you know where you're going?"

"I don't know exactly. I'm looking for a pay phone," Matty was nervously tapping his fingers on the steering wheel.

"And this woman is waiting for you at a pay phone?"

"Yes."

What a strange place to meet someone. "Are you buying drugs?"

"No."

"Why don't you just call the pay phone and ask the woman what street she's near?"

"I'd love to, but I don't have the number."

Lex reached into the pocket of his pants and pulled out his cell phone. "Here, let me see if I can pull up a list of all the pay phones in Long Beach. There can't be that many, right? Doesn't everyone use a cell phone?"

"You would think so, but there are six-hundred-thirty-five."

"What! And you're planning to drive to all of them? You *do* realize it could take hours to find her, no make that days."

"That's why I needed to leave so quickly. I don't know how I'm going to find her. April's helping as well. She's pulled up a list of all the pay phones and is calling every one of them as we speak. Hopefully, she'll call soon with the actual address of where Ann is."

"And what does her boss think about her using company

5

time to help you?" Lex felt a bit annoyed.

"Seriously?!"

"I'm just saying that making all these calls will take her away from the projects she's supposed to be working on."

Matty gave him a look that told Lex he was really mad. "You're right. Her boss wouldn't understand. He's never thought of anyone other than himself. He's never loved anyone or even been close to anyone to know what it's like to care for another person. He would rather have her spend her time working on some real-estate project to make him money that he doesn't even need or even care about, because that's more important than anything else. If he has a problem with her helping me today, then she can go work for someone else."

Lex felt the sting of his words. "I think you're being a bit harsh."

"No, I'm just being honest."

They rode in silence for a while. Lex was fuming. How could Matty say such things? What could be so important that he would risk their friendship? What was making Matty act so strangely? Lex had never seen Matty so agitated. Matty cussed several times at the traffic. Matty never cussed. His driving also had an edge to it, frantic. "What's really going on? You've never used me before."

"I'm not using you now. You invited yourself along, remember?"

"I'm talking about using April during company time."

"April took the rest of the afternoon off when she received my call. There just wasn't enough time for her to go home."

"Why didn't you tell me that?"

6

"Because I couldn't believe you reacted the way you did."

Lex picked up his cell phone. "It's Lex. April's not taking a vacation day, she's working on a special project for me. I don't want her interrupted. Pull Carman to help her." Lex hung up his phone.

"Thank you." Matty looked slightly relieved.

"What you said about me hurt, and at first I was really mad at you and seriously considered having you stop the car, so I could get out and have Charles come pick me up. But then ... I didn't know what I'd do after that. You're the only real friend I have. You don't use me like everyone else does, and I appreciate it. And you're right, I don't really care about what project April's working on. What's important is not losing you as a friend."

"You haven't. I'm sorry too. This is the most important thing anyone has ever asked me to do. I just can't fail."

"Thanks." Lex paused for a moment before adding. "Would you please tell me what's going on?"

"I'm doing a favor for Ron."

"Your brother?"

"Yes."

"When did you hear from him?"

"This morning, he's the one who called."

Lex was surprised. "He's in Iraq, I didn't think he had access to a telephone while fighting the war."

Lex didn't miss the aggravated look Matty shot him before he spoke. "Of course they have phones, they just can't use them very often. Ron's called before, he just usually calls my mom, so she can hear his voice and not worry so much about him."

"So, let me get this straight. Ron called with an urgent errand that requires you to drive all over Long Beach, California until you find a pay phone and someone named Ann?"

"Her name is Ann Kasey."

"You do realize how absurd that sounds?"

"I have no other choice. I have to find her right away. I promised Scott I would."

"Scott?"

"One of the guys in Ron's unit. I'll do anything to repay him for saving Ron's life two months ago, no matter how absurd or crazy it may be."

"So, who's Ann?"

"Scott's sister. She's in trouble, and I'm the only person who can help her."

Several hours later, April called to say every pay phone was called. While a few people answered, nobody knew Ann. At that point, the ladies started mapping out where the pay phones were, so Matty could check them all. Matty was already driving up and down the streets looking. He started along the coast and was working his way inland. When he found a pay phone, he called April to take it off the list. It was a tedious task.

At first Lex enjoyed riding around listening to the radio and enjoying the sunshine. However, the sun eventually set and the novelty of Matty's crazy scavenger hunt wore off. "Are you sure you're supposed to go to Long Beach? We've been looking for hours. It's almost nine o'clock. Why don't we stop and get some

8

dinner?"

"I'll go through a drive through and get you something. I can't stop looking, Ann's counting on me."

Matty's determination didn't make sense. Ann probably no longer needed his help which would explain why she didn't answer the pay phone when it was called. "You know I don't eat fast food." Lex complained, disappointed Matty wouldn't stop at a sit down restaurant. "Look, there's a liquor store up ahead. Would you at least turn in for a moment and let me get a drink for the road? While I'm inside, you can get out of the car and walk around the block or something to keep looking."

"Alright," Matty pulled off East 7th Street into the parking lot.

Lex got out of the car and happily walked into the store. *Matty has finally done something sensible.*

A few minutes later, he was back outside. He noticed Matty wasn't back yet, so he opened his bottle of Chivas, took a drink, and wandered down to the street. A cool breeze made him shiver. The dark night made this part of town unsavory. He wasn't sure which way Matty went, so he looked to the left and then right to see if he had come around the block yet. Lex was ready to leave.

He didn't see Matty, but a pay phone in a little cement alcove located just off the street caught his eye. Lex chuckled; *we didn't even noticed it when we turned in. This is a waste of time. There's no way we're going to find Ann. There's not enough information and too much ground to cover.*

Lex took another sip while still staring at the pay phone. His mind wandered to Matty's odd behavior. He still couldn't believe Matty threatened to have April quit or that Matty thought he was insensitive and selfish. *There's more to this story than he's sharing.*

The more Lex thought about it, the more determined he

became to figure it out, so if he needed to stay up all night looking for Ann, he would, seven-hundred fifty milliliters would get him through.

Lex glanced down to the bum asleep under the phone; *probably drunk and passed out.* Lex took another sip, still staring at the bum. He felt compelled to walk a few feet closer. This person was too small to be an adult. On closer inspection, he realized he was looking at a small girl. Her clothes were dirty and torn, showing signs of excessive wear. Her long hair was terribly matted and crooked glasses hung on her nose. Lex had never seen anyone look so destitute.

Suddenly, the realization slapped him across the face as his whole world came to a screeching halt. *Was this the person Matty was racing all afternoon and evening to help?*

He quickly walked over and squatted down next to her. He noticed her hands were covered with writing. Curious, he picked up one hand, turning it toward the street light so he could read it. The hand was very frail, bone thin, with dirt caked under the jagged finger nails. It said "Scott Kasey" with an FPO address.

This is Ann Kasey. Lex quickly walked out of the alcove and down to the street looking for Matty. He saw him turn the corner. Lex waved his arms and shouted. "We've found her!"

Matty started running.

Lex quickly went back Ann and gave her a little shake. "Hey, wake up."

She didn't budge.

Lex started to shake her harder. When he did, the beam from a nearby street light directly hit her face; she looked very pale. Impulsively, he placed a hand on her forehead and discovered she was very hot, sweating.

Matty arrived at the alcove.

"She doesn't look good. I think she's really sick."

"She's been eating out of dumpsters and probably ate some bad food."

"That's disgusting," Lex turned to look at him. "Why would she eat out of dumpsters?"

"She didn't have any money to buy food. How else was she supposed to eat?"

It was like someone knocked the wind out of him. Lex never imagined there actually existed people who ate out of dumpsters to survive. Up until this point, he didn't think poor people really existed; they were just lazy people pretending to be poor so they could live off the government's tax money instead of getting a job.

Lex looked at Ann again, her motionless body lying on the hard ground. Her clothes, her hair, thoughts of her living condition rapidly circled through his horrified mind. He suddenly became compelled to pick her up in his arms. Matty's strange behavior now suddenly made sense. He must save her, no matter what. He'd never felt this strongly or passionately about anything in his life. His hands traded his bottle of Chivas for her.

"I've never seen you lift anything over twenty pounds. Maybe I should carry her." Matty offered.

"I have her," Lex gripped her body, amazed at how little she weighed.

They walked to Matty's car. Matty opened the door to the back seat. Lex carefully laid Ann on the seat and slid in next to her, still cradling her limp body. Matty ran around to the driver's side, climbed in, and started driving.

Lex stared at Ann's sleeping face. A piece of her blonde hair was lying across her cheek. He gently brushed it aside. She looked peaceful, almost angelic despite the dirt, but Lex knew she was really sick. She was so still, he feared she might die at any moment. "I think you need to go straight to the hospital. I'll pay her bills."

"I can't."

"Why not?" Why had Matty spent all that time looking for her to now *not* get her help? Didn't he want to save her? She must be saved. There was no choice. "What aren't you telling me?"

Matty sighed. "Her parents were killed several months ago, so The State gave custody of her to her uncle. The guy was abusing her and threatened to hurt her more if she told anyone what he was doing, so she ran away. Ann's been living on the streets ever since then.

"Scott's been beside himself, Ron knew something was really worrying him. When he found out what was going on, he wanted to help. The only question was how? What could he do from halfway around the world?"

"That's where you came in."

"Ron left me a voicemail one night explaining everything. I wrote him saying Ann could stay with me until they come home from Iraq. I didn't know when or how I'd hear back, so I wasn't expecting the call today. It seems Ron and Scott got special permission from their Lieutenant to arrange things. You see, Ann's been writing Scott letters, telling him everything that's been going on. She wrote the pay phone number down in one of her letters and told him she would wait for his call today, because it's her sixteenth birthday. Scott told her I was coming."

"Wow! Why didn't you tell me you were going to do this?"

"I thought you wouldn't understand... Look, I'm sorry. I should've told you."

12

"That's alright, but what are you going to do if Scott gets killed and never makes it back?"

"Don't talk like that." There was a sharp, crisp sound to Matty's voice. "Ron's right there with him and if they come under attack, Ron could be killed as well."

Lex wished he could take back what was implied the previous moment, but he knew he couldn't, so he decided to switch subjects. He looked down at Ann's still body; she was too still. "I still don't understand why you can't take her to the hospital."

"Because she's a kid, and we're not related to her. The hospital's bound to ask lots of questions. I'm sure it'll be under legal obligation to send her back to her uncle. I promised to help protect her. I can't risk it. I'm taking her to my house."

"Matty, she's unconscious. She needs a doctor." But he knew Matty was right. How could they just walk into a hospital with her?

Matty continued to drive toward his house in L.A. They rode in silence. Lex held Ann in his arms; his mind was racing. This was not acceptable. There must be some way to get her the medical care she needed and protect her at the same time.

An idea entered his mind. Would Matty go for it? Lex softly said. "Hallie."

"What?"

Lex spoke up. "Hallie, I've always liked the name Hallie. I'm going to name her Hallie Ann McKinley. It has a nice ring to it, don't you think?"

"Yes...where're you going with this?"

"Hallie's your little sister."

13

Matty switched lanes. "Alright...then how do I explain to the doctors that I don't know why she's sick? And how do I explain her clothes?"

"I noticed the stench as well. I'm throwing them out and buying her some new ones. Let's see...oh, I know, tell the doctors a modified version of what you told me. Tell them your parents died several months ago, your sister was so upset, she ran away. Today she called, said she wanted to come home, and asked you to come pick her up. You don't know why she's sick, but you're very worried about her."

Matty switched lanes again and started tapping his fingers on the steering wheel. "That might work...I do know her date of birth... but what about Scott's name and address written on her hands?"

"Um...Let's see...Boyfriend who left for Iraq?"

"Her brother's her boyfriend?" Matty glanced back at him. "That's a bit twisted."

"Alright, then how about a good friend who was recently deployed?"

(Matty)

Matty used his navigation system to find the nearest hospital. His mind was racing. He wanted to help Ann, but he was very nervous about the idea of taking her to a hospital. He'd never told such a big lie before, but if he was going to; this seemed like a good reason. "There's a hospital about three miles away. Do you honestly think we can pull this off?"

14

"Of course we can. Once the doctors take her in to examine her, I'll have Charles pick up April and come to the hospital, having more people who know her will help reinforce the story."

Matty used the rear view mirror to look back at Lex. He was looking down at Ann, stroking her hair. He looked concerned, an expression never seen on his face. Matty sighed and ran his fingers through his hair; he was concerned as well. She appeared to be very sick; something he wasn't expecting. *This is a crazy idea. For her sake, I hope it works.*

Runaway

Matty pulled into the emergency parking lot. He turned off the car and apprehensively looked at Lex. "Now what?"

"She's your sister, you should carry her in."

Matty got out of the car and opened the back door. He was surprised at how light she was. Lex made sure the car was locked, and they quickly walked into the emergency room.

They received immediate attention, being asked to bring her into a little room where Matty laid Hallie down on a bed. Nurses and a doctor immediately started examining her. Matty gave his story.

Lex added sympathetic comments like "Don't worry...The doctors are going to take good care of her...She's gonna be alright." Lex gave Matty a reassuring pat on the back.

Matty didn't have to fake his concern for Hallie; she looked even worse in the bright, hospital lights. Lex and he stayed with her the entire time, except when the nurses needed to remove her clothes to put her into a hospital gown.

Charles, Lex's forty-four-year-old British, personal assistant, arrived with dinner and Matty's wife, April. Matty was relieved to see them. Lex immediately left the room with Charles.

April stayed. Matty noticed his wife looked more beautiful than ever. Maybe it was just knowing she was there, but under the hospital lights her chocolate hair and walnut eyes seemed to shine against her white skin. April immediately walked over and gave him a loving hug. "How's she doing?"

"She's really sick. The doctors are running lots of tests to try and figure out what's wrong. Her fever is one-o-five point eight, so they've put her on some antibiotics to try to bring it down. They've also put her on an IV to try to hydrate her. I keep thinking, 'what would've happened to her, if I didn't get the call today? What if it was tomorrow? And what if Lex hadn't found her?'"

"But you did get the call and now she's getting the help she needs." April ran her hands up and down his back. "Why don't you go out into the waiting room and get some dinner? It'll make you feel better. I'll stay here with Hallie."

Matty smiled, glad she was there; he needed her comforting support. This huge lie was very unsettling for him. Matty kissed her on the lips and headed out of the little room.

He followed the signs to the waiting room looking for Lex and Charles. While nothing his eccentric friend did should surprise him anymore, Matty was stunned to see a table set up with a linen tablecloth, fine china, and fine silverware for him to sit and eat dinner. There was even a small crystal vase full of flowers located in the center of the table.

Matty looked around the hospital waiting room and awkwardly walked over to the strange site. This was embarrassing.

"I didn't know if you were coming or not, so I hope you don't mind I already started dinner...Charles, please give Matty the first course."

"How many courses is dinner tonight?" Matty sat down at the table.

"Three."

Charles placed a linen napkin in Matty's lap and served him a bowl of soup. Matty ate his dinner without looking around the room; he could only imagine the thoughts of the other people when they looked at this ridiculous sight. Only Lex would try to turn a hospital waiting room into a five star restaurant.

17

After they finished, Matty and Lex, wandered back into the emergency room to check on Hallie. A few minutes after they arrived, the doctor admitted her into the hospital to stay for the night. Lex requested a private room. Once she was settled, Charles and April went home to get some sleep. It was almost two a.m. Matty was relieved and surprised Lex decided to stay with him.

By mid-morning, they were told her condition was slowing improving. Lex decided to leave when April returned. Knowing April was monitoring Hallie, Matty took a nap on the reclining chair in her room.

He awoke late in the day to the sound of a guitar. Matty's entire body was stiff as he stretched and opened his eyes to see Lex playing. He felt groggy. "You're going to wake her."

"She's unconscious. I can't wake her." He smiled and strummed another set of cords. "I was playing around with some ideas. What do you think?"

Matty tilted his head from side to side. April sat down behind him and started to massage his neck with her warm, soft hands. "Ahhh…that feels good, thanks." Matty let her rub him for a few more minutes before he turned his attention back to Lex. "I think you're off to a good start. Here, hand me my guitar."

They worked on the song for several hours, stopping only once for another five star meal brought by Charles. Matty was relieved this meal was private; set up in Hallie's room where only the nurse gave them a strange look.

Eventually everyone left except Matty. He chose to sleep in the reclining chair, not wanting to leave her side. He knew she had no idea who he was or anything about the story he made up about her.

(Hallie)

Consciousness came back to Ann; she recognized the familiar smell and sounds of the hospital. She groaned. She opened her eyes to confirm what she already knew.

"Hey, you're finally awake. How are you feeling?" A guy cheerfully asked.

"Fine." *Great, someone's in the room, that's gonna make escaping more challenging.*

"My name's Matty McKinley, and while I don't want to overwhelm you, there are some things you need to know before a nurse or doctor comes in. You were really sick and unconscious when I found you. Do you remember talking to Scott? Do you know who I am?"

Wait, what? She thought he was a doctor or nurse, everything was a blur. *Talked to Scott?* Ann searched her memory for the conversation. It wasn't there, *damn!* "No, when did I talk to Scott? Is he alright?"

"He's fine," Matty explained the story. "Look, I'm not really into all this lying, but I felt like I needed to protect you. I'm sorry to throw all this at you when you've just woken up."

"It's alright," Ann tried to sit up in bed, but discovered she was too weak and could barely move her arms. She needed to wrap her mind around this. *He's here to save me from the streets and hide me from my uncle? Am I dreaming?* She smelled the room again. *No, I'm definitely in a hospital, there's no doubt about that.* She knew the sterile, clean smell by heart. *This is weird, I must be in a hospital dreaming, this is an interesting dream at least, I might as well play along and see how it turns out.* "Thanks for helping me, Matty, right?"

"Yes, and you're Hallie McKinley."

19

"And I'm Lex Vanderbilt."

Ann was startled by the voice.

"Good morning, Ms. McKinley," A female nurse walked in. "Glad to see you back with us. I came to check your temperature and blood pressure." She put a thermometer in Ann's mouth while at the same time, Ann felt the cuff around her arm tighten. "It looks like your fever's dropping nicely, one-o-two point eight. I'll let the doctor know you're awake."

While they waited, Matty and Lex told her about all the people she should know to help pull off her new identity. Ann was baffled, wondering if she'd gone crazy.

The doctor came to examine *Hallie*. She was a young woman, in her thirties. She told Matty that *Hallie* was still very weak, but she anticipated a full recovery. Ann felt exhausted; all this information running through her head was wearing her out. She slipped into unconsciousness again.

It was the strangest dream. Matty and Lex were having a conversation with two other people. They were nearby, but not next to her. A man sternly asked Matty. "Why didn't you file a missing person's report when your sister ran away? She was only fifteen at the time."

"I guess I didn't think about it. I assumed she was staying with one of her friends, she just needed some space." Matty's voice sounded uncomfortable.

"How long would you have waited before filing one?" A second person, a woman this time. "You've just said she's been gone for three months. Not knowing her whereabouts is neglectful on your part. Do you realize your sister could have died?"

20

"Like I said, I didn't think about it. Now, I wish I had."

"Officer, my name is Lex Vanderbilt, I can vouch for Mr. McKinley. I've known him for five years and the past several months have been really hard. His parents recently died. His younger brother is a deployed Marine in Iraq right now. Plus, he's been worried about his sister, but honestly thought she was safe at a friend's house. He's had a lot to deal with. What else could he have done? If he'd filed a report and the police found her and brought her home, if she didn't want to be there, then she would've just run away again. She's a very, strong willed teenager. Do you have kids? Do you know how hard it is to raise a teenager? Matty's done the best he can given the situation. Please keep in mind he too is still grieving the loss of his parents....Charles, do you have everything?"

"Yes, sir, Mr. Vanderbilt." Charles's voice was in a strange accent. "I have Ms. McKinley's clothes, plus her toiletries, everything you requested I get for her. Whenever Mr. McKinley and you are ready, I have a snack waiting in the car."

"Thank you, Charles."

Ann was awoken. *That was a strange dream.* "Matty?" As much as she didn't believe it, she wanted the dreams to be true. It didn't hurt to ask for someone she thought wasn't real. What was the worst that could happen?

"It's Charles, I didn't mean to wake you, dear. I was putting some clothes into your wardrobe. Here are your glasses."

A dream within a dream? She was *sure* she was awake this time. "Where's Matty?"

"Out in the hallway talking to some police officers."

Ann immediately became alarmed. Awake or not, she must protect Matty from the police.

21

Ann pulled her body into a sitting position. The room spun twice. She took some deep breaths and assessed her attachments; inflatable leg pillows for circulation, an IV attached to her right hand, and a catheter. She reached forward to the pillows. Ann glanced nervously at Charles as she carefully pulled apart the velcro from each leg, minimizing the ripping sound as much as possible. To her relief, he seemed focused in her closet. She wondered how many things he was putting in there.

Next she reached between her legs and twisted out the tube connecting the catheter to the capture bag. Ann felt the sides of her thighs wetten. The room spun again.

Ann fought back the weakness she was feeling, determined to get into the hallway. She swung her legs over the edge of the bed and slowly slid onto her feet; her legs felt flimsy. She used the bed for support as she made her way toward the voices coming from outside the door.

When she reached the foot of the bed, her IV tube was fully extended. Ann twisted out the connection attached to her hand and quickly moved her legs, fearful they would give out beneath her. She reached the doorway without falling.

Ann leaned against the door frame for a moment to pull together some more energy. She didn't know where it was going to come from, she felt so weak, but she must save Matty. She forced herself out into the hallway. "Matty?" Her voice was so weak. Could he hear her?

"Hey, what are you doing out of bed?" He quickly walked over to her.

"Why are the police here?" Ann demanded as forcefully as she could, but it came out as a whisper.

"They have a few questions for me. It happens when someone as sick as you is brought into the hospital. They're just

22

making sure I'm not a neglectful, older brother. It's nothing for you to worry about. You should be resting."

His incredible, sweet voice gave her strength. "You haven't done anything wrong. I'm the one who ran away. I'm the one who's caused all the trouble, not you. If they wanna talk to someone, it should be me. They need to leave you alone."

Ann suddenly felt room spin out of control, her legs like spaghetti noodles. She was out of energy.

Matty caught her in his arms and picked her up, cradling her like a father would hold a young child. "It's alright, everything's going to be alright. I don't want you worrying about me. Top priority is getting you healthy again." Matty began to carry her back to bed.

He was like an angel, the way he held her. She wanted to snuggle up against his chest and stay there forever, but she couldn't make her arms move. Fearful her dream was suddenly going to take a turn for the worse, Ann battled against her fatigued body. "Matty?"

"Shhh…you rest. I'll see you when you wake up."

Everything was out of focus. Ann struggled to keep the darkness away.

(Matty)

Lex was right behind him. "Charles, buzz the nurse."

"Yes, sir."

Matty laid Hallie down on the bed. She was passed out again; just like she'd done that morning.

23

"I'll stay and tell the nurse what happened. You finish talking to the police." Lex offered.

A small time later, Matty reentered the room and closed the door behind him. He sighed as he slumped down into the chair and leaned over to put his face in his hands. "I'm sure those officers saw right through me. I can't believe I'm lying to the police. Thanks for backing me up out there. I was drowning fast."

"No problem, like I told you the night we brought her here, we're in this together. I think what I said helped, but the most convincing act was done by Hallie here, and your natural reaction to her. How could anyone doubt the close brother/sister bond existing between the two of you?"

"I hope you're right," He agreed Hallie's performance did help, but was it good enough? "What am I going to do if the police file child neglect charges against me? I can't tell them the truth."

"I don't know. It's an unexpected complication. When I insisted you bring her here, I didn't think you would be risking going to jail. Maybe you were right to avoid a hospital."

"No, you were right. She was really sick and probably would've died at my house. She needed immediate medical treatment to save her."

Lex chuckled. "And while she's getting better, you're going to be arrested for having a good heart. Don't you just love the irony?"

"Not at all."

"Don't worry, I'll pay your bail."

"You're not easing my mind. How do I get out of this trouble and protect her at the same time?"

"What would you like? I'll get you anything you want."

Ann smiled at Lex the following morning, having completely surrendered to the dream. She was thrilled beyond words; a new life, a fresh start, and a new name, Hallie. The right word to describe how she felt was eluding her. No word or group of words seemed to capture the feeling; elated, happier than any person ever was, amazed strangers could be so nice…she was full of emotions.

Hallie looked at Lex debating if she should ask for something or not. They were so kind to her; she didn't want to take advantage of them. But on the other hand, if she said nothing; she might hurt his feelings. She finally decided it would be alright to ask as long as it was small. "A book would be nice. I like to read."

"What do you like?"

"Anything will be fine, just something you have from home, I read everything."

Lex bounced out of his chair and left.

While he was gone, Hallie contently listened to Matty play his guitar. She'd never met anyone who could play. The acoustical music was so beautiful, it seemed magical to her ears.

It wasn't long before Lex returned with eight books. "I couldn't decide what you might like, so I bought a copy of every book in the gift shop."

Hallie wasn't sure what to say. "Thanks...that was really nice. I'm sure I'll enjoy all of them." She looked at the books and decided to pick one with pink on the cover. Hallie pushed up the frames which slid down her nose, because they were too big for her face. She excitedly opened the front cover and started to read.

Matty noticed the book was touching her nose. He leaned

over and moved the book an arm's length away. "Try reading it from here."

The smile on Hallie's face quickly disappeared. She was embarrassed and ashamed to admit she couldn't see the print. She knew her vision was bad, but no one had ever made her move the book away from her face.

"You can't see it, can you?" Matty asked.

Hallie silently stared at her lap.

"I think your prescription has changed. You need to have your eyes checked. I'll see if I can get you an appointment at the optometry downstairs."

"That's alright. I don't need to see a doctor. I can see fine." Hallie protested.

"I don't think you can," Now his voice was too sweet. "Getting your eyes checked is nothing to be worried about, obviously you've had them checked before or you wouldn't be wearing glasses."

Hallie wasn't sure how to respond. Dr. Bob gave her these glasses for free, a Jane Doe brought into the hospital wasn't going to need them anymore.

She played with her fingers. How could she argue against someone so nice? "I don't have money to pay for an eye exam or new glasses. What I have will have to do."

"Nonsense," Lex said. "You're getting your eyes checked. Don't worry about the cost, I'm paying your bills."

"I can't ask you to do that. You've done enough for me already."

"You're not asking, I'm offering." Lex smiled. "Matty and I

26

promised you a new life, that means some things will change. One of those changes is you'll no longer have to hold a book up to your nose to be able to read it."

Matty gently patted her shoulder. "You're in good hands now. You just focus on getting healthy and let us handle taking care of you."

Hallie continued to protest, but in the end, conceded; alright, they were concerned about her health. They were too kind. She would let them help her this time, but as soon as she was out of the hospital; they were going to stop paying for things.

Due to a cancellation, Lex was able to get her an appointment late that afternoon. Since he was at a meeting, Matty accompanied her as she was taken down in a wheelchair. After half an hour of the exam, the doctor said. "Your prescription has changed a lot since you got these glasses. They're practically useless. You're legally blind without some form of correction, but I can fix that. Have you ever thought about wearing contacts?"

Contacts? She was definitely in unfamiliar territory which was good. Pretending like she'd done this before was very difficult. Had Matty discovered her cluelessness toward all of the equipment? Hallie felt relieved; no more faking. "No."

"I want you to try them and see what you think. I can still write you a prescription for new glasses, but they'll take several days. In the meantime, the contacts will allow you to see."

"Are they expensive?"

"They've already been paid by Mr. Vanderbilt."

Hallie was stunned. "How did Lex know I'd need contacts?" She asked no one in particular.

A few minutes later, the doctor helped her put the contacts into her eyes. She looked around the room stunned for the second time.

"How do those work for you? Do you see everything clearly? Are they comfortable?"

"Yeah."

"Is everything alright?" Matty noticed the strange look on her face.

Hallie looked over at him. "Yeah," She said with a big grin. "I've never been able to see this well. This is amazing." She noticed Matty was a nice looking guy whose face was kind; just like his voice, which was memorized and ingrained into her heart. His light, brown hair and blue eyes were very clear and crisp to her. It was nice to finally put a face on the person who saved her life.

Hallie was taken back to her room to get some more rest, but she was too excited to sleep. She spent a few minutes looking around the room and then jubilantly grabbed a book. She held it at arm's length, tickled she could read it from that far away.

After seeing her pick up the book, Matty started playing his guitar again.

Hallie wasn't sure how much time passed before Lex returned to her room, because at some point, she dozed off. When she awoke, she immediately noticed how handsome he was. She'd never seen anyone like him. His wavy, jet black hair and dark blue eyes seemed to draw him to her. His clothes were very nice. She even noticed he wore a Rolex; she could actually see the letters on the face of the watch, amazing.   The nails on his white hands were perfectly manicured; obviously he'd never done hard labor. Hallie couldn't get over how smooth his hands looked. *Wow! Scott really hooked me up.*

28

After Matty and Lex left for the evening; the doctor came into Hallie's room and sat down in a chair next to her. "How are you feeling?"

"Better, thanks," Hallie smiled at the woman smiling at her.

"I'm glad to hear it. I wanted to talk with you in private about some marks I noticed on your body. Are you familiar with doctor/patient confidentiality?"

"Yeah," Hallie was suddenly alert. She felt like her back was up against a wall. How was she going to get out of this? The doctor knew about the things she kept hidden behind her clothes. Hallie swallowed hard as her tough, street kid shell surfaced.

"Then you understand anything you tell me will be kept between us, your brother will never know we talked."

Hallie knew she'd been busted.

"Has your brother ever hit you?"

"Matty's never laid a finger on me." She forced herself to smile and act sweetly; it went against every instinct in her body. The streets taught her to be hard and cold, to bury her feelings when there was a threat and to turn into an impenetrable statue. Right now, Matty and she were in serious danger. Hallie must protect both of them; must act like nothing out of the ordinary was occurring. She needed to appear like an innocent child.

"What about denying you food or making you eat a restricted diet?"

Hallie gave a little laugh under her breath as she thought about the elaborate meals Lex provided in her room. There was an over abundance of food; the wastefulness actually bothered her. "No, I have plenty. Matty's the best brother in the world." *Well,*

29

second best, Scott was the best.

Hallie couldn't tell if the doctor was buying her story or not; she was still smiling. Hallie wondered if this was her poker face. "Alright, tell me about some of the marks on your body. How did you get those?"

"I fell." A programed answer she blurted out too quickly.

"Look, I know you're trying to protect your brother. That's a pretty typical reaction of someone who's been abused. I'm trying to help you, but you need to help yourself and give me honest answers."

So, the doctor saw some things on her body; it didn't change anything. Hallie was sticking to her story. "Matty's never laid a hand on me, that's the honest truth." Hallie desperately wanted the doctor to stop asking her questions. This doctor was going to ruin her new life. Everything was suddenly at stake. Hallie scanned her thoughts for something else she could add to her story that would be appropriate.

A sudden pain in the palm of her hands startled her. Glancing down, she discovered the source; she was clenching her fists so tightly, she was digging her nails into the skin causing little cuts which were starting to bleed. Hallie quickly hid her hands under the sheets.

"Well, your body says otherwise," The doctor was no longer smiling. "Since you're not going to be honest with me, I'm obligated to file a child abuse report with the Los Angeles County Department of Children and Family Services."

Hallie was horrified. "No, please don't!" This was no longer about protecting herself; she must put Matty first. His life was more important than hers. "Look, I'll tell you the truth, just please don't call anyone and get Matty into trouble. I can prove he's never hurt me, because I only met him four days ago."

30

Hallie spent the next hour telling the doctor everything about her past. "So you see, Matty's just trying to help me. Please don't get him into trouble."

The doctor still looked serious. "As your doctor, I have a legal obligation to release you to a family member. I'm going to have to contact your uncle; he *is* your legal guardian. I'll also contact Child Protective Services."

"No!" A crushing blow overwhelmed Hallie. "Please, no! As my doctor, you have a legal obligation to make decisions on what's best for my health and well being. I almost died a few days ago, but the next time, I'll bypass the hospital and go straight to the morgue. Does that satisfy the oath you took as a doctor? You might as well kill me now and save me the pain and suffering. I can't go back there. Please, let me go home with Matty."

The doctor looked sympathetic. "You're a minor. I legally can't release you to someone pretending to be your brother. I'm sorry. Now, try to get some rest. I'll check on you in the morning. Child Protective Services can investigate and decide where you should live."

Hallie watched as the doctor left the room. She tried to fight back the tears filling up her eyes. Fear and pain ripped through her body. Hallie grabbed the business card tucked under the phone in her room. Fighting against her shaking hands, she picked up the phone to call Matty. He didn't answer. She remembered him saying something about going to work and figured his phone must be off. Hallie tried Lex's number, but again, no answer.

Panic was starting to consume her now. She took some deep breaths to calm herself; she needed to think clearly to devise a plan. She'd have to do this on her own. It was probably better this way. Matty was protected; that was good, it would be best not to involve him in her breakout.

31

She was in mortal danger.   There was no way she was going to let them send her back to her uncle. It was time to run again.

Anxious

(Matty)

Matty pulled into his driveway, tired. It was two a.m.; he was returning from work. The past three nights were spent not really sleeping on the recliner in Hallie's room. His soft, comfortable mattress was all that was on his mind the entire drive home. It was going to feel so nice to sleep in his bed, curled up with April.

As he was getting his things out of the trunk, something in the yard caught his eye. It was strange enough for him to put down his guitar and walk across the front yard toward the dark shadow. As he got closer, he recognized the shape of a person.

Puzzled, Matty decided not to take any chances. He lived in a relatively safe neighborhood, but it wasn't gated. He walked back over to his car, turned it on, and positioned it so he could shine the headlights on the person. The pink clothes caught his attention, not what he expected a potential mugger to wear. This was strange.

Getting back out of the car, he called out. "Hey, who's there?" There was no answer. Matty sighed and walked over to the person now wondering if they were drunk and passed out in his front yard.

When he rolled over the body, he was shocked and alarmed. "Hallie, Hallie, wake up!" He was unsuccessful. Now, he was worried; she was unconscious again and still burning up with fever.

Matty quickly picked her up in his arms and carried her to the car. His body no longer felt tired, concern gave him energy. He strapped her into the passenger seatbelt and drove her back to the hospital, baffled as to why she would leave and fearful her departure risked her recovery.

A short while later, he briskly walked up to the nurse's station with Hallie in his arms, relieved she was talking in her sleep. He decided to make light of the situation. "Did you lose somebody?" He smiled as he made the joke to the brunette sitting behind the desk.

The nurse looked shocked. "Mr. McKinley, we've been looking all over for your sister. Where was she?"

"At my house, I guess she's anxious to come home." Matty smiled, carried Hallie back into her hospital room, and gently laid her on the bed.

The nurse followed him and plugged the IV back into Hallie's hand. "I don't know how someone in her weakened condition made it home."

"She almost made it. I found her in the front yard. Is she going to be alright?" He was concerned she missed an important dose of the medicine they were giving her.

"She needs to rest and regain her strength. Her fever's gone up, one-o-four even."

Matty sighed as he realized he was going to spend another night at the hospital. He couldn't leave her again. A promise was a promise; he couldn't protect her if she left. What if next time she didn't make it to his house? As he sat down in the recliner, he tried to imagine it was his comfortable bed.

She didn't wake up until after lunch the following day.

(Hallie)

Hallie opened her eyes and realized she was back in the hospital. "What the hell am I doing back here?" She suddenly sat up, alarmed.

34

"I brought you back last night. You gave everyone a scare. How are you feeling?" Matty was there; and he was concerned.

"Fine. Why did you bring me back?" *Why? Why? Why?* Her escape was perfectly planned. It took her over an hour to get out, but she was successful. Now, they would be watching her.

"Because you're sick and need help." Matty's kind voice broke Hallie's heart. *Why did he have to be such a nice guy?*

"You don't understand." Hallie started to explain as panic seeped into her body. "The doctor, she came to see me last night. She was gonna call Child Protective Services on you because of me, you were gonna have child abuse charges filed against you. So, I told her the truth, I really appreciate everything you've done for me, more than you'll ever know. I couldn't stand by and let you get into trouble. Now I'm gonna be sent back to my uncle. I had to leave last night, before they took me." She could feel her heart racing and needed to make him understand. "I can't go back to him, Matty. He's a bad man, Lucifer himself."

Matty leaned over looking intently into her eyes. "If they take you, you call me, I'll come and get you. I promise."

"You don't get it," Tears filled her eyes. "I won't have access to a phone. Once I leave here, you'll never see me again, and I'll never see Scott. My uncle will guarantee it. "

"Then we'll make sure you have a phone on you," Lex said walking into the room catching the tail end of the conversation. He was instantly on his phone. "Charles, get Hallie a cell phone. I want her to have one just like mine. I need it ASAP." Lex looked back at Hallie, smiling. "See, no problem. You have nothing to worry about. You call us, and we'll come and get you."

Hallie was baffled by his actions. She studied his relaxed face and then looked at Matty's, who was anxiously studying hers. She knew they meant well and didn't want to hurt their feelings, so

35

she tried to relax. But Hallie was worried; really worried. They didn't understand the danger. A cell phone wasn't going to solve the problem; and it provided no protection.

A short while later, the doctor entered the room. "You gave us quite the scare last night, young lady."

"I wanna be with Matty." Hallie coldly stared at her.

"How are you feeling today?"

"Like I've been shot through the chest." Hallie wasn't going to fall for her games.

The doctor looked amused. "You're lucky that's all you feel. Your immune system's still very weak. Catching a small virus would make you very ill right now. What you did last night was very dangerous."

"You're right, it was. I should've kept my mouth shut."

Just then April walked into the room with a big grin on her face. "Hallie, I have a surprise for you. It's a letter from Scott. I came as soon as I saw it in the mail."

"Scott!" Hallie couldn't hide her excitement as she was handed the treasured envelope. Suddenly, the doctor and everyone else in the room disappeared. Nothing mattered more than the letter.

Hallie barely heard Matty comment. "We'll step out into the hall and give you some privacy."

Hallie wasn't sure how much time passed before Matty peaked into the room and found her crying. "Hey, is Scott alright?"

Hallie shook her head. An array of happy and sad emotions

36

was surging through her body. "Yeah, he's fine," She continued to sob. "This is the first letter I've ever gotten from him. I miss him so much."

"I know," Matty hugged her. "It's really hard having him gone knowing he's in danger. I'm right there with you. But you have to believe he'll make it back. Both our brothers are going to make it back."

"He's all I have," Hallie grabbed hold of Matty, crying. She couldn't control her emotions. It seemed irrational; she was so happy to have the letter, to have Scott close again. Up until the day he left, Hallie spent every day with her brother. She missed him terribly.

Hallie suddenly noticed the doctor standing in the open doorway. *That doctor doesn't care about anything except covering her own butt, following some stupid rule that's gonna send me back into danger. Why can't she just leave me alone?* Another gush of tears swelled and rushed out.

"He's not all you have. You have us now, and I'm going to take care of you like I promised Scott. I'm looking forward to having a younger sibling around again." Matty released his hug and looked directly at her. "Lex and I were talking in the hallway. We're not going to stand by and let you be taken back to a man who's hurting you. We'll figure out a way to keep you with us."

His words warmed her heart despite the fact she knew he ruined her only opportunity of escape.

When Charles arrived with Hallie's new phone, the tears were all dried out. She was listening to Matty, Lex, and April's various ideas, but she was convinced none of their plans would

37

save her.

Lex was excited to give her the phone. Since it was identical to his, he showed her how to use it. Hallie was amazed at how much it could do.

Lex noticed the time and told Matty. "Hey, we have to go."

Hallie tried to hide the panic which suddenly seized her body.

Matty smiled at her. "I'll be back as soon as we're done. I'll protect you."

"I can stay for a little while," April smiled at her. "It'll be nice to get to know my new sister-in-law better." She winked at Hallie. "It's going to be fun having a little sister. Matty's not into girl talk."

"Charles can stay as well," Lex turned to Charles. "Stay with her until Matty returns. If anyone tries to take her, stop them by any means you have to."

"I understand." Replied the well-dressed older gentleman.

Their conversation made part of her heart swell with happiness; they were serious about keeping her. She would not have to face the danger alone. However, a deep gnawing inside reminded her that they didn't know the danger they were facing, but she did.

(Lex)

It was mid-afternoon when Lex arrived at the hospital. He was surprised to see Matty still asleep in the chair in Hallie's room. Matty never slept this late. Lex shook his shoulder to wake him.

Matty jumped opening his eyes, quickly got out of the chair, and motioned for Lex to come out into the hallway.

"You look like hell." Lex told him.

"Hallie seems to be having a lot of anxiety about her uncle," Matty yawned. "She suffered from nightmares all night long. It seemed like every time I'd fall back asleep, she was screaming in terror. Sometime after five this morning, she became completely hysterical, she kept repeating 'he's gonna get me.' The nurse gave her something to knock her out.

"I'm worried about her. It's not healthy for her to be this stressed. She needs to be resting, so her body will get stronger. I'm also worried about what's going to happen when Child Services does show up. What if they decide to take her?"

Lex could tell Hallie wasn't the only one who was anxious. "Don't worry, I've made several arrangements."

"What do you have planned?"

"Let's just say the less you know the better. Trust me on this...Let's see if she's awake. Charles told me she was having nightmares before you came to relieve him last night. I have a gift that will hopefully help her relax. Charles spent all morning finding the perfect one."

Matty was curious; Lex just grinned keeping him in suspense.

They walked into Hallie's room; she was still asleep. They quietly watched the TV for about another hour before she woke up.

"Good morning," Lex cheerfully said when her eyes finally opened.

"Hey," She seemed groggy.

"I heard you didn't sleep well last night, so I brought you a present."

"No presents, please,"

"Oh, but you're going to like this one. Give me your hand." Lex watched as Hallie reluctantly opened up her hand for him to place the item in her palm.

She gave him a puzzled look. "You already gave me a cell phone."

"Yes, I know. This is your backup. I told Charles you needed the smallest, slimmest phone he could get his hands on today. It's already loaded with our contact information. I want you to hide this one. Don't let anyone know you have it. Stick it in your bra or something. What's important is you keep it on your body at all times. If Child Services comes to take you, they may take your other phone, but they won't expect you to have two."

Understanding touched her eyes and a little grin crossed her face.

"I can't stress this enough." Lex intently told her. "You must keep this phone on you at all times. Only turn it on when you need help and keep the ringer off. Do you understand?"

"Yes, I can do that. Thanks Lex."

(Hallie)

At one point, the doctor came to check on her. They were told Hallie's health was improving nicely; she was being scheduled to be discharged the following day.

Once everyone left except Matty, Hallie tried to get some sleep. It was another rough night. Every time she closed her eyes,

40

she could see her uncle's face. He was in the dark room, walking toward her. She couldn't move her arms or legs, couldn't scream no matter how hard she tried. He was coming toward her, going to do the thing he did every night. He was coming. She woke up screaming.

After a handful of nightmares, she finally resolved to stay awake; she didn't want the nurse giving her something to knock her out again. She wasn't going to be taken away while sleeping. She read while Matty slept.

The following day, fear that Child Protective Services or worse, her uncle, would arrive to take her away, caused her body to shake. Every time someone turned the knob to her room, she jumped and fought back the hysteria bubbling just below the surface. She was on the edge of a massive eruption. If Child Protective Services showed up, there was a chance. Maybe her hysteria would help convince them she should stay with Matty. If her uncle came, she was doomed. She played escape scenarios in her head of how she would be able to use Lex's secret phone to call for help.

Matty tried to get her to eat some breakfast, but she couldn't. She could see the concern on his face and on Lex's when he arrived. Hallie figured this was their first time watching someone go crazy. They both tried to comfort her, to reassure her things would work out; they would save her. She appreciated their efforts and wanted to believe them, but she was paralyzed in her own little hell; there was no escape. She knew the truth about what would really happen; they were clueless. She had risked everything to escape from her uncle; death on the streets was better than the hell she was returning to, one she wouldn't be able to escape a second time.

It was late afternoon when the doctor entered her room and stared at Hallie for a moment. Hallie knew she looked completely mental, the anxiety had built and festered inside her body all day long. This was it, the moment they were waiting for. Who was out in

41

the hallway waiting to take her away? Hallie assumed her eyes were wild and crazed with apprehension.

Upbringing

(Hallie)

The doctor turned to Matty, very serious as she spoke. "Mr. McKinley, before I can discharge Hallie, we need to discuss several things. She has signs of prolonged undernourishment and is going to need a very balanced diet of fruits, vegetables, grains, and proteins. I've spoken to the nutritionist on staff, he's written up a recommended diet for her to follow and an eating schedule." The doctor handed Matty the documents.

"Great! Thank you very much." Matty gave Hallie a big grin.

Hallie looked back at him, shocked. For the first time all morning, her shaking stopped.

"Also, I want to see her in my office in two weeks for a follow up evaluation." The doctor handed Matty her business card. "I expect for you to have received the letter from her real brother giving you temporary custody while he's deployed. My husband's currently deployed as well and going to miss the birth of our first child." She patted her stomach. "We military families have to stick together and help each other out during these difficult times."

Lex took the card out of Matty's hand and was immediately on his phone. "Hey, I need you to schedule Hallie an appointment. Here's the information."

While Lex was talking, the doctor told Matty. "From what I've seen so far, you're taking excellent care of her. I'm trusting this will continue."

"Of course, thank you."

43

"The nurse will be in shortly to go over the discharge procedures. I'll see you in two weeks." The doctor gave Hallie a smile.

Hallie was stunned. *Was this really happening?* She looked at Matty for confirmation. His smile was so big it touched his eyes. "How would you like to come home with me?"

Hallie's next challenge was deciding which of the beautiful new outfits from Lex she wanted to wear to her new home. She pinched herself several times to make sure she was awake; feeling very silly each time, because she figured a dream pinch couldn't actually wake her.

Sitting in the discharge wheelchair, Hallie excitedly watched the cars pull up. A shiny, black limo arrived. Having never seen one, she was very intrigued what the person riding home in the limo would look like. As her wheelchair started to roll forward, Hallie looked all around for the rider while feeling a twinge of disappointment she wasn't going to see who it was.

"What are you looking for?" Matty inquired.

"The rich person going home in the limo."

Matty chuckled. "Welcome to Lex's world."

She was stunned when the door was opened for her. Lex was sitting in the back.

Hallie absorbed every part of the inside of the limo as they rode for a while before entering a neighborhood.

"We're almost there."

Hallie noticed the cute little houses with perfect little yards neatly lined down the streets. It looked like something out of a fantasy. The houses were not much bigger than the size she was used to seeing, but they were much cleaner, no graffiti. It was a stark contrast to the world she knew.

"Wow! You're rich."

"Not rich," Matty laughed. "Just middle class."

They pulled up in front of one house with a one car garage. Hallie noticed the sign hanging over the front door. "WELCOME HOME HALLIE" it said in pink letters. Hallie was tickled, feeling very special. The limo door was opened for her; and she was offered a hand to help her out.

Hallie pinched herself extra hard. If she were dreaming, she must wake up. Reality was going to be bleaker and darker than ever before now that she'd seen this.

"Let me show you around," Matty cheerfully told her.

Hallie held her breath as she walked through the threshold bracing herself against the pain she was going to feel when she did finally wake up. This dream world was all she'd ever hoped for and knew she'd never have. Hallie looked into the house in complete awe. She wanted it so badly; she could even smell a vanilla fragrance in the air. An 11-by-14 framed wedding picture of Matty and April caught her eye.

"We got married last March." Matty whispered into her ear.

"You look so happy."

"We are, I can't put into words how much I love her, and believe me, I've tried...This is the family room."

What a nice name for a room.

"And here's our kitchen."

As Hallie turned to the right to view the galley style room, a small breakfast table big enough for four caught her eyes. It was so picturesque, a perfect home for a real family.

Come on Ann, wake up. Don't do this to yourself.

There was a hallway which led off the family room. "At the end is April and my room." He turned the knob to the door on the right. "This is the guest bathroom." Hallie glanced inside and immediately fell in love with the soft beach theme. She loved the beach. "This will be your bathroom as well." Shock stunned her body.

Hallie's breathing intensified. She was getting in way too deep; she would never be able to recover now. The dream was too intense, too real.

Lex opened the door to the room located across the hall from the bathroom. Hallie felt her heart start to race, panic set in.

"Hallie, what's wrong?" Matty gave her a concerned look.

"I can't...I can't do this...I have to wake up, now!"

Matty patted her back. "You are wake. You seem to still be wound up from this morning. Please try to relax, you're safe now."

His words jolted her. Her eyes found their way to the bedroom; she had to see it. Hallie stared in amazement at the room with light pink walls and white furniture. There was a queen sized bed covered with pillows of various shades of pink. There was a desk with a pink laptop and a bookcase containing a pink boom box. There were letters on the wall that spelled "Hallie." She now realized why Lex asked her what her favorite color was.

"Come on into your room," Lex excitedly ushered her.

Tears started streaming uncontrollably down Hallie's cheeks. She couldn't contain the overwhelming emotions she was

46

experiencing. It was like nothing she'd ever felt before.

"What's wrong?" Lex was staring at her.

"It's too much, isn't it." Matty chimed in. "Lex, I told you she wasn't a little girl."

"It's the most beautiful room I've ever seen." Hallie whispered. "You did all this for me?"

"I made sure the interior decorator was working overtime to get it done before you came home. Look, if there's anything you don't like or want changed, let me know and we can fix it." Lex was grinning.

"No, it's perfect," She whispered. "I can't believe you did this for me. Thank you." It was going to be a while before the tears stopped; her emotions were in overdrive for the second time that day.

It took over an hour and an entire box of tissues before the tears finally stopped draining. At some point, April arrived home from work along with a pleasant surprise.   Paul Swartz and Henry Greenfield came to visit her. Hallie was curious as to what Matty and Lex's frequently mentioned business partners were like. She was immediately fond of both the guys. They were silly, playful, and fun to be around. Paul was average sized with shoulder length brown hair and brown eyes. His olive skin was a light bronze shade of tan. Hallie immediately noticed his friendly smile.

Henry was a redhead with lots of freckles on his face and arms. He was slightly taller than Paul, and styled his hair so it stood straight up in little spikes.   Hallie got the impression he was the more joking of the two.

Hallie sat on the sofa eating pizza and listening to them talk. She couldn't remember the last time she'd laughed so much. Her new home was more fantastic than she could have ever imagined

47

which made her that much more fearful it would be suddenly stripped away.

The following morning, Hallie was thrown a curve as she was whisked out to a day spa with April.

"A 'sisters' day out,' compliments of Lex." April told her.

Hallie never felt so out of her element. Several times she wasn't sure about what they were doing or if she really wanted it done, but she didn't want to hurt April or Lex's feelings, so she let the staff do what they wanted with her. Facials, manicures, pedicures, waxing, makeovers, a makeup lesson, a haircut and style, new clothes, shoes, and jewelry along with the limo and a catered lunch by Charles. Hallie imagined herself as a rag doll, starting out plain and simple in a workshop and then becoming more elegant with each accessory added until at last she became a China doll. She felt like a China doll too, terrified to move because she might mess something up. It didn't help that she was required to wear heals. Hallie couldn't figure out how anyone got use to walking on such wobbly shoes.

Then, if things couldn't get worse, April asked if she were ready for her debut. *Debut? Who exactly was she presenting herself to?*

Hallie nervously rode in the limo not knowing where she was going. Her palms were sweaty as she wondered if rich people could be pimps and if she was being dressed up to entertain some man for the evening. April looked equally as made up. She just smiled and wouldn't tell Hallie where they were going.

The limo finally stopped; and Hallie was once again required to move in her dress and heels. She contemplated making a run for it, not wanting to be involved in whatever was going down. But even if she could have kicked off her heels with straps winding up her ankles, the tight skirt was sure to slow her down. Hallie was going inside whether she wanted to or not.

She held her breath as she entered through the heavy wooden doors. A sigh of relief exited when she realized she was in a restaurant. Matty and Lex were waiting for them at a table. As she approached, Hallie noticed Lex giving her a strange look. Hallie tried to figure out what was out of place. She checked her nails, clothes, and jewelry with no luck; it must be her hair or makeup. How embarrassing.

Lex got out of his chair. Hallie assumed he was going to fix the problem, but instead he said. "You look spectacular." and kissed her on the cheek. Hallie was perplexed. Lex then pulled a chair back and motioned for her to sit down. What an odd thing for him to do. He pressed his lips together as he walked around to sit across from her. Hallie could tell he was trying to suppress a laugh. She wondered why she was the butt of his joke. She felt completely humiliated.

Hallie was relieved to be handed a menu. She hid her face behind it to get Lex to stop staring at her. She fought back the tears threatening to pour from her eyes. The last thing she needed was to mess up her makeup. Hallie focused on the menu and her discomfort level increased. The food was way too expensive.

Despite the fact she was hungry, Hallie ordered the soup, the least expensive item.

Lex then ordered. "I'll have the filet minion and the lady will have the same." He smiled at Hallie whose eyes widened and quickly shot down to her empty plate.

Once the waiter left; Hallie suddenly looked up, irritated. "You shouldn't have ordered for me. Scott will be furious when he

49

finds out I spent over fifty dollars for dinner."

"Relax, I'm buying."

"I can't ask you to spend that much money on me for food. You've been more than generous. This is very unnecessary." Hallie started playing with her fingers as she began to worry what he was going to expect in return.

Lex gave her a strange look. "I appreciate you being conscious of my money, but the doctor said you needed to eat. I wanted to make sure you had enough."

"Thanks," She humbly responded and then added. "I'm not playing your game."

"Really," He was amused. "You could've fooled me."

Crap, what is he up to?

When her soup arrived, Hallie became confused. Why were their two spoons on the table?

"You use the spoon to the right of the knife. The spoon located above your plate is for your dessert." *Shit,* he was still staring at her. Hallie picked up the correct spoon and started eating.

"Hang on a minute. First, let me show you how to hold your spoon." He picked up his own spoon to demonstrate. "You hold the spoon like this. When you eat soup, you scoop it into the spoon by moving the spoon horizontally away from you. Gently tap the bottom of your spoon on the backside of your bowl to prevent drips." He demonstrated the technique. "Now you try."

Hallie realized her traitor face must have revealed her irritation at being told how to eat, because Lex suddenly looked surprised and then intrigued. Hallie sighed and executed the proper eating technique deciding to play along. Was he going to stare at

50

her all night?

"Good, now you've got it," Lex took another scoop. "Now, after several bites, you pick your napkin up out of your lap and gently touch your lips, like this." He demonstrated.

"Why?" That was one of the most absurd things she'd ever heard.

Lex was chuckling. "To make sure you haven't left any food on your face."

"Oh," She flashed a shy smile at her embarrassment.

Lex observed her carefully. When the second course arrived, he explained how to properly hold the fork and knife, how to cut the meat, and how to place the knife in its resting position on her plate. "Why are you fidgeting? You're doing a great job for your first time being taught how to eat properly. Now, sit up straight, it makes you look educated, gives you power. Slumping sends the message you're low class."

Lex appeared to be amused over her confusion as to how to use the fork and knife. She slowly turned the fork over in her hand and studied it to make sure it was in the correct position. At least if she were looking at it, she wasn't looked directly into his penetrating deep, blue eyes. She would hesitantly hold the knife, unsure whether she should continue holding it or place it down on the plate. She didn't speak and never looked up, keeping her eyes intently on the plate and silverware; contently listening to the conversation at the table.

Matty suddenly asked her a question. "Hallie, tell us about yourself."

She froze. "Um...there's not much to tell...I'm from Riverside...and I have Scott. That's pretty much it."

51

"That would be a terrible answer on a job interview." Lex informed her.

She looked straight into his eyes. "I'm not on a job interview." *At least I'd better not be.*

"One day you might be and you need to know how to present yourself."

"I'm not getting a job. Scott won't allow it."

"You don't have to work?"

"Scott provides me with everything I need."

Lex looked amused. "I don't have to work either."

Thankfully, Matty then changed the conversation allowing Hallie to go back to staring at her food.

After dessert, Lex leaned in close to her. "So, what game am I playing?"

Shit! The last thing she wanted was to be put on the spot. Hallie took a deep breath. "You're a rich pimp, and I'm not playing your game. Find some other girl to do your dirty work. I'm not for sale."

Hallie hesitantly watched him, wondering if he would actually hit her in the restaurant. But he was the one who looked like he'd been hit in the face. "What? Where'd you get that idea?"

"Why else would you get me all dolled up? You even said you didn't have to work."

"I ... I was born rich. I sent you to the day spa to make you feel special and to help pull off your new identity. I'm just trying to help you be a sophisticated, young woman. I ... I would never ask of you... I'm a gentleman."

Hallie immediately felt ashamed at her mistake.

Three weeks later, Hallie found herself in a similar situation. Matty and April were going to a show, so Lex came over to take her out, having forgiven her for thinking he was a monster.

"I'm perfectly capable of staying home by myself. You don't need you to babysit me."

"It's alright," He grinned. "I don't mind."

"Well I do."

"Then ask yourself this question. What're you going to do if you're home alone and CPS shows up?"

Hallie froze in terror as she realized he was right. There was no guarantee the doctor was going to keep her mouth shut. She could phone in a report anonymously. Hallie sighed as she grabbed her purse and headed out to dinner with him.

"What would you like to do after dinner?"

"Anything's fine." She honestly answered, very flexible. Besides, she knew he would end up getting his way.

Lex surprised her by being irritated. "Look, I don't know what girls your age like to do, so you're going to have to help me out. You want to go shopping, to the movies, let's see what else..."

"I don't need anything, so it wouldn't make sense to go shopping." Hallie quickly interjected.

He sighed. "You want to go to the movies?"

Hallie pondered this for a moment. "I don't know," She nervously answered. "I've never been to the movies."

53

"What? You've never been to see a movie? Everyone's been, it's like an American pastime ranked almost as high as baseball."

She quietly shook her head 'no' wishing he wasn't making such a big deal out of it.

"Wow, I can't believe you've never been to the movies. You're going to love it. Everyone does. Why do you think the movie industry makes so much money?"

(Lex)

At the movie theater, Lex offered to let Hallie pick out what she wanted to see. He intriguingly studied her face as she slowly analyzed the movie posters for a long time before deciding on a comedy, love story. Lex insisted on buying popcorn and drinks even though Hallie said she was full and that buying more than a person could eat was wasteful. "You can't truly experience going to the movies without eating popcorn and having a monster drink."

Lex could tell she was excited. He watched as Hallie looked all around the place with wide eyes, taking everything in and asking lots of questions. For the first time that evening, she seemed relaxed when he told her what to do. The lights dimmed down, the introduction began. Hallie jumped as the loud speakers started. She quickly placed her hands over her ears; her legs curled up tightly against her chest.

Lex, who was enjoying watching her excitement, was surprised. "What's wrong?"

"It's really loud."

"That's the point, a large screen and really loud speakers. Your ears will adjust to it."

"I don't like loud sounds." She looked painfully uncomfortable.

Lex was very puzzled by her behavior. The smile was gone from her face; this bothered him. He was having fun watching her have fun. He wanted her to enjoy her first movie experience. A few minutes passed before he leaned over again and said. "Stay here, I'll be right back."

Lex walked out of the movie theatre, down the street, and into a store he hoped had what he was looking for. Thankfully they did, and a few minutes later he was sitting back down next to Hallie, who was frozen in her strange position. Was she shaking? "Here, put these in." He told her, definitely bewildered.

Hallie looked at the pink pieces. "What are they?"

"Ear plugs, look, roll them in your hand like this and then... here, give me your ear." He gave up on the explanation. Brushing her golden blonde hair back from her left ear, he inserted the plug. Lex then placed an earplug in Hallie's right ear. "Is that better?"

"Yes, thank you," She gave him a big smile.

"Good," Without thinking, Lex gently rubbed her back for a moment. He was happy to see her smiling again. The twinkle came back into her eyes as he saw her relax and start to enjoy the movie. He placed his right arm over the back of her seat, tilting his body slightly so he was facing her. Lex wasn't interested in watching the movie; he only wanted to watch her expressions. She mesmerized him.

As they walked back to the car, Hallie excitedly talked about the movie and experience. Lex was thrilled; she was so animated. Suddenly, she noticed a man begging for money. She reached into her purse and took out twenty dollars Lex knew Matty gave her for

55

emergency money. Hallie walked over to the man and handed it to him. "Here, it's all I have."

Lex was displeased and quickly ushered her away. "You shouldn't have done that."

"Why not?" Hallie was surprised by his comment. "He needs help, Lex."

"He doesn't need help, he's a con-artist. They all come down to the wealthy part of town pretending to be poor, so rich people will give them money. They're just lazy and want a hand out."

"You don't know that for sure. Maybe he really is poor, coming to this part of town and begging for money is his only way of getting help. Not all poor, homeless people are out to scam you; some really need help and have no other way of getting it."

Lex didn't miss the seriousness of her manor and tone, or the burning passion in her eyes. "So you think that guy's legit?"

"No one with a home would allow themselves to smell that bad. You don't know what he struggles with, isn't it worth the risk to give him some money. It might buy him food he desperately needs. You don't know when his last meal was. You don't know how many times he's gone dumpster diving because it was his only option."

Dumpster diving struck a chord, smacking him right across the face. Lex knew that was what made her so sick and almost killed her. He wondered if she'd ever begged for money; she *was* homeless and living on the streets when he rescued her.

An image of her on the corner instead of the man suddenly entered his mind. It was a horrifying thought he needed to quickly shake away. "Wait here a minute," Lex told her, now compelled to do something. He walked back over to the beggar and handed him a fifty dollar bill. "Here man, I hope this helps."

56

As he walked back to Hallie, he saw her beautiful smile. "You did a really nice thing."

Lex was pleased. There was one thing she liked for him to buy for her, food for the homeless.

(Hallie)

They continued walking to Lex's red Ferrari. Lex opened the passenger side for Hallie, waited for her to climb in, and closed the door. Once he got in the car, he glanced at the clock on the dash. "It's only a little after eleven, the night's still young. You want to go dancing?"

Hallie was surprised. "How late do you usually stay out?"

"Until two or three," He pulled the car onto the street. "I know a fun club where we can go."

Hallie looked nervously at her hands. Her voice was almost a whisper when she answered. "I don't know how to dance."

"Don't worry. I'm a great dancer. I'll teach you."

Hallie remembered how humiliated she felt being taught to eat and didn't want to go through a similar situation with dancing. "Don't you have to be an adult to get into the clubs?" She hopefully asked.

"Normally yes," He turned to her smiling. "But you can get in if you're with me."

Hallie sat in silence wrestling with her thoughts, trying to figure out how she was going to get out of this situation.

Lex put a cigarette in his mouth. "Can I have one?" She excitedly asked wanting more than ever to relax the somersaults tumbling around in her stomach.

"It's 'May I have one'."

As he lit the cigarette, the flame from the lighter allowed her to see his face for a moment. It was full of disapproval. "How long have you been smoking?"

Hallie looked away from him and out the window. "Not long, a few months."

"You shouldn't smoke."

Hallie turned, incredulous. "You do."

"That's different. I'm older than you. Besides, you're a beautiful, young lady, and smoking is unattractive."

Hallie was stunned. She didn't know if she should be irritated at him or flattered; beautiful was never a word she'd use to describe herself. He handed her the cigarette; she decided to smoke in silence.

Lex pulled into a parking space announcing they were at the club. Hallie started to open her door, but Lex quickly walked around the car and finished opening it for her. He extended his hand to help her out. Lex opening and closing her car door was another bizarre, new experience. She wondered why he did it. She turned to grab her purse.

"It's a little loud inside, so you might want to bring your earplugs. You won't need your purse."

Hallie fumbled in her purse to find the pink plugs; she stuck the bag under her seat. Lex grinned and ushered her toward the side of the building. There was a long line to get inside. Hallie hoped they couldn't get in. Lex walked up to the front of the line; and they were admitted without even speaking to the bouncer.

Once inside, Hallie became very uncomfortable. There was a live band playing, lights flashing, and lots of people. She'd never been any place like it and was glad she was wearing the earplugs; she stayed right next to Lex. They walked up to the bar. Lex was immediately handed a beer. Again, Hallie was stunned he didn't have to speak to get what he wanted. She ordered a soda.

"You're drinking?" She asked him.

"It's only a beer. That's like a soda for an adult."

"But you're driving."

"Don't worry," He smiled. "I'll switch over to Coke long before we leave."

Lex's eyes scanned the room. He quickly downed the beer and turned to Hallie. "Come on." He grabbed her by the hand and led her out onto the dance floor.

It was crowded; people bumped into them as they moved to the middle of the floor. Hallie cringed and felt the panic start to build.

Suddenly, Lex stopped and turned around. "You ready?"

"No."

Lex laughed, grinning. "It's not as hard as it looks." He gently placed his hands on her hips. Hallie felt a surge of electricity shoot through her body, a new sensation. "Bend your knees a little."

She tried to focus on his instructions and not on the excited feeling charging through her. His hands were soft, smooth, warm. Normally, being this close to a guy made her very uncomfortable. However, it wasn't long before she was feeling more relaxed, swinging her hips and moving along with his body right against hers, giving in to this incredible feeling, not caring where he touched her as long as he didn't stop. Dancing was fun.

Hallie danced until she felt her legs could no longer support her. Lex waved good-bye to their very, friendly waitress who kept bringing them drinks on the dance floor and knew his name. Lex noticed Hallie giving him a puzzled look as they were walking back to the car.

"What are you thinking?"

"You didn't pay for anything, all the drinks and food we ate. How was it all free?"

Lex grinned. "I get anything I want." He leaned in and whispered; his eyes were sparkling in the street lights. "I own the place."

Hallie was speechless.

Once they were in the car, he said. "Why don't you come home with me? It's almost three, and you wouldn't want to wake Matty and April. I have a guest room you can use."

"Alright," She easily agreed, curious as to where he lived and too tired to care where she crashed.

A short while later she found herself at his condo staring at the guest bed, surprised. Laid out for her were toiletries, pajamas, and new clothes for the next day.

The following afternoon, Hallie found herself back at the club with Lex. She found out he owned three night clubs; Miaotsie, Bikinis, and Mixx. Miaotsie was the largest of the three and where Lex was holding his meeting with his managers. Hallie met Zac, the manager of Miaotsie; and found out Matty, Lex, Paul, and Henry were in a rock-n-roll band. Hallie knew Matty played a guitar as part of his work, but didn't realize he was in an actual band. It seemed that Matty was the lead guitarist; really talented based on Lex's opinion. Lex was the lead singer who also played rhythm guitar and keyboard. Paul played bass guitar and keyboard. Henry was the drummer. Their band was called Asterix; they performed every Thursday, Friday, and Saturday nights as regulars at all three clubs. There was even a gift shop where club goers could purchase the band's album and T-shirts.

Next on the agenda was to meet Matty at the music store. It felt strange she hadn't seen him in almost twenty-four hours. Hallie spent almost all her time with Matty, spending her days doing whatever he needed to do and hanging out with him on the nights he didn't work. It was like she used to do with Scott.

She was elated to see him. His smile was warm and friendly. Hallie got the impression he missed her as well.

As they started walking around the store, it felt like Lex and Matty were speaking another language; Hallie couldn't follow their conversation. Having never been in a music store before, she took the opportunity to let her eyes wander. She recognized most of the instruments, but there were many things which were foreign.

They were walking down another aisle, when suddenly there was an extremely loud series of sounds. Hallie screamed, dropping to the floor with her hands over her ears as the sound pierced through her head. She curled up in the tightest ball possible to protect herself against the menacing attack.

Matty immediately knelt down next to her. "Hallie, what's wrong?"

Secret

(Hallie)

Hallie was breathing hard and shaking. She didn't acknowledge Matty, she couldn't. The sound was heard again causing her to jump and scream once more. Her entire body was seized in terror.

"Come on, let's go outside for a minute." He pulled her to her feet putting his arm around her waist to help her walk on her shaky legs.

Hallie struggled to move. Being out of her ball was extremely distressing. She just wanted to drop back down to the ground and curl up.

Once outside, he gently sat her down on the curb. "Breathe, and try to relax." He softly said as he sat next to her. His entire face was wrinkled in distress.

Lex was standing near them; he looked bewildered.

Hallie's heart was racing; she couldn't think straight. Different images were clipping through her memory at a rapid pace; confusing her while her ears rang in pain.

Matty was gently rubbing her back when her cell phone played. She couldn't think about it; she didn't have control yet. Matty slid the phone out of her purse and answered. "Hello...May I tell her who's calling?...Hi Scott." Matty smiled giving Hallie a thrilled look. "This is Matty. She's right here." Matty handed her the phone.

Scott? The sound of his name brought her back a little.

62

Hallie gripped the phone tightly, worried her shaking hands would cause her to drop it and possibly disconnect the call.

"Scott!" She cried, her speech disturbed, her breathing rapid.

"I'm right here. Close your eyes and breathe deeply. Focus on the sound of my voice."

Matty said something about privacy; and Lex went with him back into the store.

Hallie closed her eyes, following Scott's instructions, but she was too excited to calm her breathing. She didn't remember talking to him on her birthday, and this was the first call he'd been able to make since then. As far as she was concerned, it was the first time she'd heard his voice since he left ten months ago. "Scott, Scott, I can't believe it's you. I've missed you so much."

"I've missed you, too." She could hear his smile. "And my timing was perfect. You need me right now." His voice was very calm, loving. "Now, tell me why you're upset."

"I was in the music store, and there was a sudden, loud noise. It caught me off guard. You know what happens to me."

Scott was silent for a moment; Hallie knew he was thinking. "Matty answered the phone. Was he able to help you?"

Hallie sighed with relief. "Yes. He took me outside, away from the noise."

"Does he know about you?"

Hallie was instantly alarmed. Her eyes flew open as panic entered her body once again. "No, I hope not. I've been trying so hard to keep under control. I finally made it to Dr. Neumann yesterday morning and got more pills. You know it takes several weeks before they start to fully work. Oh my gosh, what if I just

63

blew it with Matty? He's gonna wanna know what happened to me. What am I gonna do?"

"I think you should tell him the truth about you." Scott's calm voice replied.

Hallie pondered this idea for a moment. No one loved her except Scott. She knew that. It was proven time and time again. Hallie thought about what would happen if Matty found out her secret. She knew that answer.

No. She couldn't let it happen again. The secret must stay safe. She needed to start making better choices to protect herself, to keep the truth buried. She'd tried this before and failed, but the stakes were never so high. This time, Hallie was facing losing the fairytale life.

"No, I can't," She concluded. "You know what happens when people find out the truth about me. I'm finally in a safe place, a place I can stay until you come home." She didn't hide the determination in her voice, but she knew he would also detect the fear.

"I think Matty's different. He's helped you so much already. I think we should tell him the truth. I'll tell him, you don't have to." Still ever so tranquil; the most soothing voice she knew.

However, no amount of serenity was going to stop the instant panic attack. "No, Scott, please, don't! I almost died last time! I almost didn't make it to hear your voice again! No!" She cried resolved. "We must keep it a secret."

"Alright, you're the brains, and I'm the brawn. That's the way it's always been. If you think it's better not to tell him, then I won't say a word." He conceded; she knew he didn't want to upset her anymore than she already was.

"Thank you, Scott," Hallie closed her eyes so she could

imagine her brother sitting next to her having this conversation instead of halfway around the world. "It's great to hear your voice. How are *you* doing?"

"I'm doing great now that you have a phone number where I can reach you." He was elated. "I love the pictures you sent me. You look so different, I barely recognized you. You look fantastic. I assume the camera is for me to take some pictures to send to you?"

"The only pictures I have of you are in my memory. I'm worried I'll lose those."

"No problem. I'll fill up the entire camera. I also really enjoyed your last letter and the brownies you sent me. I didn't know you knew how to cook?"

Hallie smiled, starting to relax. "Matty helped me. It was from a mix. I'm so glad you liked them. I'll make you some more."

"It seems like you living with Matty is working out well."

"He's a really nice guy. I've never met someone so kind and gentle, he has very soft eyes. I feel guilty for not trusting him, but you know I can't."

"I know." Hallie heard a hit of sadness in his voice. She knew how difficult her secret was for him, and how much he sacrificed to help her. She didn't deserve him.

As they continued to talk, she could tell he wanted to hear her voice as much as she wanted to hear his. They balanced their conversation. Hallie tried to memorize the sound with every syllable he uttered. Time passed too quickly. It seemed like he was just saying 'hello' when he promised to call her again as soon as he was allowed. "I love you."

"I love you too, stay safe." She whispered back fighting tears, wishing there was more time together.

After she hung up, Hallie sat on the curb a few more minutes. Her brother was doing well. He sounded great over the phone. The call was the best gift she could have received other than him actually being home. She tried to imagine he was still with her.

When the feeling started to fade, she sighed. Hallie got up off the pavement and stared intently at the front door to the music store. She must to go back inside, to convince Matty and Lex nothing out of the ordinary happened. But how was she going to do it? She told herself she needed to be prepared for any sudden sound. If she was ready, she could stay in control. Hallie put her earplugs in her ears, took a deep breath, and walked into the store.

She found the guys looking at electric guitars. Matty smiled when he saw her. "Hey, how's Scott?"

Hallie grinned as she thought about her brother. "He's great. He enjoyed the brownies we sent him."

"Wonderful," Matty looked delighted. "You seem to be feeling better."

"I am, thanks. The sudden sound really took me by surprise."

"I'll say," Lex gave her a skeptical look. "I've never seen someone as jumpy as you. You weren't kidding about not liking loud sounds. You completely freaked when someone played an amplified guitar."

Hallie forced the smile to stay on her face, but her eyes found their way to the floor and she started playing with her fingers.

(Matty)

There was a knock on Matty's front door. It was Tuesday

66

evening; April was at her exercise class, so only Matty and Hallie were home. Hallie got up off the sofa to answer it. As she did, Matty heard.

"Hey, Hal, how's it going?" Lex greeted her. Matty rolled his eyes; Lex not only named her, but now was using a nickname?

"Great, how are you?" Well, at least she didn't seem to mind.

"Couldn't be better," Lex smiled at her. "Hey Matty, I have some things for you." He walked over to the kitchen table where Matty was sitting paying some bills. He opened a file and started pulling out papers as he spoke. "I figured you'd need some documents for Hallie, so I had these made. This is a birth certificate with her name as Hallie McKinley showing your parents as her parents. It also says she's eighteen. I thought changing her age would be a good idea, just to be safe. This is a copy of her immunizations. And, here's a copy of her school records. I thought about using your high school, but decided it would avoid suspicion if we said she was home schooled over the past several years, that way no one could discover she never attended."

"You amaze me sometimes," Matty stared at the documents, dumbfounded. "These look authentic. How did you get them?"

"Charles...I don't know his source. All I know is the guy he uses for things like this is not someone you can send a FedEx to, that's why it took so long. Charles traveled to the East Coast twice, once to drop off the information and then back again to pick up the documents."

"What's going on?" Hallie walked over to the table.

Matty gathered his thoughts as comprehension set in. "Thanks to Lex, I'm going to be able to enroll you into high school tomorrow." He happily told her.

The horrified expression that suddenly appeared on her face took him by surprise. Her expression was deep, dark. "I'm *not* going back to school! Scott says I don't have to, and *you* can't make me! There is no reason for me to go to school!"

Matty was stunned. He glanced over to Lex; he was too. Hallie never raised her voice to anyone; her hostility was shocking.

Maybe he could reason with her; find out why she felt the way she did. "Come, sit with me for a minute, let's talk about this."

"There's nothing to talk about. I'm not going." She hissed slowly moving away from the table.

"Please, sit," He watched her carefully as she wrestled with her thoughts. Her brow was crinkled as she slowly walked over and plopped herself down into one of the chairs. Her arms were crossed as she scowled at the carpet.

Well, that was a start.

What exactly should he say? How could he convince her going to school was a good idea? "It's important for you to get a good education. You need to graduate high school, so you can go to college."

"College!" Hallie suddenly looked at him in disbelief. "How the *hell* am I supposed to go to college? I can't pay for college and neither can Scott." She was on her feet again. Hallie suddenly took a deep breath. "Look," She said a bit calmer. "No one in my family has ever graduated high school. Scott never even went to middle school, he dropped out after fifth grade. I dropped out after tenth. There's nothing those teachers can teach me that I don't already know. It's a waste of my time, and I'm not going. Besides, I don't need their food anymore, there's food here. You can write Scott, he'll tell you I don't have to go."

Hallie quickly crossed the room to the hallway; stopping

68

where it began.   While looking at the floor she added. "Look, I know you're only trying to help, and I really appreciate everything you've done for me, just... let me be on this." Hallie looked directly at Matty. "Okay?"

She quickly left the room, but not before Matty noticed the tears in her eyes. He felt bad all of this upset her so much. But why? Her reaction didn't make sense.

"What are you going to do? She has to go to school." Lex's question echoed his own thoughts.

"Not much I can do. I told Scott I would look after her, but I can't force her to do something she doesn't want to do. I'm not really her guardian. I'll just have to write him and wait to see what he says about it."

"Give me Scott's address. I'll write him as well. She has to go to school."   Lex was adamant.

"In the meantime, I'm going to continue trying to give her the best life I can. I know how hard it is to have a brother in Iraq, but I can't imagine how hard it's been for her losing her parents, being abused by an uncle, and then ending up on the streets. I think all I can do right now is to continue to try to earn her trust and provide her with a safe and loving place to live."

"Have you found out anything else about her family?"

"No, she never talks about them, she just writes letters to Scott every day." This thought made him grin. "Sometimes she writes two in one day. I'm glad Scott was able to call her last week. I get the feeling she really needs him."

"I think you make a great surrogate, big brother. I'm amazed how you handle her."

Matty glanced at Lex, surprised by his complimentary

69

comment. "Thanks, she's a pretty easy kid to take care of. Tonight's the first time I've ever seen her fired up. She'll usually do anything I ask without complaining. I'm starting to get used to having her around all the time, going with me everywhere like Ron used to when we were kids. I think I would actually miss her if she went to school."

"She has to go to school."

"Yeah, I know," Matty remembered her sad look before she left. "She seemed really upset. I think I'd better go and check on her. Make yourself at home, there's beer in the fridge." Matty quickly got out of the chair and walked to Hallie's room.

He softly knocked on her door. "Hallie, can I come in?"

"Just a minute." Matty heard some faint sounds, but couldn't tell what she was doing. "Come in."

He opened the door and immediately noticed the red, puffiness in her eyes. Her knees were drawn to her chest with her arms wrapped around them. He recognized the position; it was similar to the one from the music store.

"Hey, I didn't mean to upset you." He walked over and sat down next to her. "I'm just trying to do what I think is best for you. I know you're very smart, and I feel you have the potential to do anything you want with your life, but if you don't graduate high school, your opportunities are going to be limited. I'll write Scott and do whatever he says, but I would hate to see you sell yourself short. I also get the feeling there's something you're not telling me. I want you to know, I'm on your side, you can tell me anything. I'll help you in any way I can."

She continued to stare at her comforter.

"Lex and I are going to be hanging out in the family room, you're welcome to come and join us, if you'd like." Matty got up and started to walk out of the room.

"Matty?" She whispered.

He turned around to face her again. "Yes?" He hoped she was ready to talk.

"Thanks," She didn't say anything else; she didn't join them.

Saturday morning, Matty was awakened by the doorbell. He rolled over in bed to look at the clock. Seven a.m., who on earth would be at his house this early? All of his friends knew he worked evenings. Maybe it was a neighbor.

April started to stir. "Go back to sleep," He kissed her cheek. Matty dragged himself out of bed and stumbled half asleep to the door.

He was surprised when he opened it and saw Lex. "You're up early. I thought you never got up before noon. What's going on?" He yawned.

"I want to take Hallie out for the day," He walked into the house.

Oh, this was strange, but whatever. Lex was already knocking on Hallie's bedroom door by the time Matty's brain thought to go and wake her. Matty walked back toward the hall. When he passed Lex, he mumbled. "Lock the door on your way out. I'm going back to bed."

(Lex)

Lex was on a high. His excitement energized him. He took

71

Hallie to a coffeehouse to get some breakfast, but wouldn't tell her where they were going or what they were doing. Lex loved surprises; he could tell Hallie was intrigued. After breakfast, he drove her over to a high school and stopped out front.

"What're we doing here?"

Now to put his plan into action. "I have a proposition for you. Inside that building they're holding an SAT testing session. I want you to go and take the test."

Her eyebrows wrinkled. "Why?" She was not enthused. "The SAT is for people going to college. Scott can't afford for me to go. Taking the test will be a waste of time. We've already been through this."

Lex studied her, trying to read her. "You know, you don't need to have money to go to college. If you do well on the test, you can go to college for free on scholarship."

"Really?" Her eyes widened.

Yes! Her interest was peaked.

"I could go to college for free. How?"

"Colleges want really intelligent people to attend their school. If you demonstrate you're really smart, they'll pay for you to go. Matty went to Yale on a scholarship. I think you have a chance of getting one too. I'm willing to pay for you to take the test."

Now to entice her, he pulled out his wallet. "I'll give you a $100 bill if you go in there and give it a shot." Lex held out the bill for her to see hoping she would take the bait. "What do you think?"

Hallie was silent staring at the building.

Lex anxiously waited for her response.

72

"Alright, I'll do it."

"Great! Let's go get you checked in."

He happily took her into the building. He was hoping she would take the test and realize she needed to go to high school; she didn't know it all.

After he got her signed in, he turned to her and said. "I'll be back in a couple of hours, just meet me out front. Good Luck."

Hallie smiled and suddenly hugged him. He wrapped his arms around her, enjoying the embrace. "Thanks, Lex," She gave him a quick kiss on the cheek before bouncing into the testing room.

Lex was thrilled. Not only was she going to take the test, but there was something about her kiss he enjoyed. It lingered on his cheek as he headed back to the car.

A couple of hours later, Lex was sitting in his Porsche, drinking coffee, and reading the news on his phone when he noticed kids starting to leave the building. He periodically looked up for Hallie, but didn't see her. After a while, he became concerned when the trickle of kids stopped. He looked at his watch. *The test should be over by now.*

Lex got out of the car and wandered into the school. He went to the room where he'd left her and inquired. Lex was surprised when he was told she left early.

He went back outside, still mulling over what the proctor said. *Why would she leave the test early?* And more importantly, *where was she now?*

Lex decided to walk around the school grounds, figuring she couldn't have gone far. He eventually saw her sitting on a two foot tall brick wall. Her knees were tucked up to her chest; and her head was buried into her legs with her arms wrapped over the top of her head. It was obvious she was crying.

He immediately felt guilty. *It must have been too hard for her. I didn't mean to upset her. Maybe Matty was right, it's better not to push her.*

Lex walked over to Hallie not knowing what to say. "Hey, I've been looking for you. The proctor said you left early. What happened?"

Hallie looked up at him with tears streaming down her face. "I blew it. I blew my only chance to go to college. I got one of the questions wrong. The correct answer wasn't one of the choices.

"I've never had a chance like this. For the first time in my life I actually let myself believe I could go to college and be smart like everyone else. But I blew it. I got one wrong. I won't get a scholarship, and I won't go to college." She became so choked up, she buried her head back into her knees, sobbing.

Lex started to wrap his arms around her in an attempt to give her a hug. She immediately dropped her knees and grabbed hold of him tightly, sobbing into his shirt. He patted her back. "Hey, hey, hey, it's alright."

He needed to think of something to make her feel better, anything to make her stop crying. Lex couldn't pinpoint why, but seeing her so upset really bothered him. "First off, they always put questions on the test that have no correct answer. They use practice questions to see how many people answer them a certain way, so I bet the question was one of those. Those questions aren't scored. Second, there are lots of different scholarships out there. I can help you find one. And you can take the SAT as many times as you like. I'll pay for the test. So you see, you didn't blow your chance to go to college. We'll find a way for you to go."

Hallie pulled slightly away from his chest and looked up at

him with her puffy, red eyes. "Really? I can still go to college."

"Really," He smiled at her and used his thumbs to wipe the tears off both her cheeks like a windshield wiper wipes away the rain. "What do you say we get out of here, grab some lunch, and discuss how you're going to spend your $100 bill?"

Hallie shook her head in agreement and climbed down off the wall. As they were walking back to the car Lex was still thinking about something she said. "So, you only missed one, huh?" He playfully messed up her hair. "I'm pretty impressed."

He didn't mention he felt it was pretty much impossible for a sixteen-year-old high school dropout to score that well. He was a graduate of one of the best boarding schools in England, and while his score had been good enough to get him into Yale, it wasn't close to perfect.

At lunch, Lex told Hallie there was a stipulation on the money; she must spend it that afternoon and he got to come along and watch for fun. He hoped this would help her forget about the test. A hundred dollars was not much money, Lex figured it would take her all afternoon to decide what to purchase.

"How many cars do you own?"

"Six, why?" He was intrigued by her question.

"Can we take your least expensive one this afternoon?"

"Sure, we can take the Porsche." Lex was curious by this strange request.

"That's a really nice car. It's your least expensive?"

"I like expensive cars, especially super cars. The Porsche is a 911 Turbo." Lex could tell by the blank look on her face she didn't know what that meant. He made another note in his mental file for her, *teach her about cars.* "Can I ask why?"

75

"I just think it would be the smart thing to do." She responded apparently deep in thought.

Lex was already driving the blue Porsche, so they were able to start shopping right away. Hallie provided the directions Lex followed. When she told him to pull into a McDonald's, he was surprised. "We just ate. Are you hungry again?"

Hallie flashed him a smile. "You're gonna have to come in and find out."

Lex laughed. He was filled with curiosity as he watched her purchase five $20 gift cards. She refused to tell him what she was going to do next, but started giving driving directions again. Lex was having fun playing her little game and was delighted to see her smiling and laughing again. *Wow! What a great smile!*

He became even more curious when he read the signs saying they were entering Riverside. Hallie never talked about her past; Lex felt privileged she was taking him to where she used to live. He was dying to know about her former life, but Matty advised they not press her about it; let her share when she was ready.

Despite being excited, Lex felt very strange and out of place, uncomfortable, as he looked at the rundown buildings covered with graffiti. He knew places like this existed, but this was his first time seeing one in person.

"Lock the doors." She suddenly told him.

He knew that was a bad sign. Something inside of him told him to turn the car around and leave, flee immediately. This was a dangerous place; a place he shouldn't be.

But Lex was *so* curious. "So, this is where you used to live?" He asked hoping Hallie would start gushing information about her life.

"Yeah, turn right at the next light." There was a serious look on her face.

Her manner suddenly made him think. "Is this also where your uncle lives?"

"We're gonna be careful."

"Are you sure this is a good idea?"

"Pull over."

Lex parallel parked and noticed her taking a moment to look around before she said. "Let's go."

He grabbed her arm, his instincts were screaming for him to get out of there. "Where exactly are we going?"

"To see some friends of mine, I promise we won't stay long. I know this isn't your type of place." She looked nervous.

"Is everything alright?"

"Yeah, it's great. You said you wanted to watch me spend my money, so come on. We should hurry."

Hallie quickly got out of the car and crossed the street. She turned back and motioned for him to come with her. Lex debated for a moment if he was really going to leave the security of his car. He wanted to know about her; this might be his only chance. Before he could change his mind, Lex quickly got out and followed Hallie across the street and into an alley.

What she did next completely surprised him. She started talking to some winos and handing them the McDonald's gift cards. She hugged each one of them. The sparkle in her eyes was stunning. Lex thought she looked happy, truly happy.

He listened as she explained to each person the card was

money for food. She stressed the word food each time and told them to go eat.

There was one person lying on the street who Hallie sat down next to and put their head in her lap. Lex walked closer and noticed it was a woman dressed as poorly as Hallie was the day he found her. "Essie, Essie, wake up. It's me, Ann. I've brought you some money for food."

The woman opened her eyes. "Ann, is that really you?" The woman's voice was weak, strained. "You look like an angel."

Hallie gently brushed the dirty, dark hair off the woman's face. "You're burning up." The sparkle was suddenly gone from her beautiful, blue eyes. "I need to get you to the hospital."

"Don't waste your energy, child. It's too late for me now. I'm just glad I got to see you one more time." The woman closed her eyes again.

"Don't talk like that. I'm not gonna let you die. Lex, call an ambulance!"

He fumbled in his pocket to get out his cell phone.

"Essie, Essie!" Hallie looked panicked. She grabbed hold of Essie's wrist to check for a pulse. A moment later, she checked Essie's neck and then placed her ear to Essie's mouth to feel for a breath. Lex was about to dial 9-1-1 when he saw Hallie hug the woman and heard her say. "Now you're at peace. I hope your next life is better than this one." It all happened so fast. The woman was dead.

Hallie got up and turned to Lex with a blank look on her face. "We need to leave." Her voice was as hollow as her look.

Lex started following her back up the alley. He was stunned. She stopped to talk to the ragged, drunk man whom she talked with when they first arrived. "Here, Harry," she handed him another gift card. "Essie can't use this anymore. You go and get some hot food and stay healthy, alright?"

There was no emotion on Hallie's face.

As they approached the end of the alley, Lex noticed several guys walking around the Porsche, checking it out. "Hey, get away from my car!" It was a gut reaction Lex immediately realized might not have been a good choice. There were now three pairs of hostile eyes staring at him. The men were wearing sleeveless shirts displaying their bulging muscles.

Lex quickly glanced at Hallie. The terrified look on her face told him they were in trouble. Lex felt her grab hold of his arm, pulling at him to move back toward the alley.

"Yo man, if it ain't a couple of rich folks on my turf," Responded one of the men. "Why don't you hand over your wallet, watch, and the keys to this fine car, and I'll go easy on your lady when I make love to her."

!!!!

Riverside

(Lex)

"Think again, Ramon," A large, muscular, black man suddenly said. Lex noticed he was pointing a gun at the other guy. "Ann's my girl, and anything she brings home to Daddy, belongs to me. So, you can just move away from my car, or I'll blow your fucking brains out."

What? His girl? Was he a pimp? Lex looked at Hallie; he was furious. After everything he'd done for her, she'd lured him to Riverside to be mugged, no probably killed.

"Relax, man, I didn't know this was your bitch. There's no need to get all hostile on me." The guys around the car slowly started backing down the street.

"Bring Rich Boy over here." The man called to Hallie.

She hesitated.

"Now Ann, or I'll blow him away."

Hallie put her hand on Lex's arm and quickly walked him over to the man. He grabbed her around the neck placing her in a choke hold. "Get in the car, Rich Boy, we're goin' for a drive."

Lex looked at Hallie with disgust. *What's she gotten me into? The first time I've ever tried to help someone and look where it's gotten me, dead.* Lex followed the guy's directions; what other choice did he have? Even if he could've somehow jumped into his car and flown away, he wouldn't have. A part of him still needed to save *her*. He couldn't leave her.

The man got into the passenger side with his arm still around

Hallie's neck. She was forced to sit down on his lap. "Drive."

Lex pulled the car away from the curb.

"Tyler, please, put down the gun and don't hurt Lex. He was just tryin' to help me out, that's all. Please, please, put the gun down." Her body began to shake.

Tyler removed his arm from around her neck and tucked the gun into his pants. "Relax, kid." His soft tone surprised Lex. "Take some deep breaths and calm down. I needed to make it look convincin' to those other guys. You'd gotten yourself into some serious trouble back there. You've known me long enough to know I won't hurt you. I wouldn't do that to Scott. Turn left.

"Tell me, what the *hell* are you doin' back in Riverside? I drove you to Long Beach to get you away from your uncle. What would you have done if he saw you? Huh? He's been askin' 'round tryin' to find you. He's even put a bounty. He's serious, Ann. It seems Child Services has been all up in his business since you left. Also, whata you doin' bringin' some rich boy into town, knowin' he could get his ass kicked? What the *hell* were you thinking?"

Lex was watching them from the corner of his eye, trying to figure out their relationship. So he wasn't her pimp, he was a friend? But if that was true, why was she scared when she saw him, wouldn't she have been relieved he arrived in time to save them? Hallie looked down at the floorboard. "I was bringin' some food money to the homeless winos so they could eat." She whispered.

"Look kid, you have a good heart, but those people are responsible for gettin' themselves into that position. Ain't nothin' you can do to change that. Look at you, you're wearin' nice clothes, ridin' around in a nice car. I almost didn't recognize you. You need to forget this place and never look back. You go on and live the good life, you're due for some good. Turn right. I just have one question for you."

81

"What's that?" She looked up at him.

"How'd you get hooked up?"

She smiled slightly. "One of Scott's buddies in Iraq has a brother in L.A. named Matty. Matty agreed to take me in and let me stay with him until Scott returns. Lex," she said pointing at him, "is one of Matty's friends."

Tyler smiled, shaking his head. "Your brother's always been lookin' out for you. I'm glad somethin' good finally went your way. Pull over to the side." Tyler got out of the car and turned to Ann. "Give me your hand." He pulled a pen out of one of the long, deep pockets in his baggy pants and wrote two phone numbers on her palm. "If you ever get the crazy notion to come to Riverside again, have Rich Boy here hire Domino and me to protect you from your uncle, 'cause he's lookin' to put a world of hurt on you in a father-like way. Don't trust anyone other than me and Dom." He gave her a look when he said that; Lex could tell Hallie knew exactly what he meant. "Give me a moment to pull my car out and I'll follow you out of town to make sure there's no other trouble."

"Thanks, Tyler."

"Yeah, yeah, tell Scott he owes me one."

They rode for awhile in silence. It didn't bother Lex; he needed time to think through the events of the day. Everything happened so fast. He was exhausted. Maybe it was the intensity of Riverside or the fact he'd only gotten four hours of sleep; maybe it was the combination of the two. Despite being tired, his mind was racing. He was trying to make sense of it all, like trying to put together a puzzle without all the pieces; there were many unexplained holes.

Lex glanced at Hallie; she was staring emotionless out the

82

window. "You okay?"

"Fine," she shrugged him off.

"I don't understand something. Why did you go to the trouble of purchasing McDonald's gift cards instead of just giving them the money? Wouldn't it have been more helpful for them to have cash?"

"They're addicted to booze. It doesn't matter how hungry they are, if you give them cash, they'll just buy more alcohol. If you give them anything else, they'll try to sell it for money to buy alcohol. It would be difficult for them to convince someone to purchase the gift card, so they'd have no choice but to buy food with it. They need to eat."

Lex reflected on this for a moment. What she said seemed to make sense; one hole was filled. "The woman who died, Essie, who was she?"

She remained silent, continuing to blankly stare out the window.

"Hallie, who was she?"

She didn't answer.

This irritated him. "Given what happened to us, you should at least answer my question. I just risked my life for you to bring a meager twenty dollars to the person. I want to know who she was. You owe me that."

"The closest thing I ever had to a real mom," She quietly answered empty, hollow.

Lex glanced over at her, speechless.

"Look, I'm really sorry I took you to Riverside. You could've been hurt. It was a stupid thing for me to do. Can we forget it ever happened? I don't wanna talk about it anymore." Hallie pulled her legs up to her chest and wrapped her arms around them as she continued to stare emotionlessly out the window.

Lex was clueless how to respond. Suddenly, filling the holes was no longer important. He was fine driving the rest of the way back in silence. He was still in shock over what happened to them that afternoon, and was completely unprepared for Hallie's answer.

Somehow, *he'd* hurt her. If he'd stayed out of her business, if he'd not taken her to take the SAT and bribed her; she wouldn't have gone to Riverside, almost gotten them killed, and most importantly, he now realized, she wouldn't have had someone she cared about die in her arms. It was mind boggling.

Lex stopped at a restaurant for them to get some dinner. Hallie hardly spoke through the entire meal, just stared at her plate and picked at her food. It wasn't like the time he'd taken her out and she was trying to figure out how to use the utensils; this time she looked empty, dead. When she got up to go to the restroom, an idea popped into his head as to how to make her feel better. He made a call on his cell phone. "Hey, it's Lex. Would it be possible for me to schedule an appointment tonight for two?"

"Hang on a minute, let me see if Connie can stay late…That'll be fine. What time should we expect you?" Responded the sultry voice on the other end.

"In about half an hour."

A short while later he pulled up in front of the closed

business. He told Hallie it was necessary for her to come with him. They got out of the car and walked over to the front door. The lights were off. Lex knocked on the door; a woman came to unlock it. "Come on in," She was delighted to see him.

"Hey, Barb, thanks for staying late."

"Anything for you, you know that."

Lex turned to Hallie. "Head down the hallway. Connie will tell you what to do."

Once Hallie was gone, Barbara commented. "She's a little young for you, don't you think?"

Lex chuckled. "A friend of hers died earlier today. I thought this might make her feel better."

"Aw, how terrible for her, but aren't you sweet for helping." Barbara placed her arms around Lex's shoulders and kissed him on the back of the neck.

Good ol' Barbara; he could always count on her to try to seduce him. "Will you let Connie know what's going on and tell her to give Hallie extra special treatment?"

"Sure thing, now let's go get you naked," She gave Lex a seductive smile; he laughed. Lex liked to be seduced.

A few minutes later, Lex was standing in the hallway wearing a bathrobe and talking to Hallie through a door. "It's alright. You're supposed to get naked. You can't do it with your clothes on. Look, I'll be right there with you. There's nothing to worry about. Now, please get undressed."

(Hallie)

Hallie stood horrified on the other side of the door. She trembled as she tried to keep herself composed. She didn't want to be naked. She didn't want any part of this strange sexual thing he wanted her to do. But how could she escape? If she tried to run, he could grab her and force her to do what he wanted anyway. Hallie leaned her head against the door and pleaded with him. "Lex, I don't wanna do this. Please, just take me back to Matty's."

"You're being ridiculous. I brought you here to relax you."

"I'd be more relaxed with my clothes on." She whimpered.

"No, you won't. You have to take your clothes off." She could hear the frustration in his voice. There was a short pause before he added. "I guess you could leave your panties on if it makes you feel more comfortable."

It did make her feel more comfortable. Hallie closed her eyes for a moment and sighed. She knew there was no way she was getting out of this. She reluctantly took off her clothes, put on a robe, and opened the door. Lex was waiting for her. She slowly walked out of the room keeping her eyes to the floor. She didn't want to think about what might be happening next.

Lex put his hands on both sides of her face caressing it. He gently forced her head up. He noticed the timid look in her eyes when they met his. He smiled at her. "Hey, it's okay." His voice was soft, kind. "You're going to like this. Trust me." He took one of her hands in his and walked her down the hall.

The lights were dimmed down low in the room he took her to. There was a table fountain running. Hallie noticed a pleasant smell in the room and heard soft music playing. Connie gave her instructions on how to lie down on the bed and put the warm sheets over her body. Lex, Connie, and Barbara waited out in the hallway for a moment so Hallie could get situated. *Well, this isn't too bad.*

86

At least I'm covered.

A moment later, everyone else entered the room. Lex quickly got under the sheets of his bed. Hallie stared at the floor and listened until it sounded like he was settled. She lifted her head and looked over to him. He was smiling and talking to Barbara. A few minutes later he looked over to her. "Just relax and let Connie work her magic. You'll feel like a new person when she's done. Close your eyes and focus on the music or the running water, then enjoy the sensation of Connie's hands massaging your body."

Hallie wasn't sure about this, but at least it didn't seem like *he* was going to be touching her which was a good thing. She decided to follow his instructions, closed her eyes, and tried to let her mind relax as the sound of the fountain filled her head. She suddenly felt exhausted.

(Lex)

An hour and a half later, the massage was done. Connie chuckled. "I think she's asleep."

"Hallie, Hallie," She didn't budge. Lex got up off the bed wrapping his body up in the robe and walked over to her. He tried to wake her by shaking her gently, but couldn't. He laughed. "Connie, you really worked your magic, she's out."

"Since she's asleep, can you stay a bit longer?" She loosened his robe and ran her hands up his hairy chest.

"What do you ladies have in mind?" He flirted back knowing exactly what they wanted.

A while later, Lex went to wake Hallie so they could leave. To his surprise, she still was out cold. He asked Connie and Barbara to dress her. Once clothed, he picked her up in his arms

87

remembering the night he found her. Lex thought she looked peaceful and angelic then, and now.

The ladies opened doors for him as he moved toward the car. Once Hallie was strapped in, Lex turned to them. "Thank you, ladies. I'll see you next week." He pulled out his black, leather wallet, paid them, and headed to Matty's house.

In Matty's drive way, he commented. "The whole ride back from Riverside, I kept thinking if we hadn't found her that night, it would've been her. She would've died just like her friend Essie. What does the city do with dead bodies found on the street?"

"I don't know. I guess they try to identify them, find some next of kin. That's probably why Hallie wrote Scott's information on her hands. What an awful situation that must've been for her, having to tag herself for death identification and hoping someone would notify her brother." Matty opened the passenger door and unbuckled Hallie's seatbelt.

"What a terrible way to die, all alone."

"I can't imagine it... Come on, let's get her into bed. If you'll get the doors, I'll carry her."

"I've never seen someone sleep so soundly."

"She's a growing teenager. Don't you remember sleeping a lot as a teen?"

"Yes, but you could wake me." Lex chuckled. "She's completely passed out. It's strange."

"From what you said on the phone, she's had a rough day. She must be exhausted." Matty gently laid her on the bed, took off her shoes, and pulled the sheet up over her.

Lex sighed.

"How are *you* holding up?"

"Tired, I'm glad we didn't have a gig tonight." A thought flickered across Lex's mind. "How do you understand Hallie better than I do?"

"Lex, you've lead a privileged and sheltered life. I haven't, *I* at least went to public school." He grinned. "I might have been raised middle class, but the kids at my school came from all economic backgrounds. I was exposed to lots of things. You, on the other hand, were groomed to socialize with society's elite. If I'm not mistaken, I was the first '*poor*' person you ever met."

Lex laughed. Matty was right.

(Hallie)

The limo pulled over to the side of the road at the Riverside sign. There were two cars waiting to escort it. It took a couple of days, but Lex managed to be allowed to have Essie's body and planned a funeral for her. Hallie wasn't sure what she thought of the whole thing.

First, she'd never been to a funeral. The fanfare seemed silly; getting all dressed up in expensive clothes, having your hair and makeup done, and riding in a limo. Hallie thought they should be attending some red carpet event, not a funeral. Lex had gone all out; it seemed pointless. Essie had nothing; showing up all "riched" up seemed wrong.

Second, death in Riverside was part of everyday life. She'd seen numerous people die or be killed; it was just the way it was. You didn't dwell on it, you moved on; you had to, had to stay on your guard and keep your wits. Those who dwelled or let the pain get to them usually were the next ones to die. They would go on some anger rampage to avenge the death, guns and knives were

89

usually involved. It was always bloody; the violent cycle of death continued.

Third, she forced herself to move away from the black memories starting to surface from the second reason. They would do her no good right now. Third...Third...Lex seemed excited. Hallie couldn't figure him out, but he was beaming. *Why?* Funerals were supposed to be sad.

Fourth, Hallie *was* sad, very sad; and she didn't want to share her sadness with them. They didn't understand. Essie's death hurt, but was not a surprise. However, another thought was hanging around the edges of her consciousness, one that was threatening to rip her heart out and make her fall to pieces. *His* name kept flickering through her mind. It was the memory of *him,* and the time *they* had spent with Essie; their pretend family of three. Her eyes started to water as she fought back the bleak thought entering her mind; *his* funeral.

Lex put his arm around her while handing her a tissue. *Was she crying? Lovely, so much for keeping her emotions to herself.* Hallie took a deep breath forcing herself to focus on the present moment. The limo was slowing to a stop. She glanced out the window; they had arrived at the cemetery.

Suddenly, the door was opened and Charles was motioning for them to exit. Henry, Paul, Matty, and April filed out one by one in their nice, expensive clothes. All purchased by Lex for the occasion. Lex got out of the limo and turned to give her his hand. She took it, stepping out of the car. Hallie then took Lex's arm, letting him lead the way over to the grave site. She didn't want to think, didn't want to feel.

The funeral was short with a minister saying a few words. "Hallie, would like to say anything?" She was stunned; figuring there was something she should say. A large lump suddenly swelled in her throat strangling her voice. Hallie shook her head, 'no.'

Lex kept his arm around her; she knew he was trying to comfort her. She let him.

She needed to give Lex some credit; the grave site was beautiful. Hallie'd never seen so many flowers in one place. While she wasn't an expert on caskets, she was sure this one was as expensive as it was beautiful. The funeral was perfect; Essie deserved to be pampered in the end. Hallie now felt guilty about reason number one.

Lex handed her a beautiful bouquet of flowers and escorted her up to the casket, so she could lay them on top. Hallie imagined Essie wearing a beautiful dress; Lex would not have skimped on that detail. Thanks to Lex, Essie was starting her next life off right.

There were hugs, kisses on the cheek from her friends, and expressions of sympathy whispered into her ear. Hallie's emotions were like a ping pong game. When the ball bounced on one side of the table, she was sad over losing someone she deeply cared about. But then the ball quickly bounced to the other side, and she was happy; happy Essie was being treated so nicely.

"Charles found out your mom and dad are also buried here. I thought you'd like some flowers to place on their grave. I'll walk over with you, if you'd like."

Hallie froze. *What? Her dad?* Instinctively she panicked and started scanning the cemetery. Her eyes met Tyler's; he mouthed the word 'breathe.' She took a deep breath. Tyler was there along with Domino and a handful of his brothers and cousins, a small army assembled who would protect her.

"Hallie?" A concerned whisper from Lex. He suddenly wrapped her up in his arms. "I didn't mean to upset you. I can't imagine how hard this must be for you."

91

Wait, what? "I am upset, but not the way you think. They can rot in hell. Give Essie the flowers, she deserves them more. I don't care to ever visit my parents' grave. I'll never forgive them for what they did." It came out harsh and blunt, but it was the honest truth.

"Okay," Lex was confused. Hallie hoped she hadn't hurt his feelings, but *her* feelings about her parents were deeply rooted. She was happy *they* were dead.

Matty walked over and gave her a big, comforting hug. Lex took the opportunity to place the additional flowers on Essie's grave. While he was walking back to them he said. "It's a beautiful day, let's go do something fun. Hallie, have you ever been sailing?"

"I've never been on a boat."

"Then it's settled. Charles, call the docks and have them get my Hinckley ready."

Matty interrupted him. "Lex, we're not exactly dressed to go boating."

"That's alright, we'll just stop and buy some clothes along the way. Charles, we're going to need to hit a clothing store for boating clothes and swimsuits. We're also going to need food and drinks, get someone at the dock house to pull together a catered lunch for us. Hallie, what would you like to eat?"

"Anything will be fine."

Lex was barking orders again. His world was so different from hers. "Alright, Charles, have them put together a seafood variety, calamari, shrimp, salmon, and get some fried crab claws, I know Hallie likes those." Lex got behind her and took her hands moving them like she was driving. "Hal, you're going to love sailing, the wind in your hair, the smell of sea air. I'll even teach you how to sail the boat. Would you like that?"

92

"Sounds great." She tried to sound excited. She couldn't damper his enthusiasm, not after what he'd done for Essie.

Matty suggested Lex go tell everyone else what the plans were. "He means well and is trying to cheer you up. He's never known anyone to die and insisted Charles teach him the proper etiquette and protocols. He must have forgotten to inquire about what people do after a funeral." Matty smiled. "How are you holding up?"

"Fine." It was true. However, she did feel a bit numb; too many emotions running through her body.

"Anytime you feel like talking, I'm here to listen."

Hallie nodded her head, understanding.

Matty patted her back. "We'll leave whenever you're ready."

She watched as he walked over to where everyone else was standing and talking; providing her an opportunity to be alone for a moment.

"Yo, Ann, sorry 'bout your friend," Tyler and Domino walked over.

"Not the first person in my life to leave me," She didn't have to put on a show for them.

"The people you're with seem like nice folks," Domino was staring at her. "They have you all dolled up. You look ... stunning, if that's the right word, nothin' like the street kid I've known for years."

Hallie glanced down at her clothes. She hadn't paid attention to what Lex picked out. She was wearing an exquisite black gown that showed off her soft, white arms. Two strands of pearls hung around her neck; she felt pearl earrings dangling from her ears. She mused; definitely not Riverside attire. It felt strange to have her new life and her old life come together like this.

93

"Those things real?"

"Probably," She shrugged.

"They treatin' you alright, I mean, besides the fancy duds and cars?"

"Yeah, they're great. Lex called you?"

"Sure did," Tyler grinned. "You must mean something to him for what he's paying us to protect you."

"You're protecting all of us, not just me. I think our trip into town the other day really freaked him out, he's never been anyplace like it. I don't think he knew places like Riverside existed."

"Must be nice to live such a charmed life. I heard you're goin' sailing this afternoon. You probably should go on now. My take on Rich Boy is he always gets his way and doesn't like to wait."

"You're right," She sighed, not really in the mood to have Lex teach her something new. "Take care, stay safe."

Hallie turned and walked over to Lex informing him she was ready to leave.

The following morning, Matty drove Hallie to Lex's condo to drop her off.

As they rode, she remembered the night she'd gone dancing; and she slept at Lex's. He owned the entire building and rented out apartments on all the floors except the top which was his private penthouse. The building was six stories high with the garage in the basement. The garage was gated with another gate inside. This was where Lex kept his cars, separate and locked up

94

from his tenants. Hallie wondered which car they would be taking today.

"What're we doin'?"

"I don't know, but I'm sure it will be more fun than going to the dentist with me."

Hallie thought about the top floor. There was a hallway with several doors, only two lead to residences, Lex's and Charles's. The other doors contained storage rooms.

Lex had explained, "I gutted the entire floor and redesigned the space to my specific requirements."

The inside of Lex's condo was intimidating. Hallie was afraid to touch any of his sculptures. The foyer contained the largest one which greeted her when she entered. It was taller than she was and of nothing in particular.   All his sculptures were like that, but Hallie figured they cost a lot more than nothing.

"It's modern art, very chic." Lex had commented.

"Very bizarre."   Hallie had thought.

The foyer opened to the right and behind the sculpture display wall, was the large living room. What caught her attention were the two sofas and coffee table facing a large painting on the wall. Hallie thought something seemed off. The following morning, she learned the painting rotated to reveal the largest flat screen T.V. she'd ever seen. Now the room made sense.

If the painting hung due north and the foyer wall was due south, the east wall contained paintings, bookcases, and a door.

"That leads to Charles's condo. It's an inside door, so he doesn't have to go through the hassle of coming in the front door all the time and dealing with the alarm system; both our units are wired together."

On the north wall to the left of the painting was a hallway which led to the bedrooms. Lex designed his condo with two master suites; one on the left and one on the right. The one on the left was the guest bedroom which had large windows on the far wall. This was where Hallie had slept. She remembered being amazed the bathroom seemed to be as big as the bedroom.

The door to Lex's room was further down the hallway. Hallie was surprised there were no windows in his room.

"That's why it's such a good room for sleeping. I usually don't get up before noon."

His bathroom was located behind the bedroom, where there were windows.

The west wall of the living room was all windows. Centered perfectly in front of them was a stunning, white, baby grand piano.

"I've been playing since I was four."

To the southwest was the room containing the kitchen. Its design surprised her. There were plenty of counters and cooking space, but not much eating room. She figured this was because Lex was single. There were four bar stools tucked up under one end of the counter where it was raised higher than the rest. The only other place to eat was at the small table for two, which was located next to a window.

Matty stopped the car; Hallie noticed she was at the building. She told him 'good-bye' and headed to the front door, swiping the security key to unlock it. Once inside the building, she walked down the hallway to the elevator. She pulled the special key out of her pocket as she stepped inside and activated the top floor. Only certain people had a key to get to his level. Hallie remembered how special he made her feel when he gave her one.

She rang the doorbell and was greeted by Charles. "Good

morning, Ms. Hallie. How are you today?"

Charles was so delightful; Hallie couldn't help but grin at him. "I'm great, how are you?"

"Wonderful. Did you get some breakfast?"

"I ate at Matty's."

"Lex is waiting for you in the living room."

Hallie followed Charles and was surprised to see a nicely dressed African American woman. *Who was she?*

It was like he could read her mind. Lex stood up and said. "Hallie, I'd like for you to meet Mrs. Donald. She's a school teacher who came to assess which grade you should be in."

Hallie was immediately furious. *What? What part of no school did he* not *comprehend?*

Drop it, please

"Lex, I told you I wasn't going to school. You don't listen. I'm calling Matty and leaving."

"Wait, hear me out. What about your future? You were interested in going to college. When you *do* decide to go back to school and let me help you, you're going to need some documentation, the results of today's assessments."

(Lex)

"I must admit, in all my years of tutoring, I've never come across a student like her." Mrs. Donald told Lex as they sat in the living room later that afternoon.

"That bad, huh?" Lex was smug; his suspicions were correct. Hallie was low educated.

"Quite the contrary, she's gifted."

Gifted? "What does that mean?"

"She's really smart."

"Like some type of genius?" Lex glanced over toward the kitchen where he knew Hallie was with Charles, who was fixing her a snack.

"She has the potential, yes. She has a high IQ, one hundred-sixty-five to be exact, which puts her in the top two percent. I gave her the high school equivalency exam, she received a perfect score. She also received a perfect score on all the other assessments I gave covering the subject matters taught in high school."

Hallie was smart? Perfect scores on all the tests? Really?
"So, what you're saying is when she told me she only missed one
question on the SAT, she was telling the truth?" Lex was mystified.

The woman smiled. "Well, only her test scores can confirm
that, but I'm sure she did well. What's even more amazing is she's
completely self taught. She loves to learn."

"Then why won't she go to school?" Lex was in disbelief.

"There are several possible reasons. First, she may be
bored. A brain like hers needs to be constantly challenged, the
pace at her old school might not have been rigorous enough for her.
You see, it's easy for a school to determine which students are
falling behind and need help, because it's reflected in the student's
test scores. However, sometimes gifted students go unnoticed,
especially those who are very quiet like Hallie."

Interesting. "So, instead of going to a regular high school, I
need to be looking for a private school designed to teach gifted
students?"

"That's one idea. However, I would recommend you do one
more thing before enrolling her. Now, I'm not an expert in
psychology, but I feel I ought to tell you I noticed some reactions
that are not, how should I put this, not typical of someone who loves
to learn." Mrs. Donald looked hesitant. "I don't want to make any
assumptions..."

"Say what you're thinking. I hired you to know your gut,
instinctive reaction to her."

"Alright, I think she's scared to go to school. I think you
could enroll her in the best school in the country, and she wouldn't
go, because she's terrified whatever happened before will happen
again. Until you figure out and fix the psychological component, I

don't think you should be forcing her to go anywhere.

"Now, that doesn't mean you can't be furthering her education. I would recommend you take her to one of the used bookstores in town which also buys back college textbooks and let her pick out some books of interest to her. She needs to be doing college level material, she'll naturally teach herself, because it'll be challenging to her. If you'd like, I can also start coming once a week, to offer her some direction and to further challenge her."

Lex was a bit stunned. *College level at sixteen?* Matty *had* made a comment she knew all but the pop culture answers to the Jeopardy questions. So... she was really smart, a possible genius. "Alright, let's do it." He smiled at the teacher and made arrangements for her to come back the following week. He wanted Hallie to get an education and if it meant having her home schooled for the time being; then that was what he was going to do.

After Mrs. Donald left, Lex wandered into the kitchen. Hallie was sitting on one of the bar stools. She scowled at him. Lex tried to change her mood. "I've just been told you received a perfect score on a test which allows you to graduate high school. Congratulations! I've also been told you're a genius who needs college level material. Mrs. Donald's going to come back next week, so you can be home schooled since we can't enroll you in college right now. So... how would you like to go to the bookstore to get some college books?"

Lex grinned at her skeptical expression. "Seriously, no more trying to force me to go back to high school?"

"Seriously, no more going *to* school."

Lex took Hallie to a bookstore and was intrigued by what she picked out, especially the high level mathematics books. He noticed how excited she was, talking more than she normally did, there was a sparkle in her eyes.

Before, she was just this poor, street kid who he wanted to help, because he believed she didn't have the intelligence to help herself. But now, knowing she was really smart, Lex was starting to look at her in a new light, like he was meeting her for the first time. She was an intelligent and beautiful young lady.

(Hallie)

Several days later, Hallie found herself sitting in the passenger seat of Lex's red Ferrari. Now he was furious with her. "I brought you here so you could get some help. Why on earth would you not speak for the entire hour?"

Hallie stared at the floorboard trying to keep her body under control. "Please take me back to Matty's house."

"So, that's all you're going to say. You're not going to tell me why you wasted that lady's time and my money."

She pulled her legs up to her chest and wrapped her arms around them. Hallie kept silent, gritting her teeth and focusing all her energy on breathing at an even beat.

Lex finally turned on the car and backed out of the parking space. "You know, I'm trying to help you. I don't understand why you don't want to be helped. I'm sure any other kid off the street would be thrilled to have someone like me paying for all their things."

Hallie felt the sting of the insult. As soon as they arrived at Matty's house, she asked Lex to wait a moment before leaving. She went into her room and quickly gathered up as much as she could hold in her arms. She took the laptop, radio, iPod, as well as an armful of clothes and carried them out into the family room handing them to Lex.

101

"I'm sorry I've been so much of a burden to you. I never meant to be. I'll make sure you get all your things back. Most of the clothes still have the tags on them, so you can return them to the store. Hopefully you can get enough back to pay for the appointment today. If not, let me know, and I'll pay you back as soon as I can."

"What are you doing?"

"Giving you your things back. Please don't buy me anything else. I don't need this. All I need is Scott."

"You're being ridiculous. Scott doesn't send enough money for you to have nice things like these. You need my help."

"I know how much Scott's sending, and it's enough to pay for my food and help Matty with the rent. It's plenty. As long as I have Scott, I don't need anything else."

"You need more than food and a place to stay, Hallie." Lex was glaring at her. "I'm your ticket to buying you anything. And you're just going to throw it away? You need me."

"You're wrong! I only need Scott's love. I can go days without eating and weeks without shelter as long as I have him. The money Scott's sending is more than enough. I don't want you buying me anything else."

Hallie quickly turned and walked back out of the room. She couldn't look at his face; she must stay numb and hard to trap the hurt from breaking her down.

"What's going on?" She heard Matty ask.

"I don't know," Lex responded defensively. "She wouldn't talk to the therapist. You know, I would think someone as poor as she is would be delighted to have someone as rich as me helping her out, but do I get any appreciation? No."

"Please tell me you didn't say that to her," Matty's soft voice sounded worried.

"Of course I did. It's the truth."

"So, you didn't think for a moment saying something like that might be hurtful to her?"

"How's that hurting her?"

"Lex, you threw her poverty in her face. You basically told her you're somebody, but she's nobody. That hurts."

Matty was right; it did hurt. But, Lex was right as well. *He* was somebody; and *she* was nobody. It was the first time Lex intentionally treated her like the trash she knew she was.

Hallie took another deep breath to steady herself as she entered the room again with her arms full of more things including the books Lex recently bought her. She placed it all on the sofa. "Did you buy the bedding as well?"

"Stop!" Lex yelled.

Hallie froze, cowering. He was standing right next to her.

"I don't want these things!" His voice boomed into her ears. "They're yours to keep! Put them back in your room!"

Matty was quickly in front of her, his arms lovingly wrapped around her. It reminded her of Scott's protective grip and made her miss him even more. She soaked up every ounce of his protective touch leaning her head into his chest, and felt relief knowing his body created a barrier between Lex and her. In a calm, soft tone he spoke. "Why didn't you talk to the therapist?"

Hallie lifted her head to glance up at him. His expression told her he saw the pain in her eyes. She quickly looked away and quietly said. "Because I'm a runaway. The therapist might say everything's confidential, but it isn't. If I'd said anything about my past, Child Services would've been there taking me back to Riverside and to my uncle. Lex probably would've been arrested, because I'm a minor and he's an adult male, they might've assumed he was doing inappropriate things with me. *Me* talking would've messed up both of our lives."

"You were protecting me?" Lex was dumbfounded. "Why didn't you tell me that in the parking lot?"

"I couldn't risk someone overhearing our conversation. The top was down on the car...Look, I know you're trying to help, but please stop." Hallie pulled herself free of Matty's protection and turned to walk back toward her room.

"Hal, wait," Lex called out. "These things belong in your room. I'll help you put them back." He followed her with an armful.

(Lex)

Lex studied her. Her behaviors were different. Every time he came close to her, she seemed timid of him. It didn't make sense.

As he meticulously put her clothes away, he thought back over their argument. No one ever argued with him. And while her tone wasn't aggressive, he didn't miss the fierce intensity in her eyes when she told him all she needed was Scott. While there was something refreshing about her passion and honesty; he was also baffled. He knew money bought everything he needed. He didn't have love and got along just fine without it. How could love be more important than money?

The following afternoon, Matty showed up at Paul's so the

band could practice. "You look like hell."

"I didn't get a lot of sleep," He yawned. "Hallie was having some terrible nightmares, screaming again. It reminded me of that night she had in the hospital. I think what happened yesterday must have stirred up a lot of bad memories."

"Is she alright?" Lex was concerned remembering how tormented she'd looked in the hospital.

"I guess so, she asked to go for a walk when we got here… Look, I know all you want to do is help her, *I* want to help her too, but I think we should let things slide for right now. No more talk about school or therapy or anything else. I think she's been through alot and could use some time getting comfortable with us. It would also be a good idea for you to not yell at her anymore."

"Alright…tell you what, I'll make it up to both of you. Let's all go to The Lake for a few days, my treat."

(Hallie)

Four days later Hallie found herself at a lake in Utah. Since it was early November, Lex took them to a geothermal lake. Everyone came on the trip except Charles, who was taking care of some things in L.A. At lunch, Lex suggested they all go swimming down by the dock. Hallie was less than thrilled. She didn't want to go swimming. How was she going to play along with him just enough so he felt like he was getting his way, but at the same time do what she wanted?

Hallie was in her room changing, thinking about the terrifying hurdle this past September of starting to wear shorts and T-shirts, exposing so much skin. Lex was insistent on it, purchasing only those types of clothes and being very irritated when she didn't wear what he bought.

105

She swallowed hard as she stared at the bikini she was now expected to wear.

Hallie decided the best approach was to change quickly. She pulled out the swimsuit and put it on, inspecting herself in the mirror. Despite the fact it fit her perfectly, Hallie's stomach turned. The bikini revealed practically everything. She might as well have been standing in the room naked. As she looked in the mirror, she came face to face with the shame she wore; the ugly, purple mark on her chest which was completely exposed. Hallie tugged at her swimsuit to try to cover it up, but couldn't.

There was a reason why she never dressed in front of a mirror, because if she didn't see it, then it was easier to pretend it didn't exist. Fighting the instinct to immediately cover it up, she slowly turned around and examined the other purple mark she wore on her back. The thin string of the bikini did nothing to hide the neon sign. Panic started to set in; she couldn't go through with this.

A plan, a plan, what can I do? Hallie played with her fingers as she looked around the room. *Makeup, of course*, she hurried into the bathroom and pulled out her concealer. Hallie knew she needed to hurry. Lex could knock on her door at any moment. As she started brushing it on, she quickly became horrified, the more she brushed, the more messed up it looked. She wanted to scream.

Hallie grabbed her liquid foundation, squeezing out a large glob. She smeared the foundation all over her mark. She looked in the mirror. The mark was partly concealed, but the foundation was darker than her ivory skin. *Crap.* Hallie squished out another glob and started covering her entire chest and stomach. She then moved to her back smearing and globbing wherever she could reach. Spinning around to look in the mirror, Hallie discovered a collage of colors on her back. *Damn!* She needed another plan.

What she really needed was to completely cover up her chest and back. She needed to be wearing a shirt. Hallie dug through the clothes Lex packed hoping to find something which didn't look expensive and could get wet. Of course there was nothing there. *Why can he just let me wear T-shirts?*

Of course, that's it. Hallie quickly put some clothes on over her swimsuit and headed down to the gift shop she'd seen when they arrived that morning, purchased a T-shirt with Matty's emergency money, and raced back up to her room where she discovered the red light blinking on her phone. Lex had headed down to the lake.

Hallie breathed a sigh of relief. She put the new shirt on over her swimsuit with no great speed, grabbed a book, and headed down to the dock to meet everyone else.

The walk was breathtaking. Hallie enjoyed smelling the crisp, fresh air. It smelled like nothing she ever knew; so pure and clean. As she walked along the path leading to the lake, Hallie soaked up every sight and sound. It was her first time being in a forest. She loved how green, lush it looked; a definite change from the city. She stopped suddenly when the lake came into view; the turquoise water was mesmerizing causing her to stare at it for a while. Sunlight glistened on the water. It was so beautiful like something out of a painting.

The sound of laughter broke the hypnotic trance the water held over her. Hallie recognized the voices and smiled. She hurried down the rest of the path anxious to get closer to the enchanting water.

Paul, Henry, and Lex were already swimming in the lake. Matty and April were putting their things down on the dock. "Come on in, the water feels great," Henry told them.

Hallie sat down on the dock dangling her legs over the edge to get her feet wet. The water felt nice and warm against her skin.

"Hallie, how does your new swimsuit fit?" *It didn't take him*

107

long to ask.

"Great, the perfect size for me."

"Take off the T-shirt and let me see it on you."

Absolutely not. "I'll show you later. I'm a little cold right now."

"It's unseasonably warm, you can't be that cold."

"I'll take it off when I'm ready."

It looked like he was going to protest, but something changed his mind. He went back to swimming. Hallie was relieved. She opened her book to pretend to read. She needed a reason for not swimming; however the scenery was distracting.

As the afternoon wore on, Lex grew insistent about seeing the swimsuit on her. Hallie reluctantly realized she wasn't getting out of it. She ran several different scenarios and decided it would be better to show him while he was some distance away in the water than wait until he came to her. At least from a distance, the details of her hideous marks couldn't be seen. Hallie yanked off the shirt, quickly modeled the swimsuit for him, and threw the shirt back on.

"It looks good on you."

"Hey, Hallie," Paul playfully called out from the water. "Was that a tattoo on your chest?"

"No," Hallie replied with humiliation. She needed to think of something fast. "It's a birthmark."

"Was that another one on your back?" Henry inquired.

"I have two of them." Hallie dove her head back into her book.

"Stop reading and come swimming," Lex insisted.

Hallie glanced up. "I'm not ready. I have to know what happens next."

Paul suddenly dunked Lex making her laugh and relieving her discomfort.

A few minutes later, Lex climbed up the ladder attached to the dock and walked over to her. She thought he was leaning over to see what she was reading, but instead he suddenly picked her up. "It's time to go for a swim."

"Lex, no, put me down!" She tried to wiggle free of him. *No, No, No, please no!*

"Sure thing," He said as he jumped off the dock with her.

"Lex!" Hallie screamed as they hit the water.

(Lex)

He came up a moment later, chuckling.

"Good one," Henry praised.

They were all laughing. Lex was feeling quite pleased.

"Where's Hallie? She hasn't come up yet." Matty was looking over the edge of the dock.

"What?" Lex was surprised. He started to feel alarmed. "She can swim, right?"

"I don't know," Matty dove into the water.

109

Lex took a deep breath and went under as well. His eyes frantically scanned for her. Each second felt like an eternity as he searched, and the terrifying horror worsened as he realized what he'd done.

Lex finally spotted her down near the bottom of the lake. She was already in Matty's arms, being brought up. Her body wasn't moving.

Lex surfaced and swam over to Matty as fast as he could go. He watched helplessly as Matty wrapped his arm around her chest and swam her lifeless body toward the shore. He was right on Matty's heals as he picked her up and walked up onto the beach. Paul, Henry, and April were by his side. "Is she dead?" He choked out through the strangling grip which now captured his throat. His heart was racing; he couldn't breathe as watched Matty lay her down on the sand and start administering CPR.

Trust

(Hallie)

Hallie felt someone pushing on her chest; it hurt. There was something soft against her skin. She was disoriented. Suddenly, she was violently coughing up water and gasping for air.

"Are you okay?" Matty sounded relieved.

She opened her eyes and realized he was the one pushing. "Yeah, fine," She was startled by her raspy voice. She rolled over on her side to cough up more water. Her throat burned.

"I'm really sorry," Lex was kneeling down next to her. "I didn't know you couldn't swim."

Hallie was instantly furious as she remembered what happened. "How the hell was I supposed to know how to swim? I didn't grow up at some fancy country club. Where was I supposed to have access to water? The only thing around me was asphalt. I asked you to put me down. Why didn't you listen to me?"

"I thought you were teasing. Why didn't you tell me you couldn't swim?"

"Leave me alone," She slowly got up. Her body was covered in shore sand, but she was too upset to care. She felt her shakes starting and wanted to get out of there as fast as possible, so no one would notice and ask her about them. She started walking toward the tree line, to the path which took her back to her room. Everything was a blur.

"Don't leave," Matty softly pleaded. "It was an accident."

111

Feeling horribly embarrassed and trembling at this point, Hallie yelled. "All of you leave me alone!" She then walked right into a tree. "Damn it!" She stepped back and put her hands out to feel it. She ran them along the side of the rough bark to help her navigate around it.

"Here let me help you," She heard Matty's soft voice in her ear. "You lost your contacts in the water, didn't you? And you're blind as a bat without them." Matty gently took hold of her arm.

Hallie snatched it away. "I can take care of myself, thank you." She wasn't really mad at him, just frustrated with herself. If she were in Riverside, she would be able to manage without seeing. She knew every inch of the streets where she used to live, every sound, every smell. She didn't need to be able to see to navigate there. But here, in the middle of a forest, it was impossible. Feeling helpless was a feeling she knew all too well; she hated it.

"I know you can take care of yourself," His voice was soft. "I wasn't trying to imply you couldn't. I'm just worried about the damage you're going to cause the trees if you keep walking into them. Please, for the sake of preserving the beauty of this place, can I walk with you back to your room and get an ice pack for the knot forming on your forehead?"

It was difficult staying angry at Matty's gentle voice. She knew he was just trying to help; and her head did really hurt. She couldn't risk never seeing Scott again, must protect herself. She just wanted to get away from everyone as fast as possible. Between showing her marks, almost drowning, and now shaking; she felt completely humiliated.

"If you think I'm gonna hurt the trees, then I guess you can walk me back, but you're the only one who can come."

He put his arm around her shoulder and ushered her forward. "Boy, you're really shaking. Are you cold?"

"Yes," She lied.

"I'll get you to your room quickly, so you can put some warm clothes on. Earlier, I thought you were making up an excuse not to take off your T-shirt, I didn't imagine you could actually be cold."

"I don't have any body fat," She stated to reinforce her answer.

"I guess you don't, do you," She knew he was smiling. "But I think you're looking better since you got out of the hospital. Your cheeks now have a rosy glow, and you've started gaining weight. You look healthier. It'll just be a matter of time before you have enough weight to provide you with some body fat, so you won't get cold so easily." He was trying to make her feel better. She didn't deserve him.

Hallie heard a knock at the door and grumbled. "Go away."

"It's Lex. Can I come in?"

"Why? You wanna finish the job?"

"That's not funny," He defensively replied. "Will you let me in, please? I want to take you to dinner."

"Why? You want the entire resort to laugh at the blind girl who walked into a tree and now wears a purple ball on her forehead?"

"Nobody's going to laugh at you," His voice was just above a whisper. "Please open the door."

Hallie sighed. *He never gives up. If I don't let him in, he'll probably just get another key and let himself in anyway.* She reluctantly got off the bed and slowly found her way to the door. She unlocked the bolt, cracked open the door, and turned to find her

113

way back to the bed.

She heard the door close and was startled when Lex took her arm. "Let go of me!" She angrily snatched it away from him. "I can take care of myself." She continued to walk with her hands out in front trying to find the bed.

"No, you can't. Why won't you let me help you?"

"Because you almost killed me today."

"That was an accident, and I'm so, so sorry. I'm also sorry I yelled at you the other day when you were protecting me. Hallie, I didn't mean to hurt you; I would never intentionally hurt you. You can trust me."

She couldn't see his face, but he sounded sincere. However, she wasn't about to let him off easy. Trust was something that was earned. "No, I can't."

"Why not?"

Hallie was silent. She found the bed and laid down on her stomach. She wasn't going to have this conversation with him, so she buried her head under her arms. "Go away, please."

"I'm not leaving without an answer. I want to know what I've ever done to make *you* not trust *me*?"

He was so stubborn. She sarcastically replied. "Well, for starters you threw me into a lake when I couldn't swim."

"I didn't know...it was truly an accident," His satiny voice responded full of regret. "Do you really think I would have spent thousands of dollars paying your medical bills if I planned on drowning you today?"

"I guess not," She quietly agreed feeling deflated.

"Alright, so now you trust me?"

She'd asked him numerous times to stop prying into her past, but given his history, she knew he wouldn't. Hallie sighed. The stress of the afternoon already wore her out; she felt too defeated to fight with him. Maybe, if she quietly answered his questions, he would leave her alone to deal with the agony his questions caused. "No," She whispered.

"Why not?"

"Because I can't, that's why."

"That's not a good enough answer. Why can't you trust me?"

Hallie silently contemplated telling him the truth.

"I'm not leaving until you tell me. I can be as stubborn as you are."

The truth was too painful to tell. "It's not you. I can't trust anyone."

"Why not? You trust Matty, don't you?"

"No, I can't. You don't get it, so please just leave me alone." Her voice sounded too sad. The truth, the pain that knowledge released, was starting to crush her.

"Explain it so I do get it."

"Fine." The pain burst from inside. "I can't trust you or anyone else, because there've only been three people in my life who I've ever trusted, and all three of them left me this year. That's why, now leave."

Lex was silent; Hallie wasn't sure if she wanted to see the look on his face or not. Even if she hadn't lost her contacts, she probably wouldn't have been able to anyway. The pain won; she was sobbing into her comforter.

She felt his hand gently rub against her back, through her hair, and eventually across her left cheek. His actions confused her. His lips tenderly touched her skin with a kiss. "I'm sorry," He whispered. "But I'm not going to be one of those people."

Hallie took several deep breaths. "You don't know that and neither do I. How do I know something won't happen tomorrow, and you'll abandon me? If I don't trust you, then I can't get hurt."

Lex suddenly sat her up and clasped her face in his soft hands. He put his face so close to hers their noses were touching. She could feel his warm breath on her lips; it made her body shiver with excitement. She could see clearly into his deep, blue eyes. "I know what it's like to not be able to trust. Most of the people I come in contact with are just trying to use me to get to my money. There are very few people *I* trust. But I promise you, I'll never abandon you or intentionally hurt you. I'm your friend, you can trust me." He released her face and pulled her into his chest, kissing her forehead and rubbing his hand up and down her back.

Hallie was too numb and exhausted to speak, but this felt nice. She wrapped her arms around his chest, clinging onto the hug. She could stay in his arms forever.

Eventually, he pulled away and gently took her hand. "I have something to give you."

"What is it?" She suspiciously asked quickly closing her palm.

"You're going to have to trust me to find out," He was playing.

Hallie's mind was a little clearer; she thought about what he said. She longed to trust him and Matty, but she couldn't. However,

116

she didn't want to hurt his feelings, so she opened her hand and felt the two strange, smooth rectangles with the round bump on one side. "What are they?"

"Your new eyes so you can see," He softly replied.

"Contacts?"

"Your prescription."

"How did you get them so fast?" Hallie was shocked.

"Right after you walked into the tree, I called Charles, told him we had an emergency, and to get the plane here as fast as possible."

Hallie was silent while she processed this information. He was truly amazing.

Lex helped her to the bathroom and with inserting the contacts. "Oh, and there's one more thing I forgot to mention. Charles signed you up for swimming lessons starting on Thursday. He's also working on getting the name of a good plastic surgeon to take a look at your two birthmarks. April got the impression you were uncomfortable showing them. I'll pay to remove them or cover them up, whatever is recommended. And you have an appointment on Friday to see if you qualify for Lasik."

Hallie was stunned. The amazement meter climbed even higher. She couldn't help smiling at him. "Thanks, Lex. That's really nice and generous of you."

"No problem. You forgive me?" He gave her a puppy dog look.

"Yeah," She laughed slightly under her breath. She couldn't stay mad at him when he'd done so many wonderful things for her.

"Great! I'm starved," He smiled. "What do you say we go

join everyone else for dinner?"

"Alright," Hallie grabbed a washcloth to clean her face and try to look presentable. Her eyes were red, tired. She looked terrible.

Lex heard her sigh. He gently kissed her cheek and whispered into her ear. "You look fine." He took the washcloth out of her hand placing it on the counter and wrapped his arm around her shoulders.

As he led her to the door, Hallie leaned her head against his chest and encircled her arms around his waist. She knew he didn't mind, because he gave her a little squeeze. She knew Scott would disapprove, but maybe she *should* let Lex take care of her; his body felt so good against hers.

"Oh, and one other thing," Lex lovingly told her as they started walking down the hallway. "Everyone trusts Matty."

"Hey, our survivor has joined us," Henry teased when they arrived at the table. "Are you going to do any death defying acts tonight at dinner?"

As she sat down, Hallie tried to be polite. "It's really not funny."

"Loosen up Hallie, we're just joking around. That's how we handle life." Paul was grinning. "We're glad you're alright."

Hallie picked up her menu to hide her face. Her brow furrowed in irritation. What happened was not something to joke about. She had almost drowned and had hit her head; very, very dangerous. She was lucky to be alive, again.

While she accomplished hiding her expression from the rest of the table, Matty was sitting next to her and noticed. "What's

118

wrong?"

She put the menu down; she'd been busted. "I don't think almost dying is funny. I've almost died three times this year, and each time when I realized what had happened, it scared the shit out of me. I wonder what's gonna happen next, and if the next time I'll end up in a coffin six feet under."

A silence fell over the table. Hallie knew she ruined their jovial mood.

Henry finally spoke up. "Well, your worries are over. You said you almost died three times, right? So, you're in the clear."

Hallie glanced up, puzzled.

"Don't you know things happen in threes? You had all three events, nothing else will happen now."

"Henry's right," Paul was equally as animated. "Everything always happens in threes, that's the way life works."

Hallie was skeptical and looked over at Matty for confirmation. He was grinning. She couldn't tell if they were all teasing or serious. They joked around a lot which was one of the reasons she enjoyed hanging out with them. Hallie figured they were all trying to make her feel better.

Paul said, "Here, ask the waiter. He'll tell you it's true."

The rest of dinner was very light hearted thanks to Henry and Paul. They seemed to take everything in stride; enjoying life. Hallie wondered what life looked like through their eyes; she imagined rose colored glasses.

After dinner Lex turned to the table and grinned. "Well, I'm off. Don't wait up for me."

Hallie was surprised. *Where was he going?*

"Which one are you going after?" Paul inquired.

"The redhead, she's looking mighty foxy, but to be honest, I don't really care."

What?

Lex left the table and headed over to the red haired lady sitting at the bar.

Paul and Henry commented on his actions like they were sports announcers. "He's on the move...Watch him work it...She's looking at him, checking him out...She looks interested. Come on...Come on... He's buying her a drink...He's in." They discretely exchanged high fives.

"What's he doing?" Hallie was baffled.

Paul happily explained. "Lex is our resident ladies man. The ladies find him irresistible, and Lex loves the ladies. He can charm them right out of their clothes and into his bed."

"He sleeps with them?" Hallie was shocked, appalled.

"Yeah, and gives us all the details in the morning," Henry laughed.

"But how?"

Paul explained Lex's routine. "Charm and money, a woman can smell a man with money a mile away and since Lex has millions, he smells especially ripe. He shows them a good time and then sleeps with them."

"So, he's a male whore," Hallie was now disgusted.

Paul suddenly looked at her with wide eyes and burst out laughing. "I've never thought of it that way, but I guess so. That's a good one. We'll have tease him about it in the morning."

Hallie suddenly felt uncomfortable. "Please don't tell Lex I said that."

"But it's *so* good. We have to share it. I'll tell you what. We won't tell him you said it. Alright?"

Hallie looked over at Matty. "I don't want Lex upset with me."

"Don't worry, he won't be. It's not like he doesn't already know. He's been doing this since before I met him."

"How did you meet?" Her sudden curiosity distracted her.

"We were assigned as roommates our freshman year of college. He had a girl in the room our first night. I couldn't believe it... But all the sex aside, Lex is a good guy."

Hallie looked back at Lex, who was flirting with the red head. What he was doing was sick, wrong, disturbing. She remembered when he came to see her that afternoon, how wonderful it felt to be in his arms. It was like she was thinking about two totally different people. The Lex who had held her would never treat women like a piece of meat. He couldn't, because if he did; she'd have to hate him.

The following morning brought about a lack of sleep caused by the two Lex's who starred in Hallie's dreams. It was actually the same dream which played over and over again in her mind. It started with the good Lex, the one who held her. He was holding her again on the bed, gently rubbing her back. At one point their eyes met; and he leaned in to sweetly kiss her cheek. He then softly and tenderly started kissing her lips. She kissed him back willingly, eager to be close to him. He pulled her body closer to his; his touch felt *so* good. One of his hands held the back of her head.

His kissing grew more intense, causing Hallie to want him even more. It seemed strange, but she couldn't get close enough to him. She hadn't noticed when they took off their clothes, but suddenly they were naked, and he was on top of her putting his penis into...

That's when she woke up screaming in terror.

The dream was extremely disturbing. Before leaving her room for breakfast, Hallie resolved to speak to Lex, to somehow get rid of evil Lex.

She finally saw him around one and asked to speak to him in private. They took a walk; she didn't want to talk in one of their rooms. Lex listened quietly as she expressed her views about his promiscuous behavior which included the treatment of women and sexual safety.

When she finished, he gave her a sweet smile, thanked her for her concern, and told her his dates were using him as much as he was using them; it was a mutual exchange. He also said he was very safe; he always used a condom and never kissed on the lips.

It wasn't the answer she wanted, but it did make some of her more darker thoughts go away. It also didn't help that he hugged her, causing her to once again enjoy the sensation of being in his arms.

It was now mid-November. Hallie was over at the studio in Paul and Henry's basement for a band jam session; this was where they always practiced. The studio was also equipped to record. Lex had spared no expense in designing and filling it with the latest technology. Hallie learned it was another revenue producing venture for him which Paul and Henry mostly profited.

For her, coming to the studio was routine. She was at all their practices here and all their shows in the clubs. "Asterix has their first groupie," Paul beamed one day.

They were working on a new album; today the guys were focused on one song in particular. They couldn't get it to sound quite right in one place.

It seemed strange, because she never had any real musical training, maybe it was because she hung out with them all the time, but somehow Hallie knew exactly what was wrong. She got up off the sofa and walked over to Matty. She pulled him aside. "Can I speak with you in private for a moment?"

"Yeah, sure," He put down his guitar and turned to the guys. "I'll be back in a minute."

He followed her upstairs to the family room sofa. They sat down. "What did you want to talk about? Is everything alright? You look scared."

Hallie hesitated for a moment realizing how easily he could read her face. She wanted to help him, but on their way up the stairs, she had suddenly become afraid of telling him what she knew. She needed to decide if it was worth the risk or not. She took a deep breath and then before she could change her mind, she quickly said. "I know what's wrong with the song."

"You do?" He was surprised. "What do you think it is?"

"I don't know how to explain it. I...I...I can hear it...the correct way... in my head." She started playing with her fingers.

"Oh."

Matty was silent. Hallie anxiously watched his face. He was deep in thought. "Can you sing what you hear?"

A horrible feeling suddenly grabbed her. "I...I don't sing," Her body instantly tensed.

Matty noticed. "Hey, it's alright," He lovingly smiled. "It doesn't matter how you sound, nobody's a perfect singer." He caught her eyes in his. "I promise I won't laugh."

Hallie looked at him thinking about how kind he was to her. Should she trust him? She really wanted to help, but was it worth the risk? "Alright," Her voice was shaking as she sang several lines of the song.

Matty grinned. "Can you do it again to make sure I hear the change?"

Hallie took a deep breath to steady her nerves and sang it again.

The look on Matty's face surprised her. His eyes were wild with excitement. "I think I have it. Can you do me a favor?"

Relief washed over her body. Lex was right, she could trust Matty. "Sure."

"Great, follow my voice and do some scales with me."

Matty ran her though some warm-up routines. Hallie could hear her voice becoming smoother, clearer.

After about fifteen minutes he said. "Alright, now sing the lines again."

Hallie did; an astonished look was in Matty's eyes. He was almost hyper. "I've got it. Come on, let's go back downstairs."

As they walked back into the studio, Matty announced. "I know how to fix the song. Hallie can sing it for you."

The terror seized her hard, fast. "No...I...I can't," Her body started shaking as the memory flooded her mind causing her to lose control.

Matty looked surprised, confused by her reaction. "Why not? You did it upstairs. You have a gorgeous voice, let them hear it."

"I can't," She whispered, instinctively bolting from the room.

Egg

(Matty)

Matty raced after her, puzzled by her strange behavior. He caught her on the stairs. "Hallie, what's wrong?"

She dropped onto the staircase and immediately curled up into a ball. Her breathing was quick, short. He barely heard the answer to his question. "I don't wanna get hit."

Matty was shocked. *She thought we would hit her? Why?*

He sat down next to her dumbfounded for a moment. He glanced over at Hallie; the happy, sweet kid he knew had been replaced by this terrified one. "I'm guessing the reason you don't sing is because the last time you did, someone hit you."

Hallie shook her head in agreement.

"How badly did they hit you?"

"To a pulp, I ended up in the hospital."

"I'm so sorry," He whispered. He needed to comfort her, do something, anything to make her feel better. Matty wrapped his arms around her shoulder.

It felt like someone knocked the wind out of him. *She was beaten for singing?* It was horrible; it broke his heart. And the reason behind it, made it worse. It's not like she'd committed some horrible crime. How could someone do that to this wonderful child?

And what made it worse, was she assumed they would hit her as well. The thought crushed him.

He held her in silence until her breathing was back to normal. Then he dropped his arm wanting to give her some space.

Hallie peeked out from behind her knees to glance over at him.

"You're a very brave person. You risked being hit to help me. Thank you." He sincerely smiled hoping she would come back out of her shell.

She gave him a little smile back.

"Nobody here is going to hit you, *ever*. We'd never do that to you or anyone else. We're professional musicians, we welcome anyone who loves music." He hesitated for a moment, not sure if he should say the next thing or not. "I think you have talent, and I'd like to explore it, if you let me."

Matty put his right hand out in front of her with his palm up hoping she would take it. She slowly, hesitantly, uncurled her ball and took his hand. He hugged her. "You're safe here. I'm not going to let anyone hurt you."

A few minutes later, she released her grip on the hug and softly said, "I'll sing the song for them."

Relief and excitement filled his body. "Thank you."

The first time she sang it; she was very timid. He encouraged her to sing it over and over again having her look at him to help her relax. After awhile, they took a break. He asked Hallie to go upstairs to get drinks for everyone.

While she was out of the room, Paul commented, "She has a great voice. We should start using her in some of our songs. I'd also love to test her in front of an audience and get their reaction to her."

The others agreed realizing the potential Hallie brought to

127

the band. However, Matty cautioned them. "She might not be up for it. We're going to have to ease her into it."

Over the next two months, Matty experimented with Hallie. His biggest challenge was helping her conquer her fear. He also helped her write her first song, which was very different from their usual topics. Even though she never confessed to it, Matty believed it was about some of the abuse she'd suffered and rising above it.

It was now early February. Matty, Paul, and Henry were getting anxious. They were in a back room at Miaotsie. "Have you heard from him today? It's an hour before we go on." The agitation in Paul's voice was clear.

"No," Matty sighed. "I've left several messages."

"Wonderful," Paul grumbled.

A few more tense minutes passed as they continued to get ready to perform. Matty's cell phone rang. "Lex, where are you?" He answered not making any attempt to hide his annoyance.

"Hey," Lex's voice was mumbled. "I don't feel well. I'm....really hungover. I thought I could sleep it off all day. It didn't work. I'm not going to make it. The club will still pay all of you. I've got to go, bye." Matty heard the sudden silence on the phone.

Henry and Paul's wary eyes were staring at him. "He's not coming. He's sick." They understood; it wasn't the first time he'd done this.

But Hallie surprised him. "That's terrible. Whata you think he has? I hope it's nothing serious."

Matty looked at the concern in her eyes, heard it in her

voice. He forced a smile. "It didn't sound too bad. His stomach's upset, and he has a headache. I think he'll be better tomorrow."

Suddenly, an idea flashed through his mind. He blurted it out just as quickly. "Hey Hallie, what do you think about performing in his place tonight?" Matty watched as a stunned expression crossed her face. He coaxed. "You know all of our songs."

"I don't know," She looked distraught.

Matty assessed it as nerves. He exchanged a quick glance with Henry hoping for support.

"You've already done the hard part," Henry caught on. "You've sung for us. The first song's the hardest. The more you sing, the easier it gets."

Paul seemed as excited as the others about this possibility. "Just go out there and have fun. It doesn't have to be perfect. We get paid either way."

"I believe in you." Matty said with a huge smile on his face already convinced she should be the lead singer for their band. "Please...we need your help." He was trying to take advantage of her giving nature. It was the only way he could think to entice her. He poured it on thick. "You'd be a lifesaver."

Matty watched her study all three of their faces. Her face relaxed. "Alright, I'll help you."

"Yes!" Matty grabbed her into a hug as he exploded with excitement. Hallie seemed stunned for a second, but then returned his embrace. "You're going to be great. If you get nervous at any time, just look at me."

Matty released her and watched Paul hug her. "You're a rock star, kid. You'll knock them off their feet."

Hallie sheepishly smiled. "I'll try."

129

"You're going to be fabulous." Henry embracing her. "The most important thing to remember is to relax and have fun. We'll be rocking out with you."

(Lex)

The following afternoon, Matty, Hallie, Paul, and Henry came over to Lex's condo. He greeted them in the foyer.

"How are you feeling?" Hallie was worried, everyone else wandered into the living room.

Lex smiled. "Much better, thanks." She still looked concerned. "Honestly, I'm not hungover any more."

Lex was surprised to see a shocked expression cross her face. "You were drunk?"

"I partied too hard." It was no big deal, but she looked like she'd been electrocuted. "I'm getting the impression Matty didn't tell you."

"I thought you had a stomach bug."

Lex chuckled. "Leave it to Matty to be a decent guy."

"But... they were counting on you," She murmured.

He didn't understand her glum mood. "It's not a big deal. I own the club, they were getting paid regardless. Don't take things so seriously, life should be fun."

"Lex, come here!" Paul called from the family room. "We have something to show you."

"He's sounds excited. Let's go see what it is." She didn't respond, appearing to be deep in thought. A strange, sullen look was on her face. He put his hands on her shoulders ushering her

130

into the other room.

"Matty got April to film this last night. You have to see it." Paul started the video on the T.V.

Lex watched in awe as the band performed with Hallie as the lead singer. During the second song, he glanced over to her. She wasn't watching, still deep in thought. He wondered what had her so preoccupied. He turned back to the video and couldn't help but grin. She was incredible. By the time the third song began, his mind was racing.

That evening, there was another gig. This time Lex was there. He sat in the audience with April, excited anticipation consumed him. He not only desired to watch Hallie perform, but he wanted to feel, see, and hear the audience's reaction first hand. He was not disappointed. The audience loved her. He loved her.

"Hey, Hals," Lex greeted her the following afternoon when she arrived with Matty at Paul's place. "I want to talk to you about something important." He glanced at Matty grinning. Matty's expression equally matched his. "Come, have a seat on the sofa." Paul and Henry were already waiting for them.

Lex peered into Hallie's curious eyes. "We've all been talking and we'd like to change the name of the band from Asterix to 5th Asterix." Lex enjoyed watching a puzzled look materialize on her face. "We'd like you to be the fifth member, and our new lead singer."

Hallie's face instantly became stunned. She didn't speak; and as the seconds ticked on, Lex became more anxious. Finally he asked, "Hallie?"

"Yes," She answered barely above a whisper.

131

"Will you do it? Will you join us?"

Lex watched as she slowly glanced around to see each of the band member's faces. Through his peripheral vision, he saw Matty nodding his head trying to encourage her. She finally looked back at him. He grinned extra wide hoping to entice her as well. He was confused when her eyes dropped to the floor.

"Are you sure you want me?" She asked almost too faint for him to hear.

"Of course we do," He was baffled by her reaction. "You're amazing. You're exactly what this band needs. You're the piece that's been missing."

"What about you? What will you do?"

"I'm still just as much a part of the band as I've always been. I'll still play the guitar and sing, I'll probably play the keyboard more as well. I was also hoping we could dance and do a few duets together."

Hallie quickly glanced at him. "I'd like that," She smiled.

"Then you'll do it? You'll be our new business partner?" The suspense was killing him.

Hallie nodded; Lex couldn't contain himself as he sprang forward to hug her. He saw Henry and Paul exchange high fives as Matty moved toward Hallie. Tears were flowing down her cheeks. Lex chuckled slightly as he tightened his grip. She was *so* sensitive.

He noticed a strange, worried expression on Matty's face, so he released her allowing him to have her. Matty's behavior had been odd since they returned from their vacation to visit his parents for Christmas. His usual protectiveness of Hallie had gone into overdrive. When Lex asked him about it; Matty proceeded to give him a strange analogy.

"It's like you walk into a store that sells only the most exquisite things. Your eye is immediately drawn to a glass case located in the middle. Inside you see a egg, the most beautiful thing you've ever seen in your life. You're drawn to it, have an overwhelming desire to touch it. The egg appears to have a tough shell, so you ask to hold it with no fear of breaking it. The sales person gently places the egg in your hands, but warns you this is no ordinary egg. It is delicate, extremely fragile. If pressure is applied to the wrong spot, the entire thing will immediately crumble into dust."

Lex thought about the analogy as he watched Hallie and Matty's interaction. Matty was right about one thing. Hallie *was* exquisite, the most beautiful woman he'd ever met. And Lex *was* drawn to her, desired to be in her company. But the crumbling to dust part didn't make any sense. Hallie was a sensitive person, true, but she was also from Riverside. She wasn't going to suddenly crumble.

After a few more minutes of celebrating, Lex presented Hallie with an envelope.

She was perplexed. "What's this?"

"It's your first paycheck. I thought you'd like to be paid in cash. You earned it this week with the two shows you did."

Lex enjoyed watching her eyes bulge when she saw the amount of money in the envelope. She looked up at him shaking her head in protest. "Lex, this is too much." She stammered.

"No, that's your cut."

"This is a thousand dollars."

"I know, I'm also the general manager." He watched her look back down at the envelope. "With the band's new image, I anticipate you'll be making a lot more than that really soon."

133

Lex watched her slip into a familiar expression. It was the look she got when she was deep in thought. He tried to wait patiently for her to finish thinking, but curiosity was killing him. He didn't understand her subdued reaction. "Tell me what you're thinking." It came out as a stronger demand than he meant for it to be. "Please," He tried to soften his voice.

Hallie glanced up and met his eyes. She quietly told him. "I've never seen this much money before. It's ..." she looked away again, frowning. "disturbing... It's ... not right that I should have it when..."

"Hallie, you worked hard and earned it, just like anyone else who has a job."

He observed some sort of struggle across her face. "I...I don't need this money. Scott provides for me just fine."

"It's still your money. You can spend it on whatever you wish." Lex thought it was very odd she wouldn't be excited about making the money. Surely someone with her past would jump for joy over the cash and be even more excited about the continuation of it. But Hallie looked almost tortured about it. Lex watched the struggled expression play across her face as she came to grips with her new situation. Finally, her face smoothed; she looked back at him.

"I can do anything I want with it?" She asked, but he could tell her mind was still far away.

Lex couldn't help but laugh. "Yes, it's your money."

"I wanna save it until I have enough to buy a playground. How would I find out how much a playground costs?"

Lex was stunned. He felt like he'd missed part of the conversation. "A playground?"

"I'd like to put in a state of the art one in Riverside, to give the kids a nice place to play. The streets are hard and tough, there's no happy place to go. The park playground is falling apart. It's been vandalized, the tunnel leaks when it rains. People sleeping in it get soaked through. I don't need this money, but the kids do."

The guys decided to make a donation to the cause to help her get started.

Over the next month, Lex formed a non-profit organization he named The Hallie McKinley Foundation. Since Hallie was a minor, he made himself president and Matty vice president, but Hallie retained full control. During this time, the band's popularity began to soar.

As far as Lex was concerned, life couldn't get any better. March was an even more fantastic month than February. Each of Hallie's performances out shined the previous. They started attracting the attention of some big names in the music industry. It felt like the entire country was watching to see if they were really going to be the next top band. So, when Matty and Hallie didn't show up for practice one afternoon in early April, Lex was surprised.

Neither of them were answering their cell phones; April had left work to go home. Lex knew something was wrong. Paul and Henry went with him over to their house. Both cars were in the driveway, but no one answered when Lex rang the bell. Henry checked the knob; the door was unlocked.

They walked into the house and heard the sound of someone crying. It was coming from Hallie's room. Lex glanced at Paul and Henry; they looked as worried as he was. Lex refused to let his mind wander, to think what would have her so upset.

The scene in her bedroom was ominous. Matty was sitting on the bed holding Hallie in his arms, his expression was strange like someone had punched him in the stomach. Hallie was

135

distraught; she had already soaked Matty's shirt with her tears. April seemed to be trying to comfort both of them.

Suddenly Hallie started screaming. Lex could tell she was in a horrible, agonizing pain. Seeing her suffer like that was almost too much to bear.

Matty tried to comfort her.

"No!" She screamed and jumped out of his arms onto her feet. Hallie glared back at Matty with tears gushing down her face. "No! No! No! ... Scott!" She became completely choked up and collapsed to the floor.

Matty was right by her side. He picked her up and carried her back to the bed, cradling her in his arms.

Lex couldn't believe this was actually happening.

April noticed him for the first time. She quickly crossed the room and ushered them into the hallway. She closed Hallie's bedroom door behind her.

"Scott's dead." Lex looked at her for confirmation.

"Hallie received a phone call this afternoon and became hysterical, scared the daylights out of Matty," She whispered. "When he picked up the phone, he was relieved to speak to Scott. He then called me, asked me to come home right away. They're not coming home, their tour's been extended another six months definitely, but possibly another year.

"The news is devastating to Matty as well. Another six to twelve months of worrying, hoping, and praying. It's two weeks shy of twelve months already..."

She took a deep breath. "Matty's gone numb. I think Hallie's outwardly expressing what he's feeling inside, but he won't let himself react in front of her for fear it'll make her worse. She's

136

been doing the same thing for almost two hours now. She suddenly gets angry, yells, screams, and sometimes throws things. It's usually short lived and then she crumbles. Matty pulls her into his arms, she just clings to him and cries. Then, unexpectedly, she erupts again.

"To be honest, I'm worried about Matty. He and Ron have always been close. I know the news is killing him inside, and I think Hallie's reaction is making the situation worse. She's acting like they've died."

"Don't worry," Henry hugged her. "We're here now. Let the three of us take care of Hallie while you take care of Matty."

Lex felt clueless. "What exactly are we going to do?"

"We'll be there for her, take turns letting her soak our shirts. She has to stop eventually."

"I'll grab Matty's guitar. Maybe some music will help relax her," Paul suggested.

Lex agreed and spent the next hour trying to comfort Hallie. It was hard to tell if the music helped. At one point she added a few angry lyrics to some cords Paul was playing around with. Eventually, thankfully, she passed out in his arms.

Lex held her for a while wondering what it must be like to love someone so much, you'd cry that much over them. And it wasn't even like Scott was dead; he was just going to be gone longer than expected. It seemed to him at first that she was overreacting.

But the more he thought about it, he started to wonder. He was an only child and was closer to Charles than any family member. He considered Matty to be like a brother. He remembered the trips he'd taken to visit Matty's family; how different it was from his own. There was a bond among the McKinleys; Lex

137

enjoyed spending time with them, pretending they were his family as well. He wondered what it would be like to be that close, bonded by love to someone else.

(Hallie)

Hallie woke up dazed. She couldn't breathe; her sinus cavities clogged. As she rolled over to get a tissue, her head ached. She blew her nose and was immediately seized with sharp pains all over her chest. Her heartache from the previous day was taking its toll on her body. She felt like hell.

Hallie lay in bed staring at the ceiling. Scott was still gone and would remain gone. There was nothing she could do about it. Fate had struck again.

She wondered what Matty was doing. Was he laying in bed thinking about Ron? Possibly. Matty understood her pain better than anyone else, but only to a certain extent. Matty had other family; a mom, a dad, a wife, who all loved him dearly. Hallie only had Scott.

Hallie smiled as she thought about her brother. Scott was her superhero, the one who always showed up to save the day; the one who fought off all the villains who hated her, and there were many. He could've hated her as well. But he didn't, he only loved her. And she loved him more than life itself.

Tears started to pool in her eyes making them sting. She longed to be with him, to see him again. She needed *his* strong, muscular arms to hold her and tell her everything was going to be alright; just like he'd done every night since the day she was born, like he'd done up until the day he left. The void in her heart could only be filled by Scott. He was six feet of pure, muscular power; a giant compared to her tiny frame. She wondered if he'd gotten even bigger since he'd joined the Marines. Now she'd have to wait to find

138

out. Another six months; Hallie sighed. Who was she kidding?... another year; and then they'd probably extend him again.

Hallie forced herself out of bed. Life was going to go on without Scott coming home. She couldn't stop life, and she couldn't magically make Scott appear; she would just have to tough it out a few more months. At least, she was living in a safe place.

Hallie opened her closet, grabbed the first outfit she touched, and went to take a shower. After that, she planned to find Matty, give him a hug, and thank him for everything he'd done for her. Then, she was going to see if he would like to make some brownies with her to go into another care package for Scott and Ron. It was their routine; the one they had been doing every week since she arrived, the only thing they could do to help their brothers come home safely.

In May, Hallie moved out of Matty's house and into the spare bedroom at Lex's condo. Lex told her Matty and April wanted to have a baby, but they put off starting a family, because she was staying in their second bedroom. Hallie knew Matty would never tell her she was in the way, moving was the right thing to do. Matty wasn't expecting her to stay as long as she had; she was supposed to move out in April when Scott returned. He'd already done enough for her; she couldn't expect him to put off his own family because their brothers' tour was extended. Lex offered the room; and she accepted.

Hallie wandered into the kitchen and saw Charles working away. "What're you doing?"

"Making dinner for Lex and you," He smiled at her.

"Can I help?"

"Sure, take the knife and start slicing the carrots." He

pointed to an area on the counter prepared for the task.

Since Hallie wasn't usually alone with Charles, because Lex kept him very busy, she took the opportunity to get to know him better. "How long have you been working for Lex?"

"Oh, going on twenty-one years now,"

"Wait, Lex is only twenty-three," She was surprised as she did the math.

Charles walked over to the counter where she was cutting carrots. He started shearing some chicken on another cutting board. "That's right. I was hired by his parents when he was two to be his governor. When he turned eighteen, he asked me to stay on as his personal assistant. I take care of him just like I would if he were my own son." Charles grinned at Hallie, gently nudged her arm with his elbow. "But don't tell him that."

Hallie smiled at Charles. He was so easy and comforting to be around. "Your secret's safe with me," She whispered.

"And now for the moment, I take care of you as well. You make sure you let me know if you need anything. Ah, good job with the carrots."

Lex walked into the kitchen. "Hey, what's going on?" He asked in his usual casual, cheerful demeanor.

"Charles is letting me help cook dinner."

Lex picked up one of the cut pieces of carrot and tossed it into his mouth. He leaned on the counter, his face only inches from hers. Hallie noticed him gazing right into her eyes. A tingling sensation shot through her body which she didn't understand. She also felt her cheeks flush. "Well, if you want to learn how to cook, you've come to the right place. Charles is an incredible cook." It took Hallie a moment to look away from his endless, blue eyes and focus on the carrots.

She heard Lex chuckle under his breath before he grabbed another piece of carrot and walked over to the kitchen table to sit down. "Matty tells me that you're a bit of a homebody, so I was thinking about watching a movie or two for tonight. How does that sound?"

Hallie suddenly felt nervous. "Can we watch it with the volume down?"

Lex gave her an irritated look. "What's the point in having surround sound if you don't want to use it?"

"It's alright," She didn't want to hurt his feelings. After all, she was living in *his* house. "Play the movie as loud as you want. I can wear my earplugs. It's no big deal."

Lex gave her a look she didn't understand. "What types of movies do you like?"

"Anything without sex or violence, I don't like guns or seeing people being punched." As she said the words, her stomach tightened and cramped. She took a deep breath trying to control her emotions. Living with Lex was going to be a bit of a challenge; he didn't know her secret. She stared intently at the granite countertop bracing herself against any memory that might suddenly surface.

Hallie was relieved when nothing came. She quickly glanced around the kitchen at Charles and Lex to see if they noticed her strange behavior. Charles was focused on dinner; Lex was surfing the internet on his phone, probably looking at their movie choices. Hallie took another deep breath and relaxed when she realized they hadn't been watching her.

After a delicious three course meal, something Hallie decided she was never going to get used to, she got up and started helping Charles with the dishes. "Go relax in the family room, I can take care of this." Charles told her.

"I don't mind. I'm happy to help." While it didn't bother Lex having Charles waiting on him like a servant, it made Hallie feel strange. She wanted to pull her weight.

When all the dishes were washed, dried, and put away; Hallie went to her room to get her earplugs out of her purse. She slipped them into her pocket and wandered into the family room. Lex was sitting on the sofa surfing the net over the TV. When she sat down next to him, he switched the screen and started playing the movie. Hallie began to pull out her ear plugs, but stopped when she heard the low volume. She gave Lex a questioning look.

His eyes were waiting to meet hers. He grinned. "It'd be ridiculous for you to have to wear ear plugs. Is this volume alright?"

Hallie felt touched by his selfless act. It wasn't like him to not do what *he* wanted. "This is great. Thanks, Lex."

The weeks passed; and Hallie become more comfortable in her new home. She had never been so happy. The only thing that would have made her happier would be to have Scott sharing it with her. She couldn't wait until he came home. It was now mid-July; he'd been gone nineteen months.

On the nights they weren't performing, Lex would stay home some and go out some. Hallie always stayed home unless Lex was taking her dancing, that was too much fun to pass up. Dancing with Lex's body against hers was electrifying, like bolts of energy surging through her. She loved feeling that way.

One evening, Matty and April came over for dinner. Since April worked for the property management company Lex owned, she had spent the day taking photographs of potential properties for

The Foundation to purchase as a site for the playground. She laid out a city map of Riverside on the kitchen table. Most of the properties Hallie recognized and could instantly place. It felt strange to her to be seeing these places; they were from a different lifetime, almost surreal.

April handed Hallie another photograph. Hallie froze in terror. The memories hit her hard and fast. She felt the photograph slip from her fingers, but she didn't care. She knew it was only seconds before she lost control and quickly started backing away from the table. Her voice trembled as she said, "I...I can't... get rid of it...please." As she turned to run from the room, she became completely consumed.

Memories

(Matty)

"Hallie?" Matty called to her. He saw the pain and horror in her eyes, watched her face blanch white and crumble in terror.

"That's the one you had me mark with a star." April told Lex.

Matty quickly turned to him full of anger. Lex did this deliberately. "What's that a picture of?"

"Her parent's house." Lex quietly responded.

Matty exchanged a worried glance with April, who looked just as concerned. He glared at Lex. "Why would you do that to her?"

"I wanted to see her reaction. It's for sale." Lex's voice sounded repentant. "I'll go apologize."

"No, you've done enough. Let me handle this. Just, wait here with April."

Where would she have gone? To her bedroom? He scanned the family room as he walked through. He opened the door to her room and stood in the doorway looking for some evidence she had come this way. It only took a moment before he found her sitting on the floor. She was in the corner; the furthest point from the door. Her legs were drawn to her chest, she was crying.

"Hey," Matty said as he crossed the room and sat down next to her. He noticed she was shaking.

144

Hallie looked up at him, tears pouring down her cheeks. She whispered, "He'll see me...he'll hurt me bad...please ..."

Matty recognized the terrified, pleading child. He wrapped his arms around her. "Nobody's going to hurt you, I promise. You don't ever have to go there again." He gripped her tightly in an effort to help her calm down. Her heart was racing; he thought she was on the verge of hyperventilating. She was all curled and withered up, a shell of a person.

He felt horrible this happened. Searching his mind for the information he had read, Matty remembered most discussed using "talk" therapy with a licensed professional. That wasn't going to help her at this exact moment. What could *he* do? There must to be something. He then remembered something else which said *a friend can offer emotional support, understanding, patience, and encouragement.* Well, it wasn't much, but he could do that. He could sit with her and hold her as long as she needed him, listen to her if, and when, she was ready to talk. She was not going to face this alone.

Eventually Hallie's breathing started to slow at the same time the stream of tears turned off. Her face was blank. Matty hesitantly loosened his grip. She didn't respond. He didn't know how long they had been in her bedroom, but he knew it must be getting late. Very softly he asked, "Do you want to stay at my place tonight?"

Hallie looked up at him, but he got the impression what he said didn't register. She just stared at him with an empty, blank look on her face. Matty remembered reading *feeling emotionally numb* was a symptom. He wondered if that was what she was experiencing.

Matty helped Hallie to her feet. She kept her arms curled up against her chest and was so timid. Matty kissed the top of her head as he put his arm around her shoulder. "Everything's going to be alright. I'm going to take care of you." He gently pulled Hallie along as he walked to the door.

When they got to the family room, they were greeted by April and Lex's anxious eyes. April immediately rose and walked over to him. "She's going to stay with us tonight," He quietly said.

"That's a good idea," April hugged Hallie, who didn't seem to notice the contact.

Lex was right behind her. The expression on his face was one of concern, regret. "Hallie," He tried to look into her eyes, but they were glossed over, unregistering. "I'm really sorry I upset you. I didn't mean to hurt you. Can you forgive me?" The apology sounded very sincere and genuine.

She didn't respond. Matty knew she couldn't. "I think she might be in some form of shock. She hasn't spoken to me either. Let's give her some time and see how she feels in the morning."

"Alright," Lex agreed intently studying Hallie's face. "I've destroyed the picture. If you can find out any other addresses she doesn't want to see, I'll make sure I don't have pictures of them."

"Good idea."

Lex leaned in and gently kissed Hallie on the cheek. His lips lingered against her skin for a moment before he whispered. "I'm truly sorry I hurt you. I hope you feel better in the morning."

Matty gave Lex a sympathetic smile and ushered Hallie to the door.

He anticipated a night full of nightmares. He knew Hallie experienced them frequently and was prepared. To his surprise, she was quiet. To his relief, she was back to normal the following morning. She even walked into the condo, asked Lex for the pictures, flipped through them quickly, handed one to Lex, and said, "This is where the playground should go." She didn't mention

146

anything about the previous evening; Lex seemed just as reluctant. Lex said he would take care of it for her; she nodded in agreement. She then went to her room to read a book.

(Lex)

Lex, Matty, and Charles traveled to Riverside to purchase the property. It had been two weeks since Hallie picked it out; Lex was anxious to get his hands on it. He arranged to meet Tyler and Domino at the city limits sign; Riverside gave him the creeps. Having some hired thugs for protection helped ease the extreme discomfort he felt for the place.

Charles pulled up in front of the house. It was small, very run down, dilapidated came to mind. The picture didn't do it justice; this place was a dive. It looked worse in person. The yard looked better than the house, but only marginally. The grass, or it was mostly weeds, was over two feet high.

"What are we doing here?" Matty's annoyed tone rang in his ears from the back seat.

Lex opened the door to the front passenger seat and casually called over his shoulder. "I want to see the inside. I want to know more about Hallie, specifically why this place upsets her so much."

"Lex, you need to drop this," Matty's hand was on his shoulder. Lex had never heard such a serious tone come from him. He knew Matty would be irritated about this stop, but he didn't care. Matty continued his protest. "Living here was very painful to her, she'll talk about it when she's ready."

"I'm going inside, you coming?"

Lex felt Matty reluctantly drop his hand and heard him sigh

147

as they got out of the car. They walked up to the front door and waited for Charles to unlock the realtor's box to get out the key. As Lex looked around at the nearby houses, a shiver ran down his spine. Every instinct in his body told him this was a place he shouldn't be; it was dangerous, life threatening.

He was the first of the group to enter the house and was immediately caught off guard by a horrible odor. He'd never smelled anything remotely this awful. It was so overpowering he almost turned around and walked back out. But his curiosity held him in place. "Uh, what's that stench?" He commented to no one in particular.

"Death, man," Tyler casually answered as he walked past him into the house.

"Why are all the things still here?" Matty looked puzzled. "Hallie's parents died over a year ago?"

Lex looked around the small, dingy room wondering the same thing. The furniture, pictures, everything was still in place. "I don't know, it *is* weird," He agreed as he looked around for clues to Hallie's past.

He walked over to a bookcase which held several pictures. One in particular caught his eye. It was a picture of a girl and a younger boy. The girl looked like how he imagined Hallie would look when she was seven or eight. He picked up the frame and turned toward Tyler. "Is this Hallie when she was little?"

"That's Kate and Scott." He casually commented.

"Who's Kate?" Lex was positive the picture was of Hallie. There was a very strong resemblance.

"Their sister."

Lex was surprised; Hallie never mentioned having a sister.

148

Why *hadn't her sister helped her when Scott left?* "Where is she now?"

"Dead, she was killed in an accident shortly after that picture was taken."

Well, that explained it. Lex put the picture back down and looked at the others. There were several more of Scott and Kate, but none of Hallie. Lex was very puzzled.

When he was placing one of the frames back down, he noticed some strange, large dark spots a few feet away. He walked over to investigate. "What's all over the carpet?"

"Ann's blood, you're standing right where her old man shot her." Lex froze as he heard Domino's answer. "Over there's her mother's blood." Domino was pointing and giving details like reading a list. "And that's the old man's blood. Any other blood spots you see around the house are probably Ann's."

"Wait a minute," Lex tried to shake off a sudden feeling of horror. "She was shot?!"

"Yeah, her old man put a bullet right through her chest. Don't know how she survived."

Lex was stunned. He couldn't imagine Hallie being shot. A sick, nauseous feeling came over his body as he looked down at the carpet and thought about standing in her blood stains. This horrific, disturbing feeling caused him to shutter for a split second. He fought to keep himself from vomiting.

"Lex, you need to drop this, and we need to leave." Matty's voice was firm. "Hallie would be very upset if she found out we were here nosing into her past."

Lex glanced at Matty. "You don't act surprised by this. You knew, didn't you?"

149

He nodded his head.

"Why didn't you tell me?"

"She asked me not to tell anyone. It's a very painful subject for her. Now, can we please leave?"

If Matty was going to keep secrets, then he'd use another source for information. Lex turned to Domino. "Tell me more."

"Look, man, it's not my place to be talkin' 'bout Ann's business." Domino casually lit a cigarette; this place didn't seem to bother him. "I think you should ask her. But, I'll tell you, Ann was terrified of her old man. And with good reason, that dude used to hurt her bad... Scott did everything he could to protect her from him. He would flip out every time the old man messed her up."

"Yeah, Scott's old man was one, mean son-of-a-bitch," Tyler added lounging against the wall. "I think your friend here is right, it's best to leave. No good ever came out of this place."

A man was suddenly in the doorway. He was a short, bald man with a large, round belly. He looked to be in his mid-forties; he was wearing a cheap suit. "Mr. Vanderbilt, I assume?" He was accompanied by a woman who wasn't dressed much nicer. She was younger, in her thirties, and had long brown hair.

Lex walked over to both of them, shook their hands, and introduced himself. The man was a representative from the city; the woman was a local attorney. "I have reviewed the documents for both properties and everything appears to be in order."

"Wonderful, let's get started." The woman smiled showing the wrinkles on her face. Lex noticed she looked a lot older than she should have. They walked over to the kitchen table and sat down.

It didn't take long to sign all the papers; Lex was very familiar with the procedure. The city owned both properties and was very happy to be receiving asking price. Lex knew he could have haggled it down, but why bother? He wanted possession as soon as possible, haggling would only slow things down. Besides, the properties were very cheap compared to what he usually bought. Lex gave the attorney the two checks, they both shook his hand again, and left.

"Why are you doing this?" Matty was concerned. Lex assumed he was thinking about what Hallie's reaction was going to be when she found out what he'd done. Would Matty tell her knowing it might cause her more pain?

"Charles," Lex ordered. "I want you to hire some locals to do the work on this place. I want the entire house demolished, the foundation destroyed, and the top twelve inches of dirt removed from the lot. I want all traces of what's here now, removed permanently. I then want you to bring in some landscapers to plant a thousand bulbs of all different types of flowers so the property's always in bloom. Hallie likes flowers. Make sure they plant her favorites."

Now it was time to answer Matty's question. "I can't explain it, but I feel compelled to make her happy. It's like a force driving me. I've never felt this way before, but I have to do things which will make her smile. Her smile, wow, it's an incredible smile that lights up the room. The other day when she saw the photograph of this place, I watched her face crumble. I couldn't take it. I don't ever want to see that look on her face again. I had to do something. If this place makes her unhappy, then this place will no longer exist. She may never come back here, but if she ever does, I want her to see something that will make her smile...why are you giving me that strange look?"

"I've never seen this side of you, it's nice. You're doing a wonderful thing here."

151

"Thanks, anything else you think I should do?"

"Well, you could take it a step further and embody her spirit in the place."

"How so?"

"I think you should have a permanent dedication to her. Add a sign saying something like 'Dedicated to Ann Kasey, your smile lights up my life, Love Lex.' I also think the property should be open to the public. You know, add some windy paths for people to meander down to enjoy the flowers. Some of the people who live in this community know her, I think the gardens would bring her beauty and gentleness back into a place that's dark for many. The whole idea behind Hallie's playground is to bring something positive to the community. She had no hope while living here, no place to go to make her feel good. I think by making the property a public park, you'll transform a place which was horrible for her into something positive for others."

Lex knew Hallie wanted to build the playground, but he really didn't understand why until that moment. "It's a great idea. I'm going to do it. Would you mind designing the place? You seem to be better at capturing her essence than I am."

"I'd be happy to," Matty grinned. "This is a great thing you're doing. It's just too bad she may never know about it; you can't tell her."

(Matty)

On the ride back home, Matty thought about New Year's Eve when he took Hallie to see the fireworks. She'd never seen them before and had been excited all day. As soon as the first firework hit the sky, she ran to the truck and crawled underneath it. Matty followed her, dropped onto his knees, and called to her. "Hallie,

152

what's wrong?"

She didn't answer him.

"Hallie, please tell me what's wrong." He noticed she was lying on her side, curled into a ball with her hands over her ears. He'd seen her do this before, under her bed when a thunderstorm passed. He instantly felt terrible. He had completely forgotten she didn't like loud noises; he should have told her to wear earplugs.

He tried and tried to get her to answer him with no luck. He finally decided to crawl on his stomach to her. He could tell she was repeating something, but the fireworks were so loud, he couldn't understand her. She didn't want something. He assumed she didn't want to come out from under the truck until the show was over.

Her body was violently shaking, her muscles tight and tense; he couldn't get her to move. Matty was worried if he pulled too hard, Hallie might try to sit up and hit her head on the underneath of the truck. He didn't want her to get hurt, so he reluctantly crawled back out and sat on the ground.

When the fireworks display was over, Matty could finally hear what she was saying. "I don't wanna be shot. I don't wanna be shot." It was a pleading request from a scared child.

"It's over now," He soothingly told her. "No more loud noises. Will you please come out from under the truck?"

Hallie still didn't respond, only continued her sentence.

Dad suggested they push the truck away from her. Everyone thought it was a good idea. April put the truck in neutral making sure the wheels were pointed straight while Matty, Dad, and Mom gave the truck a push. As it started to move; Matty immediately dropped to the ground to make sure Hallie was not going to be hit by the tires. He grabbed her feet to try and hold her still. As the truck started to clear her body, he moved his hands up her legs eventually grabbing hold of her arms. He placed his hand on top of her head to make sure she didn't suddenly lift it up.

As soon as the truck completely cleared her, he grabbed her tightly in his arms, determined to comfort her.

Hallie didn't appear to notice as she continued to plead. "I don't wanna be shot. I don't wanna be shot." Her eyes were unfocused.

Her shaking reminded him of the day she almost drowned in the lake. He tried to make the connection, but nothing came to him; something was missing. However, he was convinced this was a related event.

"It's alright. It's alright." He tried to comfort her without success. *Why wasn't she acknowledging him?*

Dad answered his unspoken thought. "She appears to be traumatized, son. Let's get her home."

Matty agreed, so he picked Hallie up in his arms and placed her in the back seat of the truck. The tight ball loosened slightly, but the shaking and chanting didn't stop; she appeared to be completely unaware of her surroundings. They wrapped a blanket around her to try to make her feel secure. Matty put his arms around her and held her tightly. Mom sat on the other side of Hallie and gently rubbed her hand up and down Hallie's arm and face. Hallie's head was leaned against his chest; he could hear her heavy, erratic breathing.

During the ride back to the house, the chanting started to slow, her body loosened. Eventually she was silent, still. Matty realized Hallie had fallen asleep. Relieved she was no longer terrified, he kissed the top of her head and said a silent prayer for her to sleep peacefully.

154

Once they were home, Matty carried Hallie to her room and tucked her into bed. She was completely out like the night Lex brought her back from the massage. *Was that related to this as well?*

Matty decided to join the rest of his family in the family room. He couldn't figure this out on his own. "I've never seen anything like that. Mom, Dad, what do you make of it?"

Mom spoke first. "It seems the sound of the fireworks sent her into some kind of traumatic state. Do you know anything about her being shot?"

"She's never mentioned it, but she does have a strange scar on her chest and another one on her back. She said they were birthmarks and seemed to be very sensitive about them."

They talked for a while longer, throwing out ideas, but the only conclusion they could make was they needed more information. Matty was going to have to talk to Hallie.

The following morning at breakfast, just the two of them were sitting at the McKinley kitchen table. "Has somebody shot you?"

"Yes." It was a blank, empty response.

"Is that what caused the two scars you call birthmarks?"

"The bullet went straight through."

He paused for a moment, processing the information. "Who shot you?"

"My daddy."

Matty was stunned by this answer. It took him a moment to recover. "Why would your dad shoot you?"

155

"Because he was a bastard."

"Tell me what happened."

Hallie stared down at the piece of toast lying on her plate. "I have no memory of it, but the police said the son-of-a-bitch was drunk. He tied my mom to a chair and me to another, and placed us next to each other. He shot my mom in the head and me in the chest before he blew his brains out." She looked straight into Matty's eyes. The angry street kid spoke. "*I hope he rots in hell.*"

(Lex)

Lex returned home and found Hallie sitting on the sofa. "Hey, what are you reading?"

"A new book the teacher gave me. It's a historical work about the development of suburbs from 1820-2000, so far it's very interesting. We're gonna analyze how different types of suburbs impacted or were impacted by the historical events of the time."

Lex smiled, pleased Mrs. Donald was challenging her and making her happy. He walked over to the sofa. "Would you mind getting up for a moment?"

Hallie placed the book down. As she stood up, Lex wrapped his arms around her, clinging to her in a tight embrace. He felt compelled to hold her, not wanting to let go.

"Is everything alright?" Hallie was concerned.

"I just need to hug you," He lovingly responded thinking of the horrible place he'd been, standing on her dried, blood stains. Hallie nestled in his arms for as long as he needed, and he needed it. He had never needed something so much in his entire life. She was *his* Hallie; he wanted to hold her forever, to protect her from her former life, and to feel her warm, alive body against his. He had to

156

comfort her.

But as soon as the thought was out, Lex knew it was a lie. She wasn't the one who needed comforting; he was. He had been in a horrible place, a place he didn't know existed, and it shook him to his core. The smell, the blood, the casual way Domino talked like it was no big deal, a part of everyday life; this had been *her* life, *her* every day.

Instinctively, he tightened his grip on her. Only she could take away his pain, the pain he now had because of knowledge. Maybe Matty was right, maybe he should have left the past where it belonged. Now that he knew, Lex would never look at Hallie the same way again.

"What's wrong?" Worry dominated her sweet voice.

He needed to get himself under control and release her. Lex knew the longer he held her, the more suspicious she would become, and telling her the truth about where he'd been would only hurt her. He couldn't do that, so he took a deep breath and gently kissed her on the cheek, planning to release his hold. But he couldn't.

The strangest feeling came over his body, the strongest of desires; he wanted to kiss her more. He closed his eyes and gently touched his lips to her cheek again, enjoying the sensation of *her* skin against his lips. His breathing was heavy as he continued to give her little kisses. He kissed up her cheek, across her forehead, and down the other cheek. When he brushed up against the corner of her mouth, he felt her tense.

Lex instantly opened his eyes and saw hers were wide with an unreadable expression. "Sorry," He whispered and quickly released his grip giving her a big, embarrassing grin. "What do you say we do something fun tonight? What would you like to do? Name it, we'll do anything you want."

"Sure, we can do something together." Lex saw confusion and concern in her eyes. "Are you sure you're alright?"

"I just had the worse day of my life. Thanks for the hug and the um... kisses. I really needed that. I'm feeling much better now." He gave her a reassuring smile which caused her to smile back at him. Hallie's warm, incredible smile, that's what he wanted to fill his mind with, not Riverside.

"How's it going?" Matty asked over the phone. It was the beginning of August; Lex was sitting at an outdoor café.

"How does five days of shopping hell sound?" Lex replied. "You would think if someone was told they could purchase any furniture they wanted, they'd jump at the chance. But not Hallie, she doesn't seem to like anything. I never knew there were so many furniture stores in L.A. This was supposed to be fun, now I wish I'd just sent her out with Charles." He grumbled.

"Hang in there," Matty was sympathetic. "She's never bought furniture. Maybe she's trying to get a feel for her options."

"Maybe...I'll tell you this much, if she doesn't pick out something soon, I'm going to lose the feeling in my feet."

Lex heard Matty laugh on the other end. "Stay positive, you're doing a really cool thing for her. Where are you going next?"

"I don't know," Lex exhaustedly commented. "Where ever is next on the list Charles made. Hallie has it in her purse."

"Where's Hallie now?"

"In line getting more food, furniture shopping seems to make her hungry. I've never seen her eat so much."

Matty chuckled, "She's growing. Let's see, she's grown about three inches since we got her."

"She's developed breasts as well. She looks more like a woman and less like a kid every day. Her hot body's going help us sell many albums."

He heard Matty sigh. "Do you ever *not* think about the sexual parts of the opposite sex?"

"No," Lex happily commented. "I can't help it if I'm a master at sizing up the bodily dimensions of women. It's a gift. Hallie has one of the sexiest little bodies I've ever seen, she looks fantastic in a bikini."

"I would appreciate it if you wouldn't talk about my sister that way." Matty sighed again. "April's motioning she needs me. I don't understand why we need to pick out baby furniture when she's not pregnant yet."

Lex laughed. "Better you than me. I'll talk to you later."

He'd exaggerated a bit about his displeasure at shopping with Hallie. He was enjoying every moment he spent with her; he was just sick of looking at furniture. He had already compiled a list of other things they could be doing together.

After lunch they headed to the next store. Hallie walked in; her face immediately lit up. "Wow! This is really cool."

"You like what you see?" He hopefully inquired.

"Yeah!" She responded with awe in her voice.

"Modern furniture, who would've guessed you loved modern furniture? I'll get a sales person. You start picking things out." Lex wandered to the receptionist sitting at the desk and requested assistance. He was thrilled Hallie was excited. Her radiant smile was something he couldn't see enough.

A few minutes later he was back with her. "Have you picked out some things?" Lex inquired, optimistic she would say 'yes'.

"I saw some lamps I just have to have. Come here." She grabbed his hand and led him across the room. Lex felt a surge of excitement holding her hand; it must have been Hallie's enthusiasm flowing through her.

"I should've known they'd be pink." He playfully commented.

"I want them for my bedroom." She smiled sheepishly. "I promise I won't make the entire place pink."

"I would appreciate that. Have you picked out anything else?" He wanted the condo to feel like *her* home, so he insisted she pick out all the new furniture. This was the home he wanted her to think about, not Riverside.

"Not yet."

"Well, remember you have two bedrooms, the large family room, the kitchen, and the foyer, plus any decorative pieces you want. I know you hate the sculptures, so they're all leaving."

"I don't hate the sculptures," She responded defensively. "I just think they're strange."

Lex laughed. She liked modern furniture, but not modern art.

(Hallie)

Hallie was in high spirits. She would have never thought she would enjoy picking out furniture. She remembered how disgruntled she was when Lex made the suggestion a week ago. It was the same night he'd come home acting so strangely. Suddenly, he needed to change everything in the condo. She asked Matty if he knew anything about it and was told Lex was eccentric. Hallie decided he needed really funky furniture to match his personality; what she picked out was the coolest, neatest furniture possible. She couldn't wait to see how it looked in his home.

The front door opened; Paul was surprised to see her. "Hey, Hallie, come on in."

Henry was sitting on the sofa playing the Wii. "Hi, Hal, what's up?"

"I was wondering if I could ask for a favor?" She timidly inquired knowing Scott said to never ask people for favors. She had broken this rule with Tyler. It worked out before; hopefully it would this time as well.

"Sure," Paul was curious. "Come, have a seat. Tell us what's going on."

Fearful she was going to lose her nerve, Hallie asked as she walked over to the sofa. "I was wondering if I could crash on your sofa tonight?"

Henry paused the video game, surprised. "Of course you can, but why aren't you staying at Lex's?"

She was no longer angry at Lex, just hurt, terribly hurt. The pain ached in her chest like being punched. Tears unexpectedly burst from her eyes. "Because he used me this afternoon to get sex, and I don't wanna be there tonight." Sobbing, she plopped down next to Henry and curled up with a pillow. She didn't plan to cry, but now she couldn't stop.

They both looked stunned; the room was silent. Paul quickly sat down next to her, pulling her into his arms. "Hallie, I'm so sorry." His voice was full of remorse. "We knew Lex was very charming, but we never imagined he'd use it on you. He treats you differently. He actually cares about you."

Hallie pulled away. "What are you talking about?" Now she was confused. "Lex didn't charm me."

"Did you have sex with Lex this afternoon?"

"No," Hallie quietly answered. "He told the saleslady about how he found me and saved me, so he could go out on a date with her. He's planning to bring her back to the condo later tonight and 'do it' with her."

Hallie watched as Paul and Henry exchanged a look of relief before Henry said. "Alright, so explain to us why this is bothering you. You already know Lex sleeps around a lot."

"It's bothering me, because my personal life is personal." The burn and sting of the hurt flared up again. "It's nobody's business, but mine. You should've seen how she treated me once Lex told her. I became this poor, pitiful person, it made me feel dirty and embarrassed. Lex said my past is in the past, I have a new life now. He made me feel special, but today he took it all away. I wonder how many other people know the truth and are nice only because they pity me and not because they actually like me? I'm just a big joke to him, someone he can use to his advantage to get laid."

"Did you tell Lex how you feel?"

"I tried," Hostility now seeped through her voice. "He basically told me I was his personal property, and he'd use me if he

162

wanted to. I don't like the fact he uses women for sex. It's wrong. I don't wanna be part of it."

"Look," Henry softly spoke. "It's a mutual using of each other. All the women Lex picks up are using him as well, and he knows it. They get him to buy them a nice dinner and show them a good time. At the end of the evening, they choose to have sex with him. They aren't required to. Lex would never force himself onto a woman. He's too much of a gentleman, he just likes to party and have a good time."

Paul added. "I get the feeling Lex doesn't understand how much this bothers you. He's accustomed to the world revolving around him. I think you need to sit down and have a heart to heart with him. You need to be direct and tell him what you told us. He needs to respect your privacy and your feelings. He tends to not listen, so you might have to get a little feisty with him to get his attention. You need to stand your ground and not back down from him, he needs to know you're serious."

"Do you think he'll actually listen to mc?" She felt skeptical.

"If you get in his face, he'll have no choice but to listen." Henry told her.

"I don't know," There was something about this idea that made her feel very uneasy.

Paul smiled supportively. "It's the only way to get him to stop. It'll be alright. I'll call Lex in the morning and get him to come over. You can talk to him with us in the room. How does that sound? Otherwise, he's going to keep telling people about you and using your story to get laid."

Hallie agreed to go through with the plan. She thanked them for helping her and being her friends, hoping they were right. Lex *did* listen to her when she first found out about his sleeping around. It didn't changed anything, but he had seemed attentive.

163

Maybe he would be this time as well; they knew each other a lot better now.

Henry and Paul went back to playing their video game. They offered to let her play, but Hallie declined wanting some time to think about what she was going to say to Lex. How was she going to explain how much his actions hurt her without telling him the truth about her past? No one, not even Matty, knew *that* secret; and she wasn't about to share it with them.

The following day, Lex came over about two in the afternoon. Hallie went through with the plan. She decided to keep it simple and to the point, hopefully to avoid being asked questions she didn't want to answer. She aggressively told him her two demands. "I want you to stop telling people about my personal life. You're using me, and I don't appreciate it. Also, I don't want you having sex in the condo while I'm living there. You're a male whore; it's disgusting. You should treat women with respect and not as something to fuck."

"Who the hell do you think you are?" He tore into her.

Hallie was prepared to fend off questions, but she wasn't expecting his angry response. The tone of his voice stunned her. She was immediately flooded with tremendous pain. It was no longer Lex's voice yelling at her. It was all the people who'd hurt her. She felt the hard shell she used to carry, the one which had disappeared over the past few months, quickly cover her body. It took a firm hold of her while her insides started ripping and shredding.

She could hear Lex's furious voice. "You have *no* right to speak to me like that. *I'm* the one who saved your life. *I'm* the one who paid your medical bills. *I'm* the one who's been feeding and clothing you for the past eleven months, not Scott. If I want to tell someone the true story about you, I will. And another thing, I *do* respect you. I would *never* bring a woman back to the condo with you there. I have another condo where I take all my dates to for sex. I don't want any of them to know where I really live. This entire conversation is absurd and is now over. Get your things and go home!"

The pain was raw. Since she'd been rescued, she'd slowly let her guard down, believing the fairy tale was actually going to come true; these were different people. They didn't know how to hurt.

She was wrong. The agony of Lex's anger was starting to choke her from the inside. Her knees were starting to shake; the chaos inside her body threatened to explode out at any second.

She glanced over to Paul and Henry who gave her sympathetic smiles, but didn't say anything to help defend her. She knew why and couldn't blame them; Lex was their Sugar Daddy. They needed his money; they weren't going to risk losing it.

Hallie quickly grabbed her purse and walked out of the house before the tears starting streaming down her cheeks. The all consuming pain was breaking through.

(Matty)

It was five-thirty when Matty showed up at Paul's to practice after spending another day looking at baby furniture with April. Thankfully, he'd finally found something she liked and was in their price range.

When he arrived, Paul and Henry stopped him in the family

165

room and told him what happened between Hallie and Lex. Henry confessed. "It's our fault. She came over last night, really upset. She wasn't planning on saying anything to him, but we encouraged her. We've never seen someone stand up to him before, I guess we thought it'd be amusing to see his surprised reaction, but it wasn't. We didn't think he'd react as strongly as he did knowing the way he feels about her. The look on her face when Lex started yelling."

"We've asked him to call her and apologize, but he won't." Paul was remorseful. "We feel awful. We've tried to call her ourselves, but she isn't answering her cell."

Matty stared at both of them, unsure who he was more irritated with for hurting Hallie; Paul and Henry for encouraging her to confront Lex, or Lex for being himself. He also wondered why she hadn't come to him instead.

Lex cheerfully walked into the family room. "Hey, I was wondering who was here."

"I was getting updated on the fight you had with Hallie." Matty scowled.

"Oh, that." He casually replied. "I sent her home to cool off. I don't know what got into her."

Matty sighed at Lex's cluelessness. In his calmest voice possible, he said, "Lex, please listen to me. I know Hallie's very mature for her age and we all treat her like she's an adult, but she isn't. She's a sensitive child. You can't yell at her the way you did."

Suddenly an urge to comfort Hallie caused him to turn and head toward the front door   "I'm going over to your place to talk with her. I still can't believe you guys didn't call me?" Matty finally figured out what irritated him the most about the situation. It wasn't Paul and Henry's involvement, it wasn't even Lex's obliviousness to other people's feelings; it was the fact they didn't call him, causing Hallie to hurt alone.

"I'm going with you," Paul was right behind him.

"Me too," added Henry.

"Well, it's my place, so I might as well go too. You'll need my keys to get in." Lex reluctantly decided to join them.

They all climbed into Matty's car and rode to the condo. They arrived a short while later, but Hallie wasn't there. Matty was getting worried, nothing looked out of place, her purse was even on the bed, but something was off. "Lex, are you sure she came here?"

He was equally as puzzled. Charles walked through the family room heading for the kitchen. His arms were full of groceries. "Have you seen Hallie?"

"She left a couple of hours ago."

"Left? Where'd she go?"

"She didn't say, but she was really upset you threw her out. She was deliberate to not take anything that was yours. Her wallet and your money are on her bed."

"What?!"

Now Matty was definitely worried.

Lex continued talking to Charles. "I didn't throw her out," He protested. "She was supposed to come here and cool off a bit. What exactly did she say?"

Charles sadly informed him. "That you told her to get her things and leave."

"I meant get her things from Paul's place, not here."

Matty immediately grabbed his phone as the realization she was gone finally hit him. She didn't come to him, wasn't with Paul or

167

Henry, and had left Lex's for good. The speed dial wasn't going fast enough.

Throwaway

(Hallie)

Hallie's cell rang again. She glanced down at the caller ID and stared at it for a moment. There were numerous calls from Paul and Henry which she didn't answer, but this time it was Matty. How could she not answer his call? As much as she didn't want to talk and could guess why he was calling, it pained her to think she might be hurting him. She had already started to believe the lie, to believe he was a brother. "Hey," She answered with a monotone voice.

"Hey, I heard about what happened this afternoon. Are you alright?" He was worried.

"I guess," She let the numbness she now felt keep her sedated.

"Where are you? Let me come and pick you up."

"Why?"

"So I can take you home."

A little sigh came out from under her breath as she heard the words. Thankfully, she'd spent all afternoon crying all the painful emotions out; even Matty's sweet voice couldn't touch her. Numbness was her shield. "I don't have a home," A plain fact, her voice didn't even crack.

"Of course you do. What're you talking about?"

"I was stupid. I started believing all the lies, because they were easy, but the reality is that I'm not some princess living a fairytale. I'm a street kid who just gets tossed out with the trash whenever I've used up my time. I realize that now, and accept it."

169

"You're wrong. You do have a home."

"No, I don't. I'm in the way at your house. April and you can't have a baby with me sleeping in the nursery, I refuse to be a burden to you...Lex threw me out, there's no room for me in his playboy, bachelor lifestyle. I don't know what made me start believing there was...I can't keep crashing on Paul and Henry's sofa, I've done that at other people's houses, I know how it'll end up. I have nowhere to live." Her voice cracked on the last word. Tears swelled up in her eyes as she heard the truth in her voice. She'd said too much, lost her protection. The truth burned and ripped a hole in her already fragile heart.

The soft, loving voice was in her head again. "Sweetie, April and I never wanted you to move out. We thought it was what you wanted. You're welcome to stay with us for as long as you like...And as far as Lex goes, he wants you to live with him. He wouldn't have spent the past week having you redecorate the condo in things you like, if he wanted to get rid of you...Please tell me where you are, so I can come and get you."

Hallie thought about his words, but she could only cry. How could this be true? How could Lex want her after what he said? She felt so confused; she didn't know what to do. She only felt horrible pain.

"Hallie, where are you?" The loving voice asked.

Without letting herself think, she quietly responded. "I went to the only real home I've ever had."

"Where's that?"

"Riverside."

"What?" The voice was no longer sweet and soft, but alarmed. "What happens if your uncle sees you?"

170

"It doesn't matter anymore. I can't keep believing things will be different, because they never are. I end up thrown out and abandoned every time. The only place I've ever belonged is alone on the street. So, I give up. I don't care what happens to me."

"Well, I do," His voice was firm, pleading. "Please, tell me exactly where you are. You're my little sister, I care about you. I'd never forgive myself if something happened to you. It would break my heart."

She didn't answer him.

"And what about Scott? How's he going to feel if he comes back from Iraq and you're gone? You can't do that to him. Please, give me the address where you are."

"Scott knows where I am, and you can't come. Riverside isn't safe for you. You're not like me. I appreciate everything you've done, but I've gotta go, Harry needs help. Bye, Matty." She quickly hung up the phone and buried her face into her hands as she let the pain consume her.

(Matty)

Matty hung up the phone feeling quite frantic. He looked at Lex, Paul, and Henry. They appeared to be as alarmed as he was.

"Why do I have a bad feeling she's in Riverside?" Lex inquired.

Matty nodded in confirmation.

"What the hell is she thinking? Why on earth would she go back there?"

Matty felt equally stunned and horrified. He needed to think, but there was no time. He had to get to her before her uncle did.

"She's in a lot of pain, I could hear it in her voice. I think the best thing we can do right now is for all four of us to go and show her we care about her, that no matter what happens, we're not going to abandon her and throw her out."

"You know where she is?" Henry inquired.

"No, she wouldn't tell me, just said she needed to help someone named Harry."

Lex looked directly at him. "We're taking your car."

The traffic was heavy. Matty sighed. As worried and irritated he was that this was happening, he couldn't be mad at Lex. He knew it was a misunderstanding. Lex wasn't accustomed to thinking about other people's feelings. His world had never revolved around someone else; and Hallie wasn't like anyone he'd ever met before. Her different perspective and outlook on life made her unpredictable to him.

Matty glanced over at Lex who was sitting in the passenger seat dialing on his phone. He'd already left messages for Tyler and Domino; however he was impatient enough to dial the numbers over and over again. Lex was worried.

Matty was worried, too. How safe was she? He didn't know why she'd run away from her uncle, but she must have had a good reason. What would happen if he found her? What if her memory suddenly flashed? What would happen then? What were all the dangers of Riverside after dark? The sun was setting and they were creeping down the Pomona Freeway.

There was nothing more he could do. It was a horrible, helpless feeling. Matty suddenly realized Scott must have felt the same way – being in Iraq and receiving the letter saying she was in trouble. She would have died if Matty hadn't... *Oh, please, let me be in time again.*

Lex's conversation interrupted his thoughts. "Hey, is this Domino?... Is he there?... Do you know where he is, I've been trying to reach him. It's urgent...Alright, would you please get him a message for me? Tell him Rich Boy called, Ann's in Riverside. She's with Harry on the street where the winos hang out, where Tyler found her before. I don't know the name of it. Tell Domino to get over there right away and protect her until I arrive. I'm on my way and will pay him once she has been safely returned to me...That's right...Thanks."

"Who was that?"

"His cousin."

They finally entered Riverside city limits. Lex mumbled. "This place is creepy during the day, it's even worse at night. Lock the doors." A few minutes later he added. "It looks totally different in the dark, nothing's familiar. I'm not sure I can find the street."

They drove up and down the streets for a while with no luck. "Lex, does anything look familiar?" Matty was starting to feel panicked they wouldn't be able to find her.

"No."

"Do you remember anything else from that day? A landmark or something?"

Lex was silent for a moment before he replied animated. "There was a McDonald's nearby. Here, I'll pull up all the McDonald's in the area on my phone. We'll search for her near those."

"This reminds me of the night we found her, driving to all those pay phones. She was in terrible shape by the time we got her."

"At least there aren't as many McDonald's to check. There

173

are...ten."

They heard gunshots go off in the distance. "Ten's a lot when we could come under fire at any moment." Paul nervously commented.

They arrived at the first McDonald's and drove around the streets nearby with no luck.

As they sat at a stop light near the second McDonald's, a fight broke out in the street and a guy was thrown across Matty's hood. Matty didn't wait for the light to turn green.

Each McDonald's took them deeper into the darkness of Riverside. They were propositioned several times near the fifth McDonald's.

Low riding cars with loud music playing were all over the streets. Sometimes they were in groups; Matty wondered if they were part of a gang who was going to come after their lone, normal looking car. He'd never been so terrified and was beginning to wonder if they would make it out alive.

Lex was suddenly animated. "This is it! Pull over there and park. This is where her friend Essie died. Hallie will be over there." Lex pointed diagonally across the street to an alley containing several large, round metal trash cans with garbage burning in them.

Matty anxiously parked the car wondering why Hallie would return to a place where a friend died. A horrific thought struck him. Would she still be here? Would *she* still be alive?

They got out and walked over to the dark alley. A man staggered toward them. Lex seemed to know him. "Harry, have you seen Hallie?"

Harry's eyes were glassy; he slurred as he spoke. "Don't know Hallie...Hey...you have money?... I could use a drink."

Matty immediately caught the smell of alcohol on his breath and knew he was intoxicated. He shook his head at Lex, who could be so oblivious sometimes. If this drunk knew Hallie, he wouldn't know her by her new name. "Hey mister, here's some money." Matty handed him twenty dollars. "Do you by any chance know a girl named Ann?"

"Yep," Harry almost fell over looking at the twenty. Matty caught his arm to help him regain his balance.

"Have you seen her today?" Paul inquired.

"Yep," He started to walk away mumbling to himself.

Matty quickly got in front of him. "Do you know where she is now?"

Harry gave him a questioning look. "Who wanz know?"

"I'm Matty, I'm a friend of hers, and I'm trying to help her." Matty studied Harry's face, worried he wouldn't tell him where Hallie was. He decided to add. "I told Scott I'd take care of her."

"Well, whyn't you say so?...Haven't seen Scott while...That boy do love her."

Matty smiled. "Yes, he does, and he can't come tonight. Do you know where she is?"

"Essie's," He pointed down the alley.

"Thanks, you've been a great help."

Matty turned to the others; together, they walked further down the alley. There was a figure sitting in the shadows of a large, cardboard box. Matty knew at once it was Hallie; she was safe. She was wearing blue jeans and the hood of her hoodie covered most of her head. Her face could barely be seen, but he noticed she was staring emotionlessly at the ground.

175

Matty sat down next to her. Lex followed his lead sitting down on her other side, even though he wasn't thrilled to be sitting on the dirty street.

"Hey Sweetie," Matty lovingly greeted her, relieved. "Sorry it took so long for me to get here. Are you alright?"

"Fine," She replied in a monotone voice. She was like a statue. Her guard was up; he'd seen this before.

Matty knew the longer they were in Riverside, the more danger they were in. He was going to have to break through her shell and convince her to leave, fast. "This is an interesting place. We met your friend Harry. He seems like a nice guy."

"He is."

"You want to tell me what's going on? Why'd you come here?"

Hallie continued to stare at the road. "It was my birthday, I was eight. Scott was excited all day long, said he had a surprise for me. When school let out, we didn't walk home that day, instead, we went to the store. You see, I'd never owned anything new. All my clothes were Scott's old ones, the few toys, were once his as well. I remember staring at amazement at this teddy bear store. There were two bears in Scott's price range, I liked the brown one the best, so I pulled one out of the bin and we went to the machine to have it stuffed. The sales person let us each put a red heart into the back of the bear granting each of us a wish. I remember wishing Scott's wish would come true.

"The bear was so soft and fluffy, I'd never felt anything like it. I just hugged it and squeezed it while Scott counted out the bag of coins he pulled from his backpack. It was the first time I'd ever felt special.

"When we got home, mama was waiting at the door. She

was drunk, pissed off. She said I was the reason Kate was dead, the reason my daddy was so angry all the time, the reason he was dishonorably discharged from the Marines and now couldn't hold down a job, the reason our lives were so bad. Since Kate only got eight years, so did I. She wanted me out.

"Scott protested saying I was too young to make it on my own. Mama said I was old enough and if I ever came back, she would beat the shit out of me herself. I was told I had ten minutes to get my things and go, my daddy would be home soon and he'd better not find me there.

"Scott was allowed to stay, but he chose to come with me. He knew it wasn't fair, that I had nothing to do with Kate's death. Our daddy had taken her hunting on her eighth birthday. He shot and killed her by accident. They hated me, because I looked like her, reminded them of her.

"I remember standing in the den, clutching onto Fluffy as tightly as I could. I couldn't think, couldn't move. Scott disappeared into our bedroom for a few minutes and returned with his backpack bulging. He then took my backpack, walked over to the kitchen, and crammed as much food as he could into it. I remember the instant cold I felt as he put the backpack on my back. The frozen packets sent a chill down my spine. Scott took me by the hand and led me out of the house.

"'Looks like it's just the three of us now.' He said as we walked down the street.

"'Three?'

"'You, me, and Fluffy. As long as we stick together, we'll be alright.'

"We crashed at Tyler's that night. We spent the first few weeks, bouncin' 'round Scott's friend's houses. Weekdays weren't bad, because we still went to school guaranteeing a free breakfast

177

and lunch, and school got your mind off what was really happening.

"However, we couldn't keep staying with Scott's friends. They had their own problems. I remember one night Scott took us some place new.

"'I don't know, Scott. Are you sure this is a good idea? What about what Tyler said about Child Services taking us away? I don't wanna be locked up in a kid's prison until I'm eighteen. I'll never see you again.' I was nervous about his plan.

"'Don't worry,' He took my hand in his and walked up to a lady who was standing in the line to go into the Soup Kitchen. 'Excuse me, Miss, I've heard they'll provide you more things if you have children. Would you mind pretendin' to be our mother, so my sister and I can get some food? I promise we'll be good.'

"The woman looked down at us. I studied her face, it seemed kind. 'How long have you been on the streets?'

"'Three days, Dad's mad and we're waitin' for him to calm down before we go back home, but we're awfully hungry. Would you please help us?' Scott squeezed my hand, I knew how desperately he hoped his plan would work.

"I watched as the woman look back and forth between us. 'My name's Essie. What's yours?'

"'I'm Scott, this is Ann.' I gave her a hopeful smile.

"'You look young to be livin' on the streets. How old are you?'

"'I'm ten, Ann's eight. Like I said, Dad's just mad. It takes him about a week to calm down and then we can go back home.'

"We got closer to the door of the Soup Kitchen. Essie said, 'Give me your hands.' She walked in the door with us.

178

"We ate the hot dinner and were offered a place to sleep for the night. We were even told we could stay for free for up to thirty days. We hit the jackpot. I was so excited I could've danced on the tables and sang for joy, but Scott shot me a cautioning glance and I knew I must bury my feelings.

"We were shown to a room where we would sleep. Scott walked over to his bed and plopped down, but I sat on Essie's. I liked Essie, she was sweet and kind, nothing like my real mom. 'Why are you homeless?'

"'Ann, you shouldn't butt into other people's business,' Scott immediately scolded.

"'It's alright,' Essie told him. 'I lost my job and then my landlord threw me out for not paying the rent.'

"'That's terrible!' I couldn't believe a person would throw someone else out on the streets. It was horrible, it was awful. It stunned me when I realized it was exactly what had happened to me. 'What a mean man he is.'

"Essie smiled, 'A mean man indeed.' She pulled a hairbrush out of her purse and started brushing my matted hair. My own mother had never done that. It made me feel special and I wished Essie was my real mom.

"'Do you have any other family or friends? Maybe they could help.' I wanted to help her.

"'It's just me,' Essie's voice was so loving. 'I always wanted to get married and have some children, but it never happened. Now I'm too old to have kids.'

"'How old are you?'

"'Ann, you're being nosey again,' Scott warned.

"'It's alright,' Essie affectionately replied. 'You have a very

179

curious sister. I'm forty-eight. So, tell me. Does your dad get angry often?'

"I knew I was suddenly in trouble. I shot Scott a worried glance. He gave a big smile and replied, 'Not too often. Ann, it's time to sleep.'

"'Alright,' Even though I wasn't tired, really enjoying Essie's tender touch, I knew he was changing the subject. I hugged her 'good-night' and walked over to Scott's bed climbing in under the covers. Fluffy was waiting there for me.

"'Ann, they have a bed for you. Don't you wanna sleep in it?'

"'I always sleep with Scott.' I laid down on my side, my head on the pillow with Fluffy in my arms. Scott laid his protective arm over me like he did every night.

"We milked that story for the entire month, Scott made excuses, but Essie didn't seem to care what they were. I got the feeling she was having as much fun pretending to be our mother as we were...

"At the shelter, there was a bookcase filled with donated books. There was one book, it was called *"The Island on Bird Street."* It was about a boy who survived the holocaust. I became fascinated with stories of people who were hiding from the Germans during World War Two. I would tell Scott all about them. Their ability to survive game me hope that Scott and I would also make it. Their hardships also made me feel better about my own life, because as bad as mine was, it wasn't as bad as theirs.

"The month ended way too quickly, but Scott was prepared. It seemed while I was reading books, he was making the stories come true. I was in disbelief the day we climbed into our bedroom window, and he showed me the hidden bunker he'd created under the bed. A secret hideout just like the Jews used.

180

"I would roll under the bed all the way to the wall. The board one row in was loose. I could slide it over and drop into the hole. I would then lift the loose board back over top and nobody had any clue I was under there.

"Scott kept the bedroom door locked most of the time and went out of his way to see our parents as little as possible. He told them I was dead. They bought the story, and it bought us two more years at the house."

Hallie went silent.

Matty knew this was his chance to get them out of there. The darkness was seeping in all around them making his hair stand on end. More shots were heard in the distance.

"What happened? Why did you stop living there when you were ten?" Lex's voice broke the silence. His curiosity was lulling him into a false sense of safety.

"One day, Scott was in a particularly good mood. He was working a part-time job and bought each of us a new outfit and shoes. These were really new, not something from the second hand store. They were the first new clothes I'd ever owned.

"Scott remembered eating dove with bacon wrapped around them and wanted to have it to celebrate, so he killed some birds for dinner. He made sure mama was out before we entered the house. While the birds were baking, we decided to take a shower so we'd be all nice and clean for our new clothes and fancy meal."

"I remember both of us being butt naked as the warm water flowed over us. It'd been awhile since my last shower. I felt so rich. I remembered the shampoo tingling in my hair as Scott washed it. I was so happy, I was singing. He didn't want me to sing, wanted me to be quiet. But I hadn't felt this good in a long time, so instead, I sang even louder."

She suddenly paused as a deadly silence filled the air.

181

"What happened?" Henry leaned in toward her.

Her voice softened to just above a whisper. "Our daddy heard me. He busted into the room and grabbed me out of the shower. He was full of rage. He took my body and started slamming it against the wall and mirror. Scott jumped on him to try and make him stop, but he just grabbed Scott and threw him against the hall wall. I remember seeing Scott just lying in a heap on the floor. He wasn't moving." She stopped talking.

"What happened next?" Paul gently questioned.

In a dry, monotone voice she continued. "He grabbed me again and put my head in the toilet. I remember choking on the water. The next thing I knew, I was waking up in the hospital. Scott was sitting next to me. It seemed that when he came to, he found me lying unconscious next to the toilet, and our daddy was gone. I had a concussion and was covered in bandages.

"I felt so guilty. I should've listened to him. There was a large knot on his head, and our new clothes were covered in blood. Scott said it didn't matter, but I knew it did. Every day I wore those clothes, I was reminded of what I'd done. I was so ashamed. After awhile, the dirt covered up the blood stains so others couldn't notice them, but I could always see them."

"How long did you have to wear those clothes?" Lex's voice was sad.

"Three months. Needless to say, my parents now knew I was alive. We couldn't live in our bedroom anymore, our daddy tore the door down. We were back on the streets looking for a safe place to stay. To make matters worse, my teacher wanted a parent-teacher conference. I told her mama didn't want one, but the teacher kept insisting. She even said she'd go by the house. I freaked.

"Scott, however, devised a plan. 'What we need is for someone to pretend to be your mother. I'm already signing all your forms, and they haven't become suspicious.' Scott sat down on the

182

playground swing to think. 'I know,' He finally said. 'Let's go find Essie. She's helped us before, maybe she'll help us again.'

"We spent the afternoon looking all over town. Eventually, we found her and told her our plan. She was reluctant at first, but the soft spot in her heart won out. Before school started the following morning, the three of us sat through a parent/teacher conference. It continued that way for several years. And even though Essie's drinking progressively became worse, she always showed up and pretended to be my mom whenever she was needed.

"I could always find her here. I've spent years living all over this town, one night here, a few nights there, a month somewhere if I were really lucky. Scott went through a lot of girlfriends to get us off the streets. He was picky, older women with their own place. He'd hook up with them. I hated all the sex and the using of people, but Scott would say, 'That's just the way it is.' and 'once we get out, never again.' He always said a condom was cheaper than that rat infested motel we'd sometimes end up at when the weather was bad. As much as I disliked it, I couldn't complain. I usually got to sleep on a sofa which beat the streets any night, and I knew I was the reason we were living the way we were.

"Scott could've said 'screw it' and gone back home anytime. It was me they hated, not him. But he never did. When he was between girlfriends, we lived here. It was a safe place. My daddy wouldn't find me, nobody went to be around the homeless drunks. Essie was always happy to see me. She'd spend hours brushing my hair, and I loved every minute of it.

"You wanted to know why I came here. Now you know. I always end up right back here, this street, this box of Essie's. This is my home. It's the only place I've ever lived where I'm always welcome and never thrown out. I can stay for as long as I like, and not worry about doing something stupid to screw it up. I'm gonna stay right here until Scott returns."

Matty sighed, he'd promised to protect her. "Well, it doesn't look that bad. So tell me, what's the best way to sleep? Should I try to lie down on my back or is it better to sleep on my side?"

The statue moved her head to give him a suspicious look. "You can't stay here," Her voice was firm. "The street isn't safe for you. This isn't your life."

"It's not yours either, not anymore. If you're staying, then I am too. I'm not leaving you here by yourself."

Thankfully, Paul and Henry immediately caught onto what he was doing and said they weren't leaving either. They started acting like they were trying to get comfortable to go to sleep. Matty gave Lex a 'come on' look; he reluctantly started pretending he was staying as well, although he wasn't as convincing.

(Hallie)

Hallie was surprised by their behavior. *Did they really care enough they'd actually sleep on the street with her? Even Lex?*

"What do you say?" Matty asked. "Can you make room for all of us?"

Tears started to run down her cheeks. She was too confused and tired to understand the emotions suddenly attacking her body. The one thing she did know, she was happy Matty was there. She leaned over placing her head on his shoulder.

He put his arm around her, hugging her as she sobbed. "It's alright, we're here for you."

"Why'd they extend Scott's tour? Why won't they let him come home? I haven't seen him in twenty months. I miss him so much."

"I know it feels like longer, but they've only been in Iraq sixteen months."

"Maybe you saw Ron sixteen months ago, but I haven't seen Scott since he left for boot camp. It was right after he turned eighteen, in January. He told me he'd only be gone for three months, he'd come back to get me as soon as it was over. I waited for him, but he didn't come, he was shipped to Iraq instead. And now, they won't let him come back. I want him back, I love him so much." She grabbed onto Matty overwhelmed with grief, again. Her body kept surging with pain and producing tears. She couldn't control it.

Once the gushing sobs became trickles, Matty said, "Ready to go home to a nice, soft bed?"

Hallie nodded her head in agreement. She was too exhausted to argue, and she needed him too much to send him away.

Matty helped her to her feet; they started walking toward his car with his arm around her shoulder. It felt good to be in Matty's loving and protective arms. She couldn't have a better substitute for Scott.

When they reached his car, Hallie suddenly stopped. "Wait a minute. I'll be right back. I need to get Harry some food."

Matty insisted on driving her up the road to the McDonald's. Lex purchased a three hundred dollar gift card; Hallie was touched and quietly thanked him. They then drove back down the street to where the car had been parked. The guys waited while she jumped out and walked back over to Harry.

Hallie was surprised she felt happy despite how emotionally drained she was. It felt like a ray of sunshine peeking out through heavy rain clouds. "Hey, look what I have for you." She smiled holding the card up in front of him before sliding it into the front

185

pocket of his pants. "It'll buy you hot meals. Use it."

Harry then showed her the new bottle of whiskey he purchased. "This guy just walked up me...gave me twenty. He life saver."

Hallie smiled, knowing it was probably Lex or Matty, and gave Harry a hug. "Please take care of yourself." Harry was a mess, a lovable mess.

Hallie started walking toward Matty's car, happy to be going back to her new home.

Suddenly, she was grabbed from behind. "You stupid little bitch! Where the hell have you been?" Hallie recognized her uncle's voice and screamed as he threw her to the ground and started pounding her with his fist.

Uncle

"Leave her alone." She heard Matty's voice.

Her uncle was pulled off, but his voice was still close. "Don't tell me what to do." The uncle hissed. "I'll treat her however I want, she's *my* property."

"Not any more she isn't." Hallie watched in horror as Matty punched her uncle in the face.

Hallie's uncle starting to beat him. Matty was no match for the Riverside man; he was knocked to the ground.

Her uncle started to hit her again. It was all happening so fast. Paul and Henry jumped into the fight and pulled him off her momentarily while Lex grabbed her and started pulling her toward the car.

Hallie turned around to see Paul and Henry on the ground and Matty being punched. "Matty!" She screamed. She needed to think, to fight against her own mind which was instinctively trying to protect itself. She couldn't escape into its safety; she wasn't the one who needed to be protected this time. For the first time in her life, she was going to fight back. It went against every instinct in her body. Her life meant nothing, but Matty's meant everything. She had to save him. Adrenaline surged through her; she broke free of Lex.

It was impossible to harm her uncle without a weapon. She needed one, fast. Matty would be dead in a matter of moments. Scanning the area, she spotted Harry and knew exactly what she needed. Within seconds she grabbed the almost full whiskey bottle out of his hand and ran over to the fight. As her uncle raised his fist to punch Matty again, Hallie yelled, "Leave him alone."

Her uncle turned to face her. She used all the force in her arms to crack the bottle over his head, causing him to fall to the ground.

It stunned him. Lex grabbed her while Paul and Henry helped Matty. They all sprinted to the car. Hallie jumped into the back seat with Matty and Henry. At the same time, Lex was in the driver's seat; Paul was at shotgun. Lex grabbed Matty's keys and started the engine. The tires squealed against the asphalt as the car shot away.

(Matty)

Hallie was hysterical. Matty looked at her beaten face and the tears pouring down her cheeks. The salt water must be stinging her open wounds caused by his ring, but she didn't appear to notice. Her eyes reflected a deep pain as she whispered. "I'm so sorry...I'm so sorry...I'm so sorry."

Matty grabbed her in his arms. "I'm alright. It's not your fault. Are you hurt badly?"

"I'm so sorry...I'm so sorry." She kept repeating as her body violently shook.

"Was that your uncle?" Paul inquired.

"I'm so sorry...I'm so sorry..." Was the only answer he received.

"Shh.." Matty tried to comfort her. He knew the only thing he could do was to hold her tightly until she calmed down, like she had instructed him to do. He'd promised to keep her secret, so he said, "I think she's in shock. She can't answer you right now."

The screaming of his Toyota's engine started to drown out Hallie's chanting. Lex was driving like he was in one of his super

188

cars. Matty lost count of how many yellowish-red lights he ran.

"Do you guys need to see a doctor?"

"I think I'm alright, but it probably would be a good idea to get Hallie checked out. Her uncle could throw quite a punch. Each hit felt like a twenty pound weight slamming against my body."

Paul and Henry agreed, saying they weren't badly hurt.

(Lex)

Once they were several towns away, Lex stopped at a drop in emergency clinic. They discovered Hallie was carrying a small backpack under her hoodie. It contained some sandwiches which were obviously made by Charles and her letters from Scott, her prized possession. He couldn't believe that's all she took from their expensive home.

She was a mess. She wouldn't stop crying and repeating, "I'm so sorry." They couldn't get her to respond to anything, including giving them her uncle's name. Lex was chomping at the bit to file assault charges and make him pay for what he did to her.

The only good news was that neither she nor Matty sustained any serious injuries.

Lex dropped Paul and Henry off. Hallie fell asleep on the ride back to the condo. Due to Matty's condition, Lex took her out of his arms and carried her to her room. Matty pulled back the covers; Lex gently laid her down. They took off her shoes; Lex pulled up the sheet to tuck her in. He sat down on the bed and as lightly as possible, ran his fingers over her cuts and bruises. Her beautiful face was shattered. He felt Matty's hand on his shoulder. "How could anyone beat someone like that?"

"I don't know."

189

Lex leaned in and kissed her on the corner of her left eye, one of the few places untouched.

They wandered out into the family room. "You look like you've been hit by a truck, a big one. You sure you're okay?"

"Honestly, my entire body aches. I have a bad feeling I'm going feel even worse in the morning."

"Well, I think you put up a good fight. I didn't know you knew how to street fight." Lex was impressed.

Matty smiled, causing him to wince. "That's the first time I've ever really hit anyone."

"You could've fooled me," Lex chuckled and joked. "I'm going to remember not to make you mad...But seriously, you were incredible with Hallie tonight, convincing her to come home with us and then calming her down after you guys were assaulted. I was really impressed. You're going make a great dad someday."

"Thanks, that means a lot...When I was trying to calm her down, I kept thinking she's been through so much. She's so used to being hurt, I think she expects it. I realize now, my house was probably the first stable place she's ever lived. Moving in here seems to have really thrown her for a loop, she thought I wanted to get rid of her."

"I don't get her. How could she think we wouldn't want her? We've made her the lead singer of our band."

"I think we should remind her of that in the morning." Matty groaned as he sat down on the sofa. "Do you know where I put those pain pills the doctor gave us?"

"Yeah," Lex took the pills out of his pocket. "Do you need some water?"

"No, I'm good." Matty popped two pills into his mouth and

190

swallowed them down.

"Matty," Lex quietly said as he sat down. "I've never known someone to hurt as much as she does. What else can I do to make her happy?"

"You've done a lot already. Just please try to remember she's really sensitive. If she wants to have a serious talk with you, it might be very painful to her. She's being brave to speak her mind. Other than that, I think the only thing that can make her truly happy is to have Scott come home. I really hope their tour doesn't get extended again."

Lex nodded his head in agreement.

Matty yawned; he looked exhausted.

"Why don't you take my bed tonight, I'll go and sleep at the other condo."

"That's alright, I'll just sleep on the sofa, I don't think I'm going to sleep well anyway. I want to be near in case she needs me and to make sure she doesn't try to leave again."

"Alright, then I'll see you in the morning."

(Hallie)

Hallie walked into the kitchen. Lex and Matty were already there having breakfast at the counter.

"Good morning," Lex smiled at her.

" 'Morning," She answered in a monotone voice and headed straight for the refrigerator, not making eye contact with them. The sight of Matty's face overwhelmed her with guilt. If she hadn't gone

191

to Riverside, he wouldn't have gotten hurt. She might as well have beaten him herself.

"How are you feeling?" Matty asked. *How could he sound so loving after what she did to him? She was a horrible person. He should hate her.*

"Fine," She stayed guarded, keeping her head buried in the refrigerator.

"Have you taken some pain medicine?"

"I'm fine."

"Why are you shutting me out? I know you're not fine. You're black and blue all over, don't even think about telling me it doesn't hurt, because I know it hurts like hell."

Hallie sighed. Matty was worried, and now she was hurting him again. Was Lex also concerned? She couldn't tell because she refused to look at either of them.

She wanted to tell them she was alright; no broken bones, no concussion. The beating she received was nothing compared to what her daddy used to do to her and what her uncle would have done if Matty hadn't saved her. She wanted to tell them these things and reassure them she really *was* fine.

But she knew if she told them, they would have questions and just thinking about those questions caused her considerable pain – much worse than the physical pain she was experiencing. There was no way she could talk about it.

"I'm used to it, you're not." She grabbed a fruit smoothie and quickly moved to leave the kitchen.

"Hold it," Matty demanded.

Hallie's feet froze; *damn, almost made it out.* Her back was to them; she couldn't face them, didn't want them to know the pain she was feeling. She just wanted to deal with it alone.

Matty got out of his chair, walked over to her, and tried to look her straight in the eyes. Hallie quickly dropped hers to the floor to avoid eye contact. "You're uncle used to beat you, didn't he? That's why you ran away from him, isn't it?"

Hallie thought about his words. If she said 'yes,' then maybe that would be the end of the questions. If she said 'no,' then there would be more questions she didn't want to answer. "Yes." It was true he did used to beat her, but it wasn't why she ran away.

"Sweetie, I'm so sorry." Matty encircled his arms around her in a big hug.

Hallie let down her guard and hugged him back. She felt safe and more importantly, loved, when he held her. It was the same way she used to feel when she was with Scott; she longed for that feeling again.

"He shouldn't go unpunished for what he did. We need to file assault charges against him. What's his name?"

Hallie immediately felt panicked and pulled away. No longer fearful of his face, she looked him straight in the eyes. "I can't do that."

"Why not?" Lex responded. "He should go to jail."

Hallie was trapped; she didn't want to talk about her uncle or even think about him. It hurt too much.

"Lex is right. What are you scared of?"

Tears started running down Hallie's cheeks as she lost control of her emotions. There was too much pain and only more would come. She needed to stop this conversation, immediately. She felt herself becoming hysterical. "If I talk to the police, Child

Services will find me, they'll take me away from you. I'll become property of The State, I'll get locked up in an orphanage, and I'll never see you again."

Suddenly, she was in Matty's arms again. "No one's going take you from us. I promise."

Hallie closed her eyes, gripping him as tightly as she could. Another set of arms wrapped around her; she felt a soft kiss on her cheek before she heard Lex's voice. "We wouldn't let that happen. You belong with us. No one's going make you press charges if you don't want to."

Hallie felt better after hearing this and clung on to them as tightly as she could as the terrifying images clipped through her mind.

She agreed to continue living at Lex's, but since he was leaving for a business trip to D.C., she went to stay with Matty for a few days.

Four weeks passed; Hallie and Matty's injuries healed. The wonderful, fairytale life was back on track. The band had just finished producing their first album as 5th Asterix which was exciting, but not their biggest news. They were asked to be the opening act for Carbon Dioxide, who was going on tour in the U.S. This was the break they were hoping for.

Hallie was practicing when her cell phone rang. It was the Virginia number again. "Hello?" She anxiously answered.

"Hey, little sister."

"Scott! How are you?" She excitedly asked and noticed the guys all grinning at her. She left the studio and walked up the stairs to Paul's family room to talk in private.

Hallie excitedly told him about the new album and the concert tour. Things she hadn't included in her letters, because she wanted to tell him in person. When she was done speaking, Scott said, "That's wonderful. Are you performing on your birthday? It's coming up in a week-and-a-half."

"No, we aren't scheduled to go on tour until two weeks after that."

"That's a shame. I was hoping to see you sing on the day I come home."

"What?!" Hallie was stunned, suddenly overwhelmed with joy. "Are you serious? You're coming home?" Tears started to pour down her face.

"We got the orders this morning." She could hear the smile on his face.

"Oh my gosh, you're coming home! It's finally happening! I've wished for this for so long."

"Me too. I can't wait to see you again. Look, my time's up. I love you, bye."

"Bye, I love you too. See you soon." Hallie hung up the phone with tears streaming down her cheeks. She sat and stared at the phone for a few minutes almost in disbelief. She finally got up and walked back downstairs.

When she entered the recording studio, Henry was the first to notice the tears. "Hallie, what's wrong?"

(Lex)

Lex instantly looked at her. *Why was she crying?* Hallie was looking directly at Matty. The biggest smile crossed her face. He loved that smile. "They're coming home," She choked out.

Yes, It finally happened.

"What?" Matty didn't understand.

"They got their orders this morning. Scott and Ron, they're coming home."

Lex watched as realization crossed Matty's face. "Oh my gosh, OH MY GOSH!" He crossed the room in seconds, grabbed her in a big hug, and spun her around. "Wooo...Whooo..." He yelled. They spent a few minutes embracing each other crying tears of joy. "I told you they'd make it back. I told you they would."

(Hallie)

Hallie walked into Miaotsie. She was still on yesterday's high. *Scott was coming home!* She kept screaming in her head. The news distracted her so much; it took her twice as long to get dressed. Lex laughed and asked her to meet him down at the club when she was finally ready.

Hallie bounced up to the bar to say 'hello' to Zac.

He looked concerned. "I thought you should know a guy was in here last night asking questions about you. He was a big, muscular guy with tattoos down his arms, his left arm had a huge snake. He was showing a photograph of you wearing glasses and having long hair. Something about him made me feel uneasy, so I told him I didn't know you. Do you know who he was?"

Hearing Zac's words caused Hallie to freeze in terror. He was there; her uncle, in the room. She couldn't move her arms or legs even though she wanted to run away from him. He was going to get her, and there was nothing she could do to stop him. The smug look on his face as he walked toward her, he knew she was trapped. Hallie screamed as everything went black.

Hide and Seek

"Hallie, Hallie," She heard a familiar voice. *Who was talking to her? Why did she feel wetness on her face?* She wrestled to open her eyes and eventually succeeded. Zac's eyes met hers. He was worried. "You alright?"

"What happened?" Hallie noticed she was in Lex's office, lying on his leather sofa.

"I was telling you about this guy who was asking about you and the most horrific look came across your face. I've never seen anyone look as terrified as you. You suddenly screamed and passed out. I caught you as you fell to the floor."

As Hallie realized what happened, she began to panic again. "Lex, did he hear or see me?"

"No, no one was there except me. Who is this guy, and why are you so frightened of him?"

Hallie's mind raced. She didn't want to tell him the truth, but how could she not. He'd seen her, knew about her uncle. She closed her eyes for a moment to gather her thoughts. "I moved in with Matty to get a fresh start. That guy thinks he owns me." Opening her eyes, she looked directly at Zac. "Please, don't tell Lex or anyone else he was here. I don't want Matty to get into another fight with him. I don't want anyone to get hurt." She pleaded with her eyes.

"Is that what happened to both of you a few weeks ago?"

"He and Matty got into it. If Paul and Henry hadn't jumped in to help, Matty would've ended up in the hospital." Hallie fought back her tears as she remembered the horrible night. She thought of Lex and cringed. "Please Zac, he'll hurt Lex even worse. Please don't tell him he was here."

"You should get a restraining order. In the meantime, I'll talk to the bouncers here and at Lex's other clubs. We have surveillance cameras. I'll print a still picture, so they'll all know what he looks like. I'll make sure the guy isn't allowed in. You'll be safe."

Hallie felt relieved. "Thanks, I really appreciate your help."

"No problem. There is, however, one thing that still bothers me."

"What's that?"

"The 5th Asterix posters are outside all the clubs. If this guy was paying any attention, he would've recognized you."

Lex walked into the office. "Hey, what're you two doing in here?" He looked directly at Hallie, becoming instantly alarmed. "You're white as a ghost, are you alright?"

"She's fine. She was feeling faint, so I brought her in here to lie down for a moment."

Hallie told Zac 'thanks' with her eyes for covering for her. Besides, it wasn't a complete lie, she had fainted.

Lex sat down on the sofa, worried. "Feeling faint, huh?" He removed the wet towel from her forehead and placed his hand there to check her. "Maybe I should take you to the doctor."

Hallie needed to think fast. Going to the doctor was out of the question. "I think I forgot to eat today. Low blood sugar, that's all. You know how distracted I've been since yesterday's call. I'm feeling better already."

Lex reached into his back pocket and pulled out his wallet. "Zac, go up the street and get her a sandwich." He fished out a

199

twenty dollar bill.

"Really, I'm fine." Being frightened always caused her to lose her appetite. How was she going to eat an entire sandwich?

"You're going to stay here until you've eaten. Now, what type of sandwich would you like?"

"Umm…turkey, I guess."

She watched Zac move to leave the room. At the doorway, he turned back to her. Lex didn't notice him raise his right hand to his lips. He closed them, pretending to seal them, and threw the invisible key over his shoulder. Hallie was grateful. Her secret was still safe from Lex. Now she just needed to let him coddle her for the rest of the day. That wouldn't hurt anyone.

As long as she was going to pretend to be faint, Hallie decided to close her eyes. She didn't want Lex to read anything into them as she thought about the danger they were all in because of her. There must be a way to protect her new family from her past. She couldn't let her uncle hurt them.

The early evening found Hallie reading a book on the sofa in Lex's family room. Charles passed through on his way to the grocery. She saw her chance to implement the first part of her plan, the most critical part. She needed to speak to Charles alone. "May I go with you? I was feeling faint earlier today, I thought it'd be a good idea to get some of those healthy bars to put into my purse."

She glanced over at Lex. He was working on his laptop, but had been watching her like a hawk all afternoon. She'd been resting and reading a book for several hours now. Surely, he would think this was a good idea.

"Charles can get some bars for you. Why don't you stay

200

here and rest?"

"Lex, honestly, I'm fine. I felt much better after eating the sandwich. And I'm not exactly sure what type I want. I'd like to check out my options. I promise I'll let Charles know if I even think I might be feeling faint."

After a few more minutes of protesting and pleading, he finally agreed and asked Charles to take one of his cars. As Hallie sat in the Rolls Royce, she made small talk. She wanted her important question to seem casual, so she delayed it and asked about the car.

Charles explained that owning as many cars as Lex did, it was important to drive them periodically. He didn't mind, was accustomed to this request. She found out Lex drove this car the least; it was very classy, but not fast. Lex preferred supercars.

Hallie thought it was strange Lex would own a car he didn't drive. Charles explained it was used for special occasions when he wasn't in the mood to use the limo. Hallie thought it was ostentatious and a ridiculous waste of money. Why did Lex need to own six cars anyway?

They arrived at the store. Hallie suddenly felt nervous about her question, but she needed to ask it. Charles was picking out vegetables when she made her move.

"You said Lex was like a son to you. Does that mean you'd do anything to protect him?"

Charles glanced up from the zucchini he was inspecting. Curiosity was on his face. "I suppose so."

Not exactly the answer she was hoping for, but good enough to continue. "Would you keep a secret from him if you knew it was in his best interest?"

"Best interest how?"

"He could be seriously injured if he knew the truth."

Charles was studying her face now. She gave him her most serious look. He became serious as well. "I would. What are we talking about?"

"Lex and Matty are in danger because of me. I don't wanna see either of them get hurt, but I can't protect them on my own. I need some help."

"What danger?"

"My uncle, he's found me. He was at Miaotsie yesterday asking about me. When Zac told me this morning, I freaked out and fainted. I made up the story about forgetting to eat, so Lex wouldn't be suspicious. My uncle is a terrible man, he won't stop until he gets me back. He'll kill Lex, Matty, or anyone else who might try to get in his way. That's how it works where I'm from.

"You see, my aunt had been unemployed for over a year, and he lost his job the day after I moved in. I used to be forced to do things that made him a lot of money. I was his easy ticket to income. He thinks I'm his personal property and as far as The State's concerned, I am. I was forced to lie to Child Services about my life. If I didn't, it would've been a lot worse." She shuttered as she forced the memory to stay repressed. "I'd rather be dead, than go back to him."

"If you have any thoughts of suicide, put them out of your mind right now. That *will* hurt Lex."

It took Hallie a moment to realize Charles's misunderstanding. "Of course not, that's not what I meant. Only if I were back with my uncle again would I consider that option and then only if I couldn't escape like I did before, and only if I knew Scott was never coming to get me. But he would, and he will, he'll be

202

coming home very soon and my uncle will be out of my life once and for all."

Charles was now puzzled. "Then what help do you need?"

"To find a friend of mine, he understands what we're dealing with. I've seen Lex ask you to do all sorts of things, and I was wondering if you knew how to find a missing person?"

Charles grinned; his eyes were wild with excitement. "You want me to play private investigator?" He was suddenly teasing. "I do wear many hats for Lex, but he's never asked me to be a P.I. before. I do love a good mystery, always fancied myself as a detective. I've even thought about writing a novel, maybe I'll write one about this case. *The case of the missing street kid,* it has a nice ring to it, don't you think?" But before a stunned Hallie could respond, Charles was off. "Come with me, my dear."

Hallie curiously followed him to the office supply section of the store. Charles picked up a spiral notebook, took a pen out of his pocket, and proceeded to interview her in the middle of the isle. "Now, tell me everything you know about this missing kid?"

"His name is Warren Harv. He has sandy blonde hair and blue eyes. The last time I saw him he was about five feet eight, but he's seventeen now and it's been a year, so he's probably grown some. He's built, very muscular. I don't know how you're gonna find him. He moved, I don't know where. The house was abandoned. They just disappeared one day."

"They?"

"His mother and brother. His brother's probably in jail. Ray was bad news. Warren tried to stay clean, but Ray was into drugs, guns, and stealing cars. I guess it's possible Warren could be in jail as well. I sure hope not." Hallie's mind started to wander.

"So, Ray, how old is he?"

"Umm….he's either nineteen or twenty."

"And his mother?"

"Her name was Penny. I think she was sixteen when she had Ray, so she's thirty-four, thirty-five."

"What about Warren's father?"

"Dead, killed in a street fight when Warren was two."

Charles studied his notes and shook his head in agreement as he thought. "I have some ideas of where to check first. Don't worry, I'll find your missing friend."

"Thanks, Charles," Hallie felt completely relieved. He was going to help her and keep it a secret from Lex. It was exactly what she wanted.

They finished grocery shopping. Charles reminded her to pick out some bars, so Lex wouldn't be suspicious. After paying for the food and spiral notebook, Charles didn't head straight home. He stopped at a specialty store and purchased a detective's hat.

Hallie was delighted he was having so much fun with her problem. It made her feel less anxious; she was glad she confided in Charles.

Hallie walked out of Matty's house the following afternoon. She was on top of the world. First, she couldn't believe she actually had her driver's license; Lex took her that morning to take the test. Second, she couldn't believe Lex let her drive the Lamborghini to Matty's. It was so much fun showing up and surprising him.

Now she was heading back to the condo. Lex loved surprises and had one waiting for her. Hallie was so happy; she danced and sang her way down the front steps and toward the car.

She tossed the keys up into the air and as her eyes tracked them into her hand, something in her peripheral vision caught her attention.

There was an old, brown station wagon parked a little bit up the road. Hallie stared at the car for a moment. There was something about it that seemed familiar. It suddenly struck her, she knew that car and the driver.

Panic instantly set in. She needed to get him away from Matty, who would get hurt. Hallie quickly glanced at the shiny, yellow Lamborghini next to her. This car could easily out run that one. However, the handling was sensitive and if she were driving fast or worse, if she flashed, she could easily lose control, wrecking the car. She would become an easy catch.

Her breathing accelerated as her uncle got out of his car and started walking toward her. This was it. Instinct kicked in. She bolted down the street away from him. When she came to the first corner, she turned left and kept running.

The car was following her. She could hear the loud, piercing sound it made. It was close by. She sprinted across someone's yard, cutting the next corner. *What are you doing? You're making a circle and taking him back to Matty. What if Matty's outside wondering why he didn't hear the Lamborghini's engine?* She darted across the street to switch directions.

Her throat was starting to hurt due to the amount of oxygen she was forcing into her lungs. The pounding of concrete under the thin soles of her sandals make her knees ache. But she continued to run, going as hard and as fast as her body could move her.

Suddenly, she was flying through the air. She hit the asphalt with a thud skinning the palms of her hands and both her knees. It took her a stunned moment to realize she tripped. A quick glance behind her showed her uncle getting out of the car only a few yards away to come and grab her. *MOVE!* Hallie scrambled to her feet and took off again.

What was she gonna do now? She was running out of steam and could feel her body slowing down, straining against her efforts to flee. There was a bus that had just pulled up on the other side of the street. She bolted across the street again.

A car horn blared. "Watch where you're going! You trying to get yourself killed?"

Hallie's heart stopped for a second as she realized she'd almost gotten hit, but she kept moving. The bus door closed as she reached it. "Please!" She cried and banged on the door.

It opened.

"Thank you," She told the driver as she paid him and the bus jolted away from the curb. The bus was about half full. Some of the passengers were staring at her, but Hallie didn't care. She walked to the back and slumped into a seat still breathing heavily. At least now she could sit and think of a plan.

The sound of her cell phone ringing caused Hallie to jump. "Charles, I'm in trouble! He found me!"

"What happened?" He was alarmed.

As Hallie recapped the events, she was able to think a little clearer. "And then I did something really stupid, I jumped on a bus."

"That was actually a smart move. I'd be willing to bet he's not going to attack you with witnesses."

"I'm not so sure...I can't out run him in a bus. All he has to do is follow and wait for me to get off. Then he can grab me. What am I gonna do?"

"Stay on the bus," He was firm.

206

"What about when it pulls into a depot? I'll have to get off then."

"We'll figure that out if and when we need to. Can you look out the window and see if he's still following you?"

"Um…Let me see. It looks like we're gonna be turning at the next intersection. Hang on," Hallie switched seats to the other side of the bus so she could look back once it made the turn. She waited anxiously for the light to change. Finally, the bus was moving around the corner. Her eyes caught sight of the brown car. "He's still following me."

"Alright, sit tight while I work on a plan to get you. Do you have the second phone Lex gave you, the emergency one?"

"I always keep it with me."

"Good, turn it on."

"Okay," Hallie reached down her shirt and took the phone out of her bra. A moment later, she returned it. "It's on and hidden."

"Great! Now sit tight, I'm on my way to get you."

Hallie could hear the rev of the car's engine and wondered how fast Charles was driving. He was coming to get her, but would he get there in time? Hallie looked at the bus map to determine where she was. Her body tensed. "Charles!" She was now panicked. "I'm almost to the depot."

"Go to the depot. It should be crowded with people which will help you lose him."

Hallie swallowed hard, not sure she was able to do this. She'd tried to run before, but had never been very successful. It was one thing to run around Matty's neighborhood, she knew it well. But, the bus depot was unfamiliar. How was she going to be able to look, think, and act so quickly?

207

"Are you still there?"

"Yeah...Charles, I'm scared."

"I know...When you get off the bus, head towards a crowd of people, preferably one getting on another bus. You'll be able to move faster if you're not talking to me, so call me back when you're on the next bus."

"Alright."

As they pulled into the depot, Hallie slipped her phone back into her purse which hung diagonally across her chest. She was completely on her own now. She looked out the window for the crowd of people she needed. To her horror, the depot looked fairly empty. Where was she going to go?

The bus came to a stop and the doors opened. Knowing she needed to move quickly, Hallie bolted.

She ran three stalls over to another bus. The sign on the front said 'Out of service.'

The panic started to seize her. Hallie turned around looking for any bus boarding. There weren't very many buses there. A few people were sitting on benches waiting, but none were gathering their things.

Hallie ran over to the bus departure board. The red letters said it was two minutes after two and the next bus would be leaving at two ten.

Her heart was racing. Hallie knew if she didn't keep moving, she would become paralyzed with fear and her uncle would easily get her. In eight minutes, it would all be over, her entire life.

RUN! The voice in her head commanded. Hallie started sprinting as hard as she could across the empty depot. She saw a sign directing people to a mall. Hallie knew she couldn't out run his car on foot, but she could try to hide in a mall. All she needed to do was get across the street and wait for Charles to come and get her.

Hallie bolted toward the bus parked in the first stall. The street she needed to cross was on the other side of it. *Almost there. Almost there.*

As Hallie cleared the bus, the squealing of a car's tires made her stop dead in her tracks frozen in complete terror.

Plans

"Get in!" The voice yelled. It wasn't the voice she was expecting. Hallie opened her eyes to see Lex's sleek, black Koenigsegg right in front of her. "Hurry, Hallie!"

She was stunned, but quickly jumped into the car.

"Put on your seatbelt and hang on. I'm going to lose him." Charles slung the car around a corner.

Despite the fact they were in traffic and not on an open road, Hallie took some comfort in knowing she was sitting in one of the fastest cars in the world. Charles wove around the other cars smoothly, effortlessly, like he was out for a leisurely Sunday drive in the mountains not racing away from someone.

"How did you find me?"

"Your emergency phone has a GPS tracking feature. It was a backup plan in case Child Services took custody of you while you were in the hospital. We weren't going to let you go back to your uncle. There were even plans to take you out of the country. Lex's parents own an island off of Nicaragua. He was going to hide you there. Luckily, it was an unnecessary precaution, because it would've been illegal."

Hallie was shocked. "Lex barely knew me then, and he was willing to go to so much trouble? Why?"

"Lex trusts Matty. He knew how important your safety was to him."

Oh my gosh! Matty! "Matty and April are in serious danger. My uncle knows where they live." Hallie was suddenly panicked

210

again.

"I know. I have a plan."

Hallie realized they were in Matty's neighborhood. Charles was explaining what she needed to do. Within seconds, they were in front of Matty's house.

She jumped out of the car, ran to the front door, and turned the knob. She bolted into the house startling Matty, who was playing his guitar on the sofa. "Come quickly, I have a big surprise for you."

He chuckled, putting down his guitar. "I think Lex is wearing off on you. Two surprises in one day?"

"Here, take the keys to the Lamborghini and go to April's office. Call me once you get there and I'll tell you what to do next." Hallie knew she needed to get him out of the neighborhood immediately.

He laughed again. "That's sweet, but I have the plumber coming to fix the leak in my shower. He'll be here sometime before five. Your surprise will have to wait until then. I've already waited two weeks for this appointment."

Five! That was almost three hours away. Her uncle was only minutes away. What else could she say or do to get Matty to leave? Her uncle would kill him this time. And what about Charles? Would he try to fight him as well? How badly would he get hurt? They were sitting ducks.

"What's wrong?"

"Huh?" His question startled her.

"You're biting your nails and have a horrible look on your face. Why are you so upset?"

"I...I...I just need you to go now."

"It's that important to you?"

"Yes, please," Hallie begged while glancing over to the front door, fearful her uncle would be there.

Matty got up off the sofa, walked over, and gave her a hug. "Alright, I don't want you this upset." He kissed the top of her head and softly said, "Stop biting your nails. Lex's going to flip when he sees them. You know how he feels about that." Matty released the hug. "Do I need to bring anything with me?"

It took Hallie a second to register he was going. "Um...no, you don't need anything. Just the car." She started pushing him toward the front door.

"Hang on a minute," He laughed and then turned around and walked over to the kitchen counter. It felt like an eternity as he slowly put his wallet, keys, and cell phone into his jean pockets. He then sat down on one of the kitchen chairs and slipped on some sneakers.

"Come on," Hallie grabbed him by the hand and led him out of the house. As he locked the front door, she scanned the street for her uncle's car. He would be showing up any second now.

Hallie stayed right next to him as they walked down the walk and over to the Lamborghini. Matty stopped. "Is that Charles?"

"He's giving me a ride back to Lex's. Now, get into the car and go."

Matty laughed and opened the door. He started to get into the car when he suddenly stopped again. "What happened to you?" He was staring down at her skinned knees.

The fall had completely escaped her mind. Minutes were passing like hours. She needed to think fast. "I went for a walk, I

212

miss this place. I flashed and tripped. It's no big deal. I'm fine. But you have to go now." She kissed him on the cheek. "Go, I'll talk to you soon."

"Alright, I'm going," He grinned at her and climbed into the car.

Hallie bounced back over to the Koenigsegg relieved when she heard the roar of the Lamborghini's engine. As the door swung up, Charles commented. "Good job. Do you see your uncle's car anywhere?"

She nervously looked up and down the street. "No."

"Good. We'll follow Matty for a while just in case. Keep watching for your uncle and let me know the minute you see him. We'll make sure he follows us and not Matty."

Charles was then talking on his BlueTooth. First he called April's office and told her boss Lex needed her pulled for a special assignment which would require her to be out of the office for the next week. Then he called the airport and told them to get Lex's plane ready to go to Aspen, Colorado. His third call was to some person who could get Lex's chalet ready for visitors and give them the five star treatment.

Hallie was so busy listening to Charles's conversation and looking out the window for her uncle's car, she wasn't watching where they were going. They were now pulled up to a bank teller window; Charles was talking to the woman on the other side of the glass. "Hello, Susan, how are you today?"

"Wonderful, and you Charles?" She cheerfully replied.

"Couldn't be better." He smiled. "I need to get five thousand dollars, cash."

"Sure, the bills the usual way?"

213

"Yes, please."

"I'll be right back."

Charles turned to Hallie. "Are you alright? You've had quite a terrifying afternoon."

"Yeah, I'm fine," She was on purpose not processing what was happening, knowing her family was in danger because of her, made her feel terrible. She needed to focus on saving them; she'd punish herself later. "I'm amazed at how easily you can call and request things, and they get done instantly."

He chuckled. "I've had years of experience arranging things for Lex. This is what I do every day, I manage his life. He calls me, demands something, and expects me to handle it for him, which I do. I take care of him, and I take care of you."

"Thank you," She sincerely told him. "I don't know what I would've done without all your help. You saved me today, and Matty and April. There are no words to express how grateful I am to you."

"Thank you is plenty enough," He smiled and turned his attention back to the teller window.

Charles handed Hallie the cash while he pulled away from the bank. She stared at it, still not accustomed to her new lifestyle. It was a lot of money to suddenly have in her hands. "What's the money for?"

"They won't be able to go home and pack, so it's to purchase clothing and anything else they'll need while they're away."

"They're going to Aspen?"

"You're sending them on a romantic getaway for a week. All we need to do now is stop and purchase some beautiful flowers and a card to put the money in. I know just the place, it's on the way to

214

the airport. When Matty calls, have him take April to Lex's private jet. Make sure you tell him he must go directly there."

The plan worked perfectly. April and Matty were surprised, thrilled. Hallie hugged and kissed them good-bye.

As she watched the plane take off, relief washed over her body. They were safely out of L.A. and wouldn't be back until Scott returned. Hallie climbed into the Lamborghini and followed Charles back to the condo. She suddenly felt tired. But she couldn't relax. Knowing her uncle was definitely tracking her, kept her tense. He'd been to Miaotsie and to Matty's house. How did he find her? He must know her new name. Could he find her at Lex's place? Or Paul's? How much danger were they in? She couldn't let her uncle hurt any of them.

She thought about the band's schedule. They would perform on her birthday for Scott and Ron, but not again until they started the tour in Houston. They were busy making the numerous final arrangements. Lex might be upset she sent Matty away. What would she say to explain her actions? Could she also talk him, Paul, and Henry into leaving town as well, until Scott came home? It wasn't likely with all the work they needed to do. How was she going to protect them without telling them what was going on? Hallie figured she'd better get some extra protection.

She pulled the car into the garage. Lex was waiting for her, smiling. She felt terrible as she realized she'd completely forgotten he said something about a surprise for her. She hoped he hadn't been waiting long. She was just supposed to go to Matty's and come right back; not play a dangerous game of hide and seek with her uncle. At least, he looked like he was in a good mood.

He opened the door of the car for her and gave her his hand. "Hey, I was beginning to wonder when you were going to return." His voice suddenly changed. "What happened to you?"

"Huh?" Hallie glanced down to see what he was so alarmed about. "Oh...I fell."

"Good grief...you skinned your knees," He lifted up her arms to inspect them. "Your arms, and you've messed up your nails."

"Sorry."

"I thought your days of being clumsy would end with the Lasik. I see I was wrong. Are you alright?"

"Yeah, I'm fine," She quietly told him. "It's just some scratches."

He suddenly smiled. "I heard you surprised Matty and April by sending them on a romantic trip. Very classy, I like it."

"Thanks," She smiled back, relieved he wasn't upset with her. She took some comfort in knowing they were not only safe, but off on a nice trip they deserved after everything they'd done for her.

He kept chatting. "Maybe they'll get lucky, and April will get pregnant. You know it's going to be hard once we go on tour. They'll be in different cities most of the time." His smile suddenly widened. "Speaking of the tour and surprises, while you were out playing love maker, I was getting a special surprise for you."

"Lex..."

His hand was suddenly over her lips. "Before you can protest, hear me out. Now that you have your driver's license, you need a set of wheels, so a bought you a car. However, there's a stipulation. You have to share it with the band while we're on tour. It's more discrete than my normal cars, so we can go sightseeing without drawing attention to ourselves."

Hallie was speechless as he took her hand and led her over to the black Ford Mustang which showcased a picture of a cobra on it. While the car was a gift, it was also practical and functional for

216

everyone else. It was not one of his usual, frivolous splurges.

"Well?"

"I don't know what to say,"

"'Thanks' is usually appropriate, I like hugs as well." He playfully smiled.

Hallie grinned and laughed. "Thanks, Lex," She threw her arms around his neck.

Lex squeezed her close to his body and whispered, "You're welcome."

Hallie was going to let him hold her for as long as he wanted. It felt good to be in his arms. The fear of her uncle was washed away by the electricity flowing through her body His touch was having this effect on her more frequently; and she desired it like a drug. Eventually, he loosened his grip, kissed her gently on the cheek causing a stronger surge of electricity, and released her.

The next few hours were a blur. She wasn't exactly sure what they'd done, just that she'd been with *him*; and it felt magical. Eventually, they went to bed.

Lex was holding her and kissing her. This time it wasn't her cheek that was kissed, it was her lips. His were moist and soft against hers. He kissed her gently, tenderly. He loved her.

Hallie awoke still feeling dazed. She rolled over expecting Lex to be lying beside her and was surprised when he wasn't. Realization struck hard. It'd all been a dream; she hadn't really kissed him. She sat up quickly, her mind was clear now. Her uncle was a danger; she must to protect Lex at all costs.

Hallie grabbed her phone and made the call she meant to make last night, before she was sidetracked by Lex hugging her. She couldn't think of him that way; it was wrong. She was sixteen,

217

he was twenty-three. Of course, he didn't think of *her* that way, she was a poor street kid he was helping; that was it. He could have any woman in the world, there was no reason he'd pick a plain, nobody like her; besides she was just a kid, and he was an adult. It was ridiculous.

Hallie focused on the call; the one which might save Lex's life as well as her own. She got the information she needed, the cost.

Now, for step two, she sent a text message just in case Lex was on the other end listening. "Charles, I need seven hundred and fifty dollars."

"Why?"

Hallie panicked. What would she tell him? He might not approve, and she needed to have it. "Extra insurance to make sure Lex stays safe. I won't risk his life for mine." Texting was a good idea. This was her first time asking Charles for money. Her stomach twisted and turned inside with nervousness. He would probably notice a change in her voice. The text message protected her from discovery.

"Do you need cash or check?"

Hallie sighed with relief. Charles was an incredible ally. "Cash."

"I'll have it within the hour."

"Thanks :)" Hallie flopped back down on her bed; and let out a big sigh. Now for step three, make arrangements for the rendezvous.

Her morning went quickly. By the time she finished dressing and eating breakfast, Charles was back with the money. She distracted Lex by asking some questions about the motorhome he was purchasing for the band's tour. Lex didn't want a tour bus, because he wanted to be able to tow her car in a trailer. He was looking at the most luxurious motorhomes money could buy and one that he could get in less than three weeks. Hallie inquired about the features while Charles slipped the money into her purse.

It was now eleven thirty. Hallie was in Beverly Hills at a crowded shopping center with the money. She was meeting Domino on "her turf," as he called it. This was a good plan. She knew she couldn't handle going to Riverside right now. She still felt uneasy and was constantly looking over her shoulder for her uncle, fearful he found her again. Going to Riverside would have probably sent her over the edge.

Hallie took a deep breath. She knew she could relax a little once she was holding the item Domino was bringing. She couldn't actually bring herself to say what *it* was, even in her mind. The word was too disturbing to her and could possibly make her flash, a risk she wasn't willing to take. Luckily, Domino knew exactly what she wanted without her saying *the word.*

She anxiously searched over the parked cars looking for one which was out of place. His run down car should stand out from all the fancy ones. A terrible thought entered her mind. What if he got pulled on the way to meet her? Yes, his car would stand out in a place like this. Oh no, he would go to jail if he was caught with the item. How could she have been so stupid to have him meet her here? She should have met him near Matty's house instead, but at the time she was worried her uncle might be still looking for her there.

As the anxiety quickly built up inside and threatened to overwhelm her, she spotted his car turning into the lot. However, she wasn't able to relax because a police cruiser pulled in right behind him. Her fears were going to come true right in front of her.

She must protect Domino; he was doing her a favor.

219

It suddenly hit her. She was Hallie McKinley, multi-millionaire, well technically Lex was, but she knew how to act the part. He'd been grooming her for almost a year. Could she pull it off? Could she be as convincing and confident as he?

Domino pulled into a parking space; the police car pulled up behind him, blocking his exit. Hallie quickly walked toward them and watched as the police officer got out of his car. What if the police officer didn't believe her? What if her uncle filed a missing person's report on her? Was she in some database for runaway children? Could she be taken away?

Hallie swallowed hard as she continued to walk toward them. She was terrified of the police, had been her entire life. Did she actually have the nerve to walk up and talk to an officer? Everything instinct in her body was telling her this was a terrible mistake, to run and hide.

But what about Domino? He'd been arrested before and didn't deserve to go back to jail, because he was breaking the law for her. How was he going to react to the police officer? This was an extremely dangerous situation for both of them.

Hallie continued walking toward his car. She couldn't back down and leave him hanging. If they went down, they would go down together. She would take the blame and get arrested. She would lie and say Domino knew nothing about the item. Her stomach was doing so many somersaults, she thought she would vomit.

Domino got out of his car acting incredibly cool, pretending not to notice the officer like he wasn't doing anything wrong.

It was her cue. "Dom!" She called and waved, smiling as sweetly as she could. Hallie excitedly bounced over to the car. She hoped her fake enthusiasm would hide the panic erupting inside. Henry once told her nervousness and excitement felt the same to your body. Hallie was testing that theory now. "You made it!" She threw her arms around his neck giving him a hug and kissing him on the cheek.

Domino instantly played along. He hugged her back, smiled, and commented. "Sorry I'm late. I hope you weren't waitin' long."

Hallie turned to the police officer who was scrutinizing the situation. It was time to play Charles. "Good morning officer, does he have a tail light out or something? I'll get it fixed right away. I'll call the garage and have them send someone right over. It will be fixed before the car leaves the lot." She innocently smiled while taking out her phone to make a call, hoping the officer didn't notice her shaking hands.

"Uh, no, that won't be necessary. I was just making my rounds. I don't see many cars like this in *this* part of town, so I was making sure everything was alright."

Hallie watched as the officer eyed Domino suspiciously. She wrapped her arms around Domino's waist and laid her head into his chest. Domino hugged her back, kissing the top of her head. "I've missed you so much, baby." He told her.

Hallie couldn't tell if the officer was buying their story or not. He scrutinized them and Domino's car. Hallie tried to breath and kept telling herself, *for all he knows, I could be the daughter of some high powered lawyer.* She knew she was dressed well enough.

"You two have a nice day," The officer eventually said.

"Thanks, you too." Hallie squeezed Domino, grabbed his hand, and led him away from the car.

"Good thing you showed up when you did," He commented when they were out of earshot. "The bacon was getting ready to come up with some law I'd violated. I don't look like I belong here. I was gonna be 'rested for no reason."

"I know."

He was then chuckling. "You see the look on his face when you walked up to me, gave me a hug and kiss? He was thinking, 'What's a rich, white girl like her doing with a poor, black man like him? Bet she's doing it to piss off her folks.'"

"I don't care what he thought. I just had to make sure he didn't search your car. Did you bring what I asked for?"

"I have it. There's a secret compartment where I keep special items."

"Good, let's move it to my car in case yours gets towed." Hallie turned to him and smiled, relieved. It felt strange to be with Domino like this, as a friend. As one of Scott's closest friends, he'd always been good to her. Now it was her turn to be good to him. They were on her turf where money, not muscles, was power. Hallie felt a strange satisfaction in knowing for once she was taking care of him. "Then I'm taking you out for lunch, and we're going shopping. *You* need some new clothes. I want to get Tyler some as well. I'm having a big party in seven days, you're both invited. Scott's coming home."

Hanging with Domino was a lot of fun. His facial expressions kept her laughing. They reminded her of how she felt the first time she saw the fancy clothes Lex bought. Having someone else dress you *was* a bizarre experience, but Domino took it in stride at the men's shop. He seemed to be enjoying it as much as she was. Maybe Lex felt the same satisfaction when he bought clothes for her.

Hallie was waving 'good-bye' to Domino when Charles called. "Where are you?" There was excitement in his voice.

"Heading home, what's up?"

"I found Ray Harv. I thought we could go and see him this

afternoon."

"Great!"

"I'll be waiting for you in the garage with my hat on. I'm going with you, we're taking my car."

He was as anxious to see Ray as she was. Hallie complimented him and played their game. "You make a fabulous detective, Sir Charles."

"Thank you, my lady."

As she drove home, her mind raced through all the questions she wanted to ask Ray. She was so preoccupied that as she clicked the remote to open the gate, Hallie suddenly realized she didn't know which car was Charles'. She pulled into her parking space and got out. "Charles?" She didn't see him.

"I'm over here. Come on, let's go."

Hallie followed the sound of his voice to the far end of the garage. She stopped when she saw his car. It was stunning; white exterior, beige leather interior, and a silver jaguar on the bonnet. Suddenly Hallie became conscious she was gawking. She looked up at him, embarrassed. "Sorry, I've never seen a car so beautiful. Okay, that sounds silly, I've never thought of a car as beautiful before."

"She is exquisite, isn't she?" He endearingly replied.

Hallie looked at Charles, amazed he thought the same as she did. Hallie then picked up on the one word. "She?"

"Like a sophisticated woman."

Umm, Hallie speculated. "Are there any other sophisticated women in your life?"

Charles responded with a knowing grin. "You're not the only one with secrets."

Hallie was thrilled. Not only did Charles have a life outside of Lex, but he shared a confidence with her. "My lips are sealed."

"Come on, Ms. Hallie. Let's run our errand and see where this mystery leads us next, shall we?"

Hallie laughed as she climbed into the passenger seat of his car. Charles was having fun helping her. She liked the way he made it sound like a mystery novel. So, they were off to interview a suspect. A man who could hopefully help her find the missing street kid and help them crack this case.

They were gone for several hours and during that time Lex called wanting to know where they were. Charles told him they were running some errands. When they returned home Lex was sitting on the sofa doing something on his phone. "What did you buy?"

"Nothing," Hallie plopped down next to him, happy as could be about what Ray knew about Warren. She wasn't lying. She didn't *buy* anything, but she got some great information.

"Nothing? You were out all day. What were you doing?"

"We were just out and about."

"Why are you being so vague? You can tell me what you did."

Curiosity danced across his deep, blue eyes, so Hallie decided to have some fun with him. "You really wanna know?" She asked playfully.

"Yes."

"Fine, I'll tell you. I went to the California Institution for Men in Chino to pick out a rough, tough convict, but they wouldn't let me have one. I thought you said money could buy anything. It wasn't fair." She pouted. "That's why I came back with nothing. Oh well," Hallie shrugged her shoulders, gave Lex a little smile, and glanced over to Charles who was trying to keep a straight face.

"Cute, very cute. Fine, don't tell me what you did today." As he spoke, he leaned in and was only inches from her face. Hallie felt a surge of electricity bolt through her body as she stared into his gorgeous eyes. He playfully whispered. "You can keep your little secrets, I'll find out eventually."

Hallie blushed, causing Lex to chuckle before he got off the sofa and walked out of the room. He called from the kitchen. "I'm ordering dinner." Hallie heard him open the drawer that contained all the restaurant menus.

Charles quietly told her. "I want you to wait and go tomorrow, it's too late tonight."

Hallie agreed. She didn't want Charles to worry about her; she'd put enough stress on him already with her uncle problem. She also didn't need Lex becoming more suspicious; and she needed him to stay home to keep him safe.

She was up half the night replaying the information Ray gave her. She was ready to fly out the door first thing this morning when Charles reminded her Lex would be suspicious if she wasn't home when he woke up. Hallie reluctantly stayed. She very dutifully ate brunch with Lex and hung out around the condo like nothing was going on, like she wasn't studying the map on her phone while she waited to leave.

Thankfully, Lex decided to go look at motorhomes with Paul and Henry. Charles thought it would be a good idea for them to all

225

go in the Rolls Royce; he would drive them. Lex agreed and left. Now, he wouldn't notice she was gone.

It was a little after four. Hallie nervously and excitedly rang the doorbell of a beautiful house in Laguna Beach.

A girl around the age of thirteen answered. She was nicely dressed with her hair pulled back into a neat ponytail. She smiled with friendly eyes; Hallie noticed the braces on her teeth. "Can I help you?"

"Is Warren home?" She anxiously inquired hoping Ray was correct about the address.

"He's in the family room playing video games. Are you a friend from school?" She led Hallie through the house.

Not sure how to answer, Hallie decided to tell the truth. She didn't want to start off on the wrong foot with Warren's new family. "Yes, but he hasn't seen me in a while. I'm from Riverside."

The girl gave her a strange look, but she didn't have time to interpret it, because they walked into the family room. There he was, sitting on the sofa, Hallie could hardly contain herself. "Hi, War," She said about to explode with joy at seeing her best friend.

Confession

(Warren)

A very surprised Warren Harv stopped playing his game and stared at her. There were only three people who called him War; his mother, his brother, and "Ann?" He couldn't believe his eyes. He knew her voice, but standing in front of him was not the street kid he'd grown up with. No tangled long hair, no glasses, no worn clothes, Warren barely recognized her. The gorgeous blonde with chin length hair, beautiful blue eyes that he never noticed in all the time they'd spent together and designer clothes; she looked amazing.

"It's really me. Look," She held out her arms. "No sleeves." She commented referring to the fact she was wearing a tank top with spaghetti straps; something she never would have done in Riverside, because there were always bruises on her arms.

He got up off the sofa and walked over to her, still stunned. "I can't believe you're here." A huge grin was on his face when he gave her the biggest bear hug he possibly could; overjoyed to see a friend who he thought was dead. There was a hole in his heart he didn't know existed; it was suddenly filled with warmth.

Warren stood there embracing her, not wanting to let go. Ann hugged him back; he knew she was elated as well. Neither one of them spoke for a long time, caught up in the moment of the reunion. Eventually he spoke, his voice shaking. "The last time I saw you…you were in a coma … the doctors didn't think you'd make it." His voice cracked when he said this. "And here you are." He tightened his grip, so relieved and delirious with happiness. A tear ran down his cheek.

227

She noticed. "Hey now, I'm the sentimental one."

Warren pulled back and looked into her eyes. He could see the pools of tears hanging on her bottom lids. He laughed, "That's true. I can't believe you're here. You look amazing. You know I'm *not* gonna let go."

"I don't want you to," She sweetly replied.

He hugged her again. "I've missed you so much."

"Me too, I had to see you again."

This caught his curiosity. "How'd you find me?"

"I went to the prison, spoke with Ray. He told me you were living here. I hope you don't mind me just showing up."

"Are you kidding? You're welcome anytime. How've you been? And where'd you get such nice clothes? Is Scott back? I have so many questions, I don't know where to start."

"Scott's not back," She quietly responded, but then her voice lightened. "However, he's coming home in six days. While he's been away, I was sort of taken in by a multi-millionaire, it's a long story."

Burning with curiosity, he wanted to hear all about it. He put his arm around her shoulder, ushering her to come with him. "Would you like something to eat?"

"A snack sounds great," Ann hesitated; Warren knew something was up. He could read her body language as well as Scott. "Can I ask you a question first?" Since when had she ever been timid around him?

"What's wrong?"

"Ray said your guardian's an attorney. Is that true?"

228

"Samantha is. Why? Are you in some sort of trouble?" He dropped his arm off her shoulder and peered deeply into her eyes.

"I don't know... maybe...yeah... I kind-of am. I'm just not sure how much. Can I trust her?"

"You can," Now he was concerned. "Why don't you tell me what's going on?"

"Like I said, it's a long story. I'd like to tell Samantha and you at the same time, if that's alright. I don't think I could tell it twice."

"Alright," He conceded, wondering what sort of trouble she'd accidentally gotten into; trouble had a habit of finding her. "I'll call Samantha and find out when she's coming home." Warren pulled Ann into his arms and hugged her again. "Whatever it is, we'll get through it together. I'm not gonna lose you again."

"Thanks, War," She squeezed him back and held him. A few minutes passed before Ann pulled away, giving him a smile. "While we're waiting, why don't you tell me all about yourself, and how you ended up living here?"

They sat at the kitchen table munching on potato chips. "I came to visit you every day after you were shot, I'd sit and read that book Dr. Bob said you liked. One day, I was with Ray, he started a fight. I jumped in to help and was arrested for assault. Samantha was my state-appointed attorney, she got me out.

"Ma was furious, threw me out. I didn't know where to go, no one would let me crash with them, so I stayed in your hospital room. Three days passed, I decided to go back home to see if Ma would take me back. The house was abandoned, she just split on me, I couldn't believe it. I stayed with you another few days until I needed to show up at court. Samantha questioned where Ma was, I told her the truth.

"The next thing I knew, I was staying with the Harris'. Samantha and Mike became my legal guardians. I've been living with them for just over a year now.

"They have three other children they also adopted, they're all siblings. Tom's our age, you met Claire, and Ashley's ten. Their mother was on drugs, Child Protective Services removed them from their home. Their mother overdosed shortly after that. Samantha and Mike can't have kids, so they adopted them. This was nine years ago.

"When Samantha brought me home, I was welcomed into the family. Tom was especially thrilled to have a brother his own age...I'm really sorry I never came back to see you. To be honest, everything happened so fast, I forgot about everyone back home." He felt horribly guilty. No matter how true, it was a terrible excuse. How could he have ever forgotten about her? He was all she had; and he abandoned her.

"I understand."

Ann always forgave him, even when he really didn't deserve it. It was her kind, loving nature that had gotten him through some really tough times. "Still," Warren sincerely told her, "I shouldn't have forgotten you. I'm a terrible friend."

"Hey, I should've looked you up sooner as well. I hate that I've shown up with a problem. I've thought of you often, wondered where you were, what you were doing. It wasn't until I needed you that I even thought about trying to find you."

"Warren?" A familiar voice called.

"We're in the kitchen."

A moment later she walked into the room. "Hi, I'm Samantha Harris," She said extending her hand to shake Ann's.

230

Ann stood up. "I'm Hallie McKinley."

"Hallie?"

"Yeah," Ann sheepishly replied. "The new life came with a new identity. Everyone thinks I'm eighteen, and I'm known as Hallie Ann McKinley. Everyone calls me Hallie except you, Scott, and the people back in Riverside."

"Your initials spell HAM."

"I know," She rolled her eyes. "It was unintentional, Lex finds it to be very amusing."

He had so many questions for her, but before he could decide which one to ask, Samantha interjected. "Warren told me you wanted to talk, that you might be in trouble."

"Yes," Ann nervously glanced down at her hands as she spoke.

Warren stood up, put one hand on each of her shoulders, and looked directly into her eyes. "You can trust Samantha. Why don't you tell us what's going on?"

"Come, let's sit out by the pool," Samantha suggested, smiling.

They walked out into the back yard. "Wow! What an incredible view of the ocean. I can't believe you get to see this every day."

Warren smiled, still amazed *he* was seeing *her.*

He sat next to her, wanting to be close in case she needed help. Samantha sat across from them still smiling casually.

Ann took a deep breath. "When I woke up in the hospital, I didn't know what was going on. The police wanted my statement,

231

but I didn't remember being shot. Dr. Bob was gone. You were gone." She said glancing over at him.

Warren cringed as he realized how much it must have hurt her to be abandoned by both of them at the same time. Being abandoned was a horrible, hollow feeling; one of the worst things he'd ever experienced. And he'd experienced a lot growing up in a violent, hopeless place like Riverside. The only thing which had topped being abandoned was holding Ann in his arms the night she was shot and thinking she was going to die, because he hadn't protected her like he promised.

"Everything had changed. Child Services came to see me. They told me since both my parents were dead, they'd found an aunt and uncle living in Riverside who'd agreed to let me stay with them. I had no idea my mom's sister was living there.

"My aunt came to the hospital one day, she seemed nice. However, I could see part of my mom in her face. My only memories are of her being drunk and hitting me with beer bottles, so seeing someone who looked similar to her, made me uncomfortable.

"Instead of being anxious about my aunt, I should've been concerned about my uncle..." Ann paused, her eyes dropped down to the patio. She took several deep breaths.

Wondering if she'd suddenly flashed, Warren took her hand in his and started gently rubbing it. "Hey, it's alright," He softly said. "Tell me what happened."

Ann looked up with tears in her eyes; her legs were suddenly pulled up against her chest with her arms wrapped around them. He knew her protective ball. Her face was crinkled in pain. She was definitely fighting the flashes.

"He was raping me, War, and selling me for sex. He'd tie me to the metal framed bed he had set up in the room where I slept,

232

guys would pay him to take turns with me. They were mean and rough, usually drunk, my insides used to hurt so bad when they were done." Tears started to run down her cheeks. "I'm sorry. This is the first time I've said it aloud. It's harder to talk about than I thought." Her brow furrowed in agony.

Warren quickly wrapped his arms around her and held her as she crumbled. Her words ripped his insides apart. He'd promised to protect her, and instead, he'd left her. He should have been there to prevent this from happening. Warren held her as tightly as he could, to somehow absorb some of her pain.

Between sobs she continued the story. "I could take being hit, I was used to that, but not being raped. I couldn't handle it. In the seven years I'd lived on the streets, I'd never felt as dirty as I did when I was at his house. I felt trapped. Every time Child Services came to visit, I was forced to act like everything was alright. It seemed my aunt and uncle were getting money from The State to help support me. He would spend it on drugs and booze, and she started buying herself things. I never saw a penny of it. I was kept locked in the room except when he wanted to show off my naked body to some customers.

"Finally, the first day of school came. He had to send me or get in trouble with Child Services." She tightened her fists. "What he said next is too horrible to repeat."

"It was my only chance to escape. Deep down inside, I knew I wouldn't make it, that I'd die on the streets, but I decided I'd rather take my chances. I needed to get out of Riverside, so I went to Tyler and asked for a favor. I told him what was going on, asked him to drive me to Long Beach. I didn't have any money, so I offered my body to him as payment. What was one more guy having his way with me if it meant getting out? Thankfully, he declined, said the ride was on the house. He drove me all the way to the ocean.

233

"It was a beautiful sight. Scott used to take me there whenever he had a little extra cash. Seeing the beach made me happier than I'd been in a long time. The water was so peaceful, the waves seemed to wash all my troubles away." She paused reflectively for a moment before continuing.

"Tyler gave me forty-five dollars, said it was money he owed Scott. I didn't believe him, but thanked him anyway. I walked down to the beach and sat on the sand. I stayed there for a couple of weeks, rationing out the money.

"Since I was used to having little food, I was able to stretch it pretty far. During that time, I found the local library and would go there to drink water, bathe in the bathroom sink, and climb up into the ceiling to sleep at night. The library had a better selection than the one in Riverside, so I spent a lot of time sitting by a window reading. Life was good until I ran out of money. I tried to get a job, but no one would hire me. I started eating out of restaurant dumpsters and eventually got sick."

She suddenly stopped the story. "I forgot to mention that when I first arrived in Long Beach, I found a pay phone and wrote Scott to give him the number, asking him to call me on my birthday, if he could... I started feeling ill several days before then, I knew I wasn't gonna make it. I couldn't ask for help, I was afraid I'd be sent back to my uncle. So, I sat next to the phone waiting for it to ring. At that point, all I wanted was to hear Scott's voice one last time before I died. I don't actually remember speaking to him, but he says I answered and talked for a few minutes. The next thing I remember is waking up in a hospital with Matty and Lex by my side."

Ann continued telling them what her life had been like since she was saved. Her eyes lit up with pleasure as she talked.

Despite the terrible guilt he felt for leaving, Warren was happy for her. "Wow! Your life sure took a one-eighty. It sounds like you're with really nice people now."

234

"Yeah, they're great, wonderful. I've been really lucky… that is until recently."

"What happened?"

Ann told him about running away to Riverside and her uncle's attack. "War, he's found me. First he showed up at one of Lex's clubs. Then, I was at Matty's house two days ago, and he was there." She explained everything that happened next. "I would never forgive myself if they got hurt. When Ray told me you were adopted by an attorney, I knew I had to come and try to get help."

Ann turned to Samantha. "Mrs. Harris, I'd like to hire you as my attorney. Right now, my uncle still has custody of me. I want Scott to have it. He comes home in less than a week. He's nineteen now, and the only real family I have. I'll pay whatever it costs."

"Of course, I'll help you," Samantha gave her a very serious and concerned look. "After listening to your story, I think there are several other things we need to do as well. For starters, as your attorney, I can take temporary custody of you until Scott arrives. I'll also file a restraining order against your uncle which will prevent him from ever being allowed near you again."

Ann looked at her with astonishment and hope in her eyes. "You can do all that?" Warren felt her body instantly relax.

"I think you should consider pressing charges against him. You can put him in jail. You shouldn't let him get away with what he's done to you."

"Will I have to see him again to do this?"

"In a special situation like this one, I can ask the judge to allow you to testify in a closed courtroom without your uncle present. They can tape your testimony."

"You should do this," Warren encouraged her. "You need to make him pay for what he's done." His blood boiled. If he ever saw her uncle, he'd definitely make him pay. Warren would kill him.

Ann agreed, thanking Samantha for her help. "War, are you alright?" She knew him well.

"I'm glad you're safely with me."

"Me too," She smiled and squeezed him. "I feel so much better knowing that soon Scott'll be my guardian, and my uncle'll be in jail, never able to touch me again. I've spent the last year living in fear of being sent back to him and now, I don't have to worry anymore. Promise you'll stay with me until this is all over. I don't want you running off and doing something stupid."

Warren gave a little sigh under his breath and smiled at her. "I promise." It was the least he could do. He would never abandon her again. He would keep her close, safely protected from any harm.

They ate dinner out on the patio since Ann loved the view so much. While eating, she told Warren's family about her plans for the new playground in Riverside. "I'm really excited about it. We're taking over an entire city block and adding skateboard ramps, a spray paint wall for people to graffiti without worrying about getting arrested, a huge climbing jungle gym for the little kids, lots of swings and slides. It's a place designed just for the kids, so they have a safe place to go and hang out."

Wow! "That's a really cool idea. I'm amazed that after all the bad things that happened to you there, you wanna give such a nice gift to the community."

"When I lived in Riverside, it was such a dark place for me, I know there're others who have no hope, just like I had none, like *we* had none. I wanna bring something good into their lives."

Warren was deeply touched. He'd left Riverside and never looked back. As far as he was concerned, it was hell on Earth. Ann's life was worse than his and she was spending her money trying to make it a better place for those who lived there; those who hurt her. Warren seemed to fall even more in love with her. How was that possible?

Dinner continued with Warren watching and listening to her in awe. At one point, they started sharing stories about when they lived in Riverside. It was like the year of separation never existed. They were best buds, comrades. Ann laughed, "I don't think your Ma ever figured out I was living in your bedroom."

"You were living in Warren's bedroom?" Tom was surprised.

"Yeah," Ann was beaming. "After Scott left and the girlfriend he planned on me staying with threw me out, ran off with his money; Warren let me crash with him. I used to hide in the closet or under the bed when his Ma wanted to come in."

"Ann used to clean Ma's house as a way to pay her back for the food we stole out of the cabinets for her to eat. Ma thought she was crazy, and I ate a lot. Ann used to climb in and out of my bedroom window to get into the house." Warren turned back to her. "We used to do some crazy things to keep you hidden."

Ann's cell phone rang. "Excuse me, please. I need to take this. Hey, Lex, what's up?.. I'm visiting a friend....I'm not telling you...because I don't want to. I'm just taking care of some things before Scott comes home...Yes, I'm safe...No, I'm not in Riverside, I promise. I'm in Laguna Beach...Yes, I'll talk to you later, Bye.

"Now that he's figured out I'm not home, let's see how many times he calls to check up on me," She chuckled. "Charles is the only one who knows my uncle's after me. Outside of you, only Scott knows the truth about what my uncle did when I lived with him. I

237

was too ashamed to tell anyone else. I trust you'll keep it a secret."

"We will."

The phone rang again. Ann answered it without looking at the caller ID. "What now?" She jokingly asked while rolling her eyes.

Warren watched as a horrified expression crossed her face. "No, you listen to me, you son-of-a-bitch. You're gonna pay for what you've done. I hope you rot in hell."

She stood up, hurling her phone into the pool. Her body started trembling; her breathing accelerated. "Warren, I'm so sorry, I shouldn't have come here. I've put your nice, new family in danger. I'm so sorry, I've gotta go." She ran into the house, grabbing her purse off the sofa.

Warren jumped up and ran after her. Something was terribly wrong; and he was not about to let her leave. He was shocked to see her tuck a handgun into the back of her shorts. "Where're you going? And what're you doing with a gun?"

Assault

"I don't know. Away." Ann started backing toward the front door. "And if he finds me, I'm gonna shoot the bastard. I'm gonna blow his fucking brains out, War. I can't go back." Her shaking was intensifying.

His heart was racing. He knew she was in serious danger. "I'm not letting you go," He said moving quickly toward her, determined to make her stop.

Ann backed to move away and ran into a wall. Warren took the opportunity to quickly push his body against hers, successfully pinning her. She struggled to wiggle free, but he stood firm. He wasn't going to lose her again.

"He's gonna touch me. He's gonna touch me." She screamed as tears started pouring from her eyes; she stopped struggling.

Warren knew she was gone. She either flashed or just became completely overwhelmed. It didn't matter which. He wrapped her up into his arms giving her a tight, comforting hug, helping to support her weight as her legs momentarily gave out. "Everything's gonna be alright. I'm not gonna let him hurt you. I promise." He held her and loved her with all his heart, relieved he had her.

But there was still the problem of the gun. He couldn't believe she actually had one. He needed to get rid of it before someone got hurt. Slowly, he leaned her away from the wall, reached down her back, and slid it out of her shorts. "You're not on the streets of Riverside anymore. We'll serve justice correctly, legally, this time."

The rest of Warren's family had followed him into the kitchen and witnessed what happened. Warren reached back and carefully handed the gun to Mike, who quickly left the room with the weapon.

Warren held Ann until her breathing and shaking slowed. He peered straight into her eyes. They were dazed. He didn't know her mental state, but decided to try to talk to her anyway. "Do you trust me?" He whispered, searching for any sign of acknowledgement she heard him.

Tears were still trickling down her face, but there was a slight shift in her eyes. "You're the only person I do trust," She whispered back.

Relief washed through him. He had somehow stopped her before she completely shut down. "I want you to do exactly what I tell you. Alright?"

Ann nodded her head in agreement.

"You're gonna stay here until Scott returns, I'm gonna take care of you. Will you let me do that?"

"Yes," Ann whispered, closed her eyes, and leaned her head against his chest. Warren held her tightly.

After she was completely calm, he said, "You need to call Charles and tell him what happened to your phone."

There was alarm in her eyes.

"You can do it. Just remember to smile, so he won't detect anything in your voice." He handed her his cell.

She stared at it. Suddenly, Ann took a deep breath, grabbed it, and dialed. "Hey, it's Hallie. Things are going great with Warren, we've been catching up on old times. His mom's gonna take care of my legal issues, but that requires me to stay here until Scott comes home... Yeah... Um, I had a little accident with my phone, it fell into

240

a swimming pool...Yeah," She sheepishly grinned. "I'll go buy a new one tomorrow...I still have it. I'll turn it on in a few minutes. Would you please not tell Lex it's on? I don't want him tracking me down. He needs to stay in the condo where it's safe. Will you be able to keep him there?...Alright, thanks."

When she hung up the phone, Warren gave her another hug. "Good, now there's no reason for them to be worried about you."

"I am."

"Why?"

"Because Charles said to keep my old number, so Lex can call me and not be suspicious...so Scott can reach me."

"Not a problem," Warren was determined to make her feel safe. "It a call comes in and it's not a recognized number, I'll answer your phone. I'll also set up different ringtones for your friends. I'll screen all your calls if you'd like, including the ones from Lex." He jokingly added to try and lighten her mood. Giving her a smile and another hug he said, "See, everything's gonna be alright. Now, I need to know. Where'd you get the gun?"

"Domino."

He should've known. "Did you go to Riverside?"

"He came to Beverly Hills."

"Does he have your cell phone number?"

"Yeah," She gave him a puzzled look.

"Who else in Riverside knows it?"

"Only Tyler, but neither of them would give it to my uncle, they're Scott's best friends. They're happy I have a new life. They wouldn't rat me out." She was positive.

Warren, on the other hand, wasn't so sure. But he knew she was mentally fatigued, so he dropped the questions. She needed to rest, and he needed to talk with Mike and Samantha alone. He wasn't sure what their reaction was going to be his inappropriate request.

He signaled to Tom for help. "Hey, Hallie, would you like to play the Wii? It'll get your mind off things."

Warren smiled. The rest of his family called her by her new name, which was good. However, he knew and loved her as Ann, calling her by a different name didn't feel right to him.

She seemed a little reluctant to leave his side, but he reassured her he would join her in a minute.

Now, what exactly was he going to say to Mike and Samantha. Warren could feel the sweat on his palms. "I hope you don't mind I invited her to stay without checking with you guys first. She's running scared, I was really worried she was gonna get herself killed."

"Of course not," Samantha smiled. "She needs help and is welcome to stay as long as she likes."

"Thanks, I really appreciate it. Um..." Warren's stomach felt raw. "I don't want you to take this the wrong way, but Ann needs to stay in my room with me. I promise nothing'll happen. As you've already heard, she used to live in my bedroom and sleep in my bed. However, I've never had sex with her, we've never dated or anything.

"The reason I'm asking for your approval is because she has terrible nightmares. When she sleeps with someone, she feels more secure. She's spent most of her life sleeping with Scott. When she was a baby, he used to climb into her crib and lie with her. When she started staying with me, I found she slept a lot better curled up next to me instead of across the room.

"As shook up as she was a little while ago, I can promise she'll wake up screaming numerous times if no one's there."

"Let us talk about it in private." Mike suggested to Samantha. "Wait here."

Warren watched them walk back out onto the patio. What if they said 'no', then what? It was too dangerous to let her sleep alone. What if she flashed during night and tried to leave? What if her uncle actually knew where she was? Would he try to come into the house after her?

They came back in. Warren anxiously looked at Mike. "It's unusual, but we trust you. However, you must keep the door to your room open, and you must sleep fully clothed. We'll tell the girls you're having a sleepover."

"You got it. Thanks guys. And thanks again, Samantha, for all you're doing to help her out legally."

"One other thing," She told him. "Just to be extra careful, I think you should pull her car into the garage."

""Hey, Ann, can I have the keys to your car? And how'd you get a driver's license?"

"Lex is a club member over at Auto Club Speedway. The guys race his four super cars on certain days when the track's open. On one of those days, he taught me to drive his 911 Turbo, so I could pass the driving part of the test. We weren't worried about the book portion."

"Did you drive his car over here?" Warren asked as the surprising image of Ann sitting behind the wheel of a Porsche entered his head.

243

She got up and started walking toward him, smiling. "I drove the new Mustang he bought me two days ago. He wants to bring a car with us while we're on tour. He didn't want anything too flashy, but he loves fast cars, so he bought a Shelby Cobra GT and gave it to me." She sheepishly grinned. "I know it only has four seats, but Lex insisted on having a 500 horse powered engine and figured I could sit in someone's lap if all five of us wanna go somewhere. Anyway," She shrugged her shoulders. "He told me to drive it around to break it in." She handed Warren the keys. "You know, I probably should've brought the Lamborghini, you'd really like that car."

Warren just smiled at her and shook his head in disbelief. *Lamborghini, Porsche, Mustang; this from the girl who used to be so poor she only had the clothes she was wearing.*

After Charles delivered a suitcase to Ann, she climbed into Warren's bed and curled up in his arms. It felt different from when they lived in Riverside. She was more than his best friend, his comrade; he loved her. Warren knew he'd do anything for her.

He laid in bed thinking how suddenly his life changed. When he woke up that morning, he never would have imagined the day would end like this. Living with the Harrises afforded him the luxury of thinking about and planning for the future. Ann's presence negated that; he was back to living moment by moment. Warren had spent a year breaking himself of his old habits; he was amazed how instantly they all came back. Maybe it was a good thing, maybe it wasn't. Either way, it was necessary.

Bright and early the following morning, Warren and Tom took Ann out for pancakes at a diner they liked to hang out in before school. They bumped into Danielle and Carmen.

"Hey, can we join you?" Danielle, the tall, slender brunette, gave him a curious look.

"Sure," Warren agreed, but felt awkward. Danielle was his former girlfriend; they were trying to be 'just friends'. They had dated for ten months; the breakup was hard. Despite the fact he knew how much he loved Ann, Warren still had feelings for Danielle.

Carmen, a shorter brunette, was Danielle's best friend, and a girl Tom was crushing on. The five of them sat in a large booth in the back of the diner.

"It's so nice to hang with kids my age," Ann smiled. "Matty and Lex's friends are all in their twenties."

As they finished eating and started making plans for the day which included Ann hanging out in the school library while they went to class, getting her a new phone, and showing her around town; she suddenly dropped under the table. Warren felt her grab his leg.

"War, it's him. He's gonna touch me."

Warren was immediately alarmed. "Where is he?"

"At the front, please don't let him touch me."

Warren looked across the room and saw a man going out the door. He needed to act quickly. "Alright, here's what we're gonna do. Danielle, please take Ann to the bathroom. Lock yourselves inside and don't come out unless it's for me or Samantha. Tom, get your mom on the phone, tell her what's happened, ask her to come over right away." Warren took Ann's hands from around his leg and started to get out of the booth.

"What are you gonna do?" Tom inquired.

"I'm going after the guy," Still holding her hands, Warren gently pulled her. "Come on." She crawled out from under the table. Warren looked straight into her terrified eyes. "Go with

245

Danielle, quickly now."

Danielle put her arm around Ann's trembling body and rapidly walked with her to the bathroom. Once Warren heard the lock click, he bolted out the front.

Adrenaline and anger were racing through his body. He ran toward the parking lot scanning the area, but the man wasn't there.

Warren ran to the end of the block still searching. He wanted more than anything to find her uncle, to beat him to death for touching her. He searched and searched, but couldn't find anyone who looked like they were from Riverside.

About twenty minutes later, Warren reluctantly gave up. The man was long gone. "Damn!" He slapped the side of the diner.

His heart was still racing, so he paced back and forth outside for a few minutes to calm down. Ann wouldn't handle his anger well.

A few minutes later, he knocked on the bathroom door. "It's Warren, open up."

Ann burst out and into his arms crying and shaking. He consoled her, holding her tightly.

Warren looked at his ex-girlfriend. "Thanks for staying with her."

"You're welcome," Danielle's expression told him she noticed how much he cared for Ann.

He gave her a sympathetic smile, not wanting to hurt her and mess up the friendship thing. He would have to explain Ann's special situation to her later.

Samantha walked into the diner. "Is everyone okay?"

246

"We're fine. Ann's really shook up, but no one got hurt. I tried to find the guy, but I lost him."

"Good," Samantha looked relieved. "A friend of mine, who's a police officer, will be here in a moment. It's his day off. He's going to escort Hallie back to the house and stay with her. The judge just approved the restraining order, I have some officers going with me to Riverside to personally deliver it to her uncle." Samantha turned to Ann and gently said. "Once I get this delivered, your uncle won't be allowed within a hundred yards of you. If he tries, he'll be arrested.

"I want the rest of you to get to school. You're already late for first period. Here, I'll write you a note." Samantha pulled a pad and pen out of her purse.

Warren noticed a man enter the diner. Samantha also saw him. "Hey Frank, thanks for coming so fast. Hallie, go with the officer."

"Stay at the house until I get home," Warren peering directly into her eyes. "Until Scott comes back, I'm your personal body guard."

Ann shook her head in agreement. Warren walked with her to Frank's car. He hated he had to be separated from her, but knew Samantha wasn't going to let him skip school, and Ann would be safe with a police officer. Warren decided to call the house and check on her every break he got during the day.

Warren raced home from school. Tom joked about him getting a speeding ticket and messing up his probation if he didn't slow down. Warren didn't care; he had to see Ann. He sprinted into the family room and saw her curled up on the sofa reading a book. The officer was watching TV. Warren felt instantly relieved.

Danielle and Carmen arrived at the house a few minutes after he did. Earlier, when Tom told them about Ann, they offered to help. Warren was glad he didn't have to explain things to Danielle. Tom didn't know his deep feelings, so Danielle wouldn't find out and possibly get hurt.

Warren really appreciated them coming over. Ann needed some distractions and had never hung out with girls her own age. Danielle and Carmen would be good for her.

They were all starting to get a snack in the kitchen when Samantha returned home. Everything was taken care of - the restraining order and the temporary custody.

Now that it was safe for Ann to leave the house, the five of them headed out for the remainder of the afternoon in Ann's car. Ann gave Warren the keys; he was thrilled. She sat in the passenger seat. Danielle, Tom, and Carmen squeezed into the back. Carmen sat on Tom's lap; Warren hoped they would be dating soon. He headed straight for the cell phone store and then they took Ann on a tour of Laguna Beach.

(Hallie)

The next day, Hallie went to school with Warren. Samantha had made arrangements for her to be a visiting student. Hallie was thrilled to be in all of Warren's classes. He attended a nice, private school; school wasn't nearly as intimidating with him by her side.

That night, she took The Harrises out to a nice dinner to thank them for their hospitality. She gave the waiter her credit card to pay for the bill. A short while later, he returned with a security officer. "Miss, I'm going to need you to come with us."

248

"Why? What's going on?"

"This credit card's been reported as stolen."

"What? That's *my* credit card."

The security officer grabbed her arm. "Come on Miss, tell it to the police."

"Let go of her," Warren immediately jumped to her side. Hallie wasn't surprised. She knew his temper and how protective he was; it was why she felt so safe when she was with him.

"Warren calm down," Samantha was firm. "Gentlemen, I'm Miss McKinley's attorney. Let's talk about this."

The security officer released his tight grip from her arm. Hallie immediately grabbed her phone. "Lex, what's going on? I took Warren's family out to a nice dinner, and now they're gonna have me arrested for stealing the credit card you gave me." She didn't hide the panic in her voice.

"I'm sorry, sweetheart," He sounded tired. "I was getting ready to call you. I needed to report all of them as stolen and freeze my accounts. This guy jumped me outside of Miaotsie, punched me in the face, and stole my wallet."

"Oh my gosh, are you alright?" She turned to everyone at the table. "He was mugged a little while ago."

"I have a new appreciation of how Matty and you must've felt when your uncle hit you. I've just arrived at the police station. They want me to look at mug shots, but to be honest, I didn't really see the guy. I just remember he had a big snake tattoo on one of his arms." Lex sighed. "The part I don't understand is why he didn't steal the Ferrari. I'd just gotten out of the car."

Hallie was frozen in terror. Snake tattoo, only stole his wallet which had his home address, didn't take the car; this was not a

249

regular mugging. Her uncle attacked Lex. He was sending her a message.

"Are you still there?"

"Lex," She whispered. "Don't go home tonight, please. Stay at the other condo, or get a hotel room, please don't go home."

"Don't worry, Charles agrees with you and has already booked us in a hotel. The locksmith's on his way to the condo to rekey all the locks. I'll bring you new keys and credit cards in the morning. Are Warren's parents with you?"

"Yes," She was still stunned. She felt horribly guilty Lex got hurt. It was her fault.

Hallie felt Warren's arm wrapped around her shoulder. He must have been reading her facial expressions, worried about her reaction.

"Let me speak to his dad. Don't worry, I'll get all of this straightened out. If they take you to the police station, call me, and remember to stick to your story about being Hallie McKinley. I'll be there as fast as I can to bail you out. Everything's going to be alright."

Warren was worried about her. Lex was worried about her. They had heard the concern in her voice, but misread it. Going to jail was the furthest thing from her mind; she was worried about Lex. How had she been so stupid to leave him unprotected? Her uncle could have killed him.

"Hallie?" Lex interrupted her thoughts.

"What?" She felt dazed.

"I promise you everything's going to be fine," His voice was so sweet. How could he be nice to her after what she did? "Hand the phone to Warren's dad."

250

"Okay," She was too shaken up to think about anything but Lex.

At some point, Mike handed the phone back to her.

She heard him talk to the waiter and security officer. "Gentlemen, this is all a big misunderstanding. When the police arrive, have them call this officer at the LAPD and she can confirm Miss McKinley's story. As for the bill, I'll pay it myself."

The rest of the evening was a blur. At some point she told Warren her uncle attacked Lex. She was consumed with guilt; numbness controlled her. All she could remember was Warren holding her and taken care of her like he promised.

(Lex)

Lex arrived at the house around eight the following morning. He enjoyed using the GPS tracking feature on Hallie's phone. He was going to see *her*, her infectious smile.

He rang the bell; a man answered. Lex noticed he was nicely dressed - the neighborhood was classy enough as well, a gated community. *Good*, she was staying somewhere tasteful. "Hi, I'm Lex Vanderbilt. I'm looking for Hallie McKinley."

The man smiled sticking out his hand to shake Lex's. "I'm Mike Harris. She's in the kitchen, follow me."

Lex picked up a pink suitcase and followed. He thought it was strange he was as excited as he was. Knowing he was only seconds away from her made his heart race.

251

Hallie was sitting on a bar stool at the end of the counter. She looked up when they entered the room. He expected her to smile.

"Oh, my gosh," She jumped up and ran over to hug him.

Lex dropped the suitcase and wrapped his arms around her. Alright, not the smile he'd been anticipating, but the hug was nice. It felt great to hold her in his arms. Lex held her tightly enjoying the attention his black-eye caused.

"Are you alright?" She leaned back and looked at the bruise on his eye.

Lex knew he wasn't going to get a smile until she stopped worrying about him. "Yes... it hurts a lot. I've never been hit before."

She was still concerned.

He decided to try to lighten the mood. "I was thinking I'd ask Scott to teach me how to throw a punch." He made a fist with his right hand, but kept his left arm wrapped around her waist. "That way the next time I get mugged, I can hit the guy back." Lex punched the air like he was a boxer.

"No!" Hallie pulled out of his arm. "Don't ever try to hit anyone. As soon as you hit them, they'll hit you back harder, then you'll really get hurt like Matty did." She took his hand, opened his fist, took his thumb out of the middle, and closed his fist back with his thumb on the outside. Her hands were soft and gentle against his. "You don't even know how to properly make a fist. You could break your thumb puttin' it in the middle like that. No, don't ever try to hit anyone. You're a musician. How are you gonna play the guitar with a broken thumb? Promise me if you ever get hit again, you'll go down and give them whatever they want, so you won't be seriously injured."

252

"Don't worry," Lex could tell Hallie was really rattled. "I promise I'll never *ever* hit anyone. You're right, I probably would end up getting more injured. Hey, come here," He put his hands on her waist and gently pulled her to his body. He looked directly into her gorgeous, blue eyes. "I was trying to make a joke about learning how to fight. You know I'm not like that. If it's not light saber fighting, I'm not interested." He grinned at her.

Hallie smiled back. It was like someone just turned on the sunshine, the brightest sunshine ever with sunbeams expanding out in all directions. Lex's heart stopped for a moment as he soaked in her glorious rays. He definitely loved her smile, it was better than he remembered; he could have stayed mesmerized in it all day. However, her words forced him back. "I'm gonna kick your ass next time we duel."

"Oh really," He let go of her waist, pleased this joke relaxed her. "You think you can become the master, my young padawan?" He teased back. "You still have a lot to learn."

Hallie gave Lex a playful look and walked back over to sit down next to a guy her age. He had dirty blonde hair about two shades darker than Hallie's. However, his eyes were a lighter shade of blue. Lex figured this must be Warren and his thoughts were confirmed a second later when Hallie introduced him. When they shook hands, Lex noticed his firm grip and bulging muscles. He was dressed nicely, but something about his built reminded Lex of Tyler and Domino. He wondered how Hallie knew Warren, but now wasn't the time to ask.

Lex pulled out his wallet. "Before we do anything else, let me get you situated. I could tell you were upset last night, so here you go." Lex started laying items out on the counter. "Charles keeps a second set for emergencies, so I didn't have to wait for new cards; MasterCard, VISA, AMX, $500 cash for you, and," Lex reached into his pocket pulling out a wad of bills. "$500 in twenties for your favorite charity of helping the homeless. Now, who do I owe for dinner last night?"

"Mike paid the bill," Hallie put the money into her pocket.

Lex turned to Mike to pay him, but was told it was not necessary.

Lex looked back at Hallie. "Since I was coming, I brought you some new clothes." He handed her the pink suitcase.

Lex watched her brow furrow; the smile disappeared from her face. "Lex, I don't need any new clothes. My closet is overflowing with the ones you've already bought me. Over half of them still have tags."

"Oh, well that can be easily fixed," He picked up his phone and rang Charles, "Get an architect out to the condo. Hallie's closet is too small. I expect to have the plans by the time I return from my trip."

Hallie tried to grab the phone from him. He swung it out of her reach.

"That's not what I meant," She jumped on his back which surprised and amused him. She was successful in getting the phone out of his hand. "Charles, don't call an architect. I don't need a bigger closet. I need Lex to stop buying me clothes. There aren't enough days in the year to wear all the outfits he's purchased for me."

Lex playfully wrestled the phone away from her, laughing at the fun they were having. "You sure you don't want a bigger closet? I can make it happen."

"I'm sure, please don't waste your money on that."

He sighed. She never wanted him to do anything for *her*. He thought he'd found something she would agree to. "Alright," He put the phone back up to his ear. "Cancel the architect."

He turned his attention back to her, noticing her outfit for the first time. "Speaking of clothes, what exactly *are* you wearing?" Lex looked her up and down, appalled.

Hallie glanced down at her oversized T-shirt and jean shorts which were frayed at the bottom. "It's comfortable, I like it."

"Yeah, I didn't buy that for you. You look cheap, I won't have you dressing that way."

"I can dress however I want."

"No, you can't. When I rescued you, I promised to give you a better life which means nice clothes."

She sighed. "I get tired of you dressing me every day. Some days I just wanna wear whatever."

He thought about that for a moment. He didn't want to fight with her. She didn't smile when she was fighting, so he thought of a compromise. "Alright, you can wear whatever," he crinkled his face to make sure she knew he still disapproved, "when you're inside the condo. But when you're not, I'll dress you. Right now, you need to go change, because you can't wear *that* to Oahu."

"I'm not going to Hawaii."

Lex chuckled, *surprise*. "Yes, you are. It's Saturday, I'm taking you and your friends sailing and snorkeling today, so go get changed, we have a plane waiting for us."

"Lex! I'm visiting a friend. You can't just show up and make me go with you. You're not my guardian, you can't tell me what to do."

Lex was surprised and hurt by her reaction. "What's going on? You've never talked to me like that. I know *legally* I'm not your guardian, but I've been taking care of you for a year now." He paused for a moment waiting for some rebuttal about Matty taking

255

care of her, but she didn't respond. "Look, you've been acting strange and a bit stressed out lately. After what happened last night, I thought you could use a relaxing day sailing and snorkeling some coral reefs. I'm not trying to take you from your friends. If you remember, I invited them to come along."

He could tell she was thinking; there was a specific expression she had. Since she still hadn't spoken, Lex tried to entice her. "Come on, Hal, it'll be fun. You've never seen a coral reef before, I think you'd enjoy it. You like those three Zen beta tanks mounted on your bedroom wall. Imagine hundreds of gorgeous fish swimming around your body."

A black haired boy sitting at the kitchen table suddenly spoke up. "I love sailing," His brown eyes were wide with excitement. "Dad, can we please go?"

This boy was an ally Lex hadn't expected. Maybe *he* would convince Hallie. Lex anxiously turned to Mike to see his response.

(Hallie)

"It's fine with me. I trust you kids."

Lex did it again, charmed people into getting what *he* wanted. Now Tom wanted to go, and Mike approved. Hallie looked at Warren. "Do you wanna go?"

He smiled at her. "It sounds like fun. I've never done anything like it, and it might not be a bad idea to get out of town for the day." He gave her a knowing look. "But I'll do whatever you wanna do."

"Come on, Hal," Lex pleaded. "You haven't been yourself lately. A day out on the boat might be just what you need. Besides, you wouldn't really make me go sailing all by myself, would

256

you?"

Hallie contemplated her choices. She was angry at Lex for making plans without asking her, but she knew his heart was in the right place; he was being really nice. Warren also made a good point; her uncle couldn't bother her or Lex if they were in Oahu. "I'll go."

"Great! Now, go and change quickly. You guys are going to want to bring your swimsuits as well. I have everything else we need."

Lex enthusiastically turned to Mike. "Mr. Harris, I promise to take good care of your kids. We'll be back by tomorrow morning. Here, let me give you my cell phone number." He pulled out one of his business cards.

Hallie got off her seat. As she walked pass Lex, he said, "Put on some sunscreen, you're getting a tan."

She stopped, puzzled. "What's wrong with that?"

"Don't you know ivory's the new bronze?"

She rolled her eyes at him. "Lex, guys like girls with tanned skin."

"Not smart ones."

She gave him a skeptical look.

"Haven't you ever noticed older women who have dark brown spots on their skin and look like they stayed too long in the oven? That's what the sun'll do to your skin." He ran a finger down her cheek and smiled. A bolt of electricity shot through her body causing her to tingle all over. "I won't let that happen to you. I'm keeping you gorgeous. Wear your sunscreen."

"Alright," She muttered suddenly dazed.

They flew in Lex's private jet over to the Hawaiian Islands where a chartered sailboat was waiting. Hallie loved swimming in the water looking at all the beautiful fish and seeing a sea turtle. They spent the entire morning and early afternoon in the water.

On the way back to the harbor, Hallie saw Lex light up a cigarette and immediately became furious with him. Her blood boiled. She snuck up behind him, grabbed it, and took off running to the other side of the boat. She started taking quick, little puffs on it. She'd show him.

"Hallie!" He yelled as he chased after her. "What are you doing? You promised you were going to quit."

"Yeah!" She yelled back. "We made a pact to quit together. I trusted you, and you lied to me." The words burned through her skin.

"I *am* trying to quit. It's a hard habit to break. But you have a beautiful singing voice. You're going to ruin it if you keep smoking."

"Awe...now wouldn't that be a shame," His concern couldn't touch the fire now raging through her body. "I guess that policy you took out on me would become worthless wouldn't it?"

"Policy? You mean the life insurance policy?"

"I saw it on the kitchen table. You get a million dollars if I die. It's too much." She knew the truth; she was a worthless street kid. He was wasting his money again on stupid stuff.

"Hold on a minute. First thing, the policy's a standard one I took out on all five of us. If something happens to one member of the band, the remaining members could be out a lot of money professionally. Matty, Paul, and Henry have their entire life savings

258

wrapped up in the band. You're the key ingredient to making the band successful. If something were to suddenly happen to you, the three of them risk being financially ruined." He gave her a serious look. "The second thing, you're worth a lot more than a million dollars. I don't understand why you always sell yourself short. You're smart, funny, and beautiful all wrapped up in a sexy little body with an incredible voice. There's no dollar amount that could replace you."

Hallie handed the cigarette back to Lex. She couldn't find a hole in his argument. Of course she wouldn't want Matty, Paul, and Henry to lose everything. And while she should have felt flattered he thought so much of her, she couldn't. She was still fuming. "You don't get it. You never will."

"Then explain it to me, so I do get it," He was irritated. "You know, you've been acting strangely the past few days. What's up with you?"

"Forget it. Just go back to L.A. and leave me alone."

"And what are you going to do?"

"I'm staying with Warren."

"Warren? You can't just start staying with some random guy. What is he, your new boyfriend? I've never heard you mention the guy before last night. How could you want to stay with him instead of me?"

Hallie saw the hurt in his eyes, but she was too agitated to give in. The anger inside was erupting. She laid into him as if she was stabbing him with a knife. "Warren knows me a lot better than you do."

"How's that possible? I've known you for a year, you've just met the guy."

"Lex, let it go!" She warned him. She could tell the knife was successful in wounding him. She needed to stop before she hurt him more; the fire was raging out of control.

"I want to know the truth."

"Fine," Before she thought it through, Hallie dug the knife in as hard and as fast as she could.   "Warren's my best friend! Warren grew up in Riverside with me! I'd trust Warren long before I'd trust *you!*"

She was successful. Lex had been stabbed through the heart. The injury and sting of knowledge, that after all he'd done for her; she still didn't trust him, was clear on his face. It was more than Hallie could take. He extinguished her fire.

She felt horrible. Wasn't it bad enough she'd gotten burned? Why did she take him down with her? She was a terrible person. Hallie didn't know what to do, so she shut him out, preventing herself from hurting him anymore. "Please, just leave me alone," Her final, quiet request before she turned and walked away, heading to the front of the boat to deal with her misery alone.

Truth

Warren walked over to where she plopped down. "Can I join you?"

"Sure," She sadly told him while she stared down at the deck.

"I couldn't help but overhear what happened."

"I didn't mean to hurt him," She sighed and shook her head thinking about the stupid fight. She shouldn't have told him the truth. He didn't deserve to be hurt like that. Why did she let herself get so out of control?

Warren's voice interrupted her thoughts. "I can't help but wonder if Lex is the one you're really mad at, or if you're just so comfortable with him that it's easier to yell at him instead of the person who really deserves it."

Hallie pondered for a moment, "The latter."

"That's what I thought. From the way you've been talking about the guy, I got the impression he's a good friend. You trust him."

"No, I don't."

Warren chuckled. "Yes, you do. Last night when the waiter accused you of stealing, your immediate instinct was to call Lex. You trusted he'd take care of you. You also trust he'd never hit you. If you didn't trust him, you wouldn't have argued with him. I've never seen you stand up to someone the way you just did with Lex. You trust him, completely. That's why you were so upset when he broke a promise.

"Having quit myself, I can sympathize. It's not easy. You never really smoked, not like I did, and I'm guessing, not like he did. Cut him some slack. He cares about you, and you care about him, the look on your face this morning when you saw his, the sound of your voice on the phone when you found out he was mugged…

"Look, coming from where we've been, it's hard adjusting to a life where there are people around you who you *can* trust. You keep waiting for them to suddenly pull the rug out from under you, the fairytale has now ended. It was a difficult transition for me, and I'm sure it's been hard for you. You're comfortable now, you finally have a chance to speak your mind, but in the process, it seems like Lex is taking the blame for everyone who's ever hurt you. I think you need to trust him, tell him the truth about what's going on. Your uncle's caused enough pain, don't let him ruin your friendship with Lex."

Hallie looked at Warren. She was glad he was there. She laid her head on his shoulder, and he automatically wrapped his arm around her. She knew he would. Being with Warren was the best. She let him comfort her for a few minutes. But she knew what she needed to do, and she wanted to get it over with.

She sighed. "You're right. Lex is a good friend. Thanks, War."

"Hey," He gave her a hug. "What are best friends for? I'll be here if you need me."

Hallie got up and went looking for Lex. She found him at the back of the boat standing at the railing, looking out at the horizon. "Can we talk?"

"I don't know, can we? The last time I tried to talk to you, you took my head off, and I don't know why."

Fighting against her instinct to run away, escape the anger directed toward her, Hallie stood her ground. Lex had a reason to

262

be mad at her. This was her mess; she must fix it. She fought against the fear trying to consume her. Lex was not going to hit her. Warren was right; she did trust him. "I'm sorry," She finally choked out, her breathing becoming uneven as she fought the anxiety trying to cripple her. Even though her eyes were down on the deck, she was aware of Lex turning to look at her.

Hallie glanced up at his face and noticed he didn't look as angry as she imagined. Instinctually, she quickly looked back down. She realized her body had started shaking; she fought for control. She must make this right. "I...I..." Her voice was cracking; the shakes weren't helping. "I guess I'm a bit messed up right now." She finally spit out. Hallie's legs were wobbling; the shakes were winning the battle. She grabbed the railing in an attempt to support herself. Just thinking about the next sentence was sending her over the edge.

She was no longer scared of Lex's reaction; she was terrified of the memories. She was being crushed by them. Pulling together every ounce of strength she could, Hallie forced the sentence out. "My uncle showed up at Miaotsie, asking questions about me. Two days later, when I was at Matty's, he chased me, which is how I fell. Now he's calling me, and I swear I saw him in Laguna Beach."

"What!"

Hallie lost control. As she collapsed to the deck to curl up into a ball, to let the memories paralyze her completely, Lex caught her in his arms. She was consumed by the terror.

Once it ended, she leaned her head into his chest trying to focus on his breathing and comforting arms. He waited for her to get calm; his voice lovingly asked, "Why didn't you tell me?"

Hallie choked through the tears now pouring down her face. "Because after what he did to Matty, I didn't want you or anyone else to get hurt. I figured the less you knew, the better. I would just die if my uncle hurt you trying to get me. So, Charles went with me to the prison to talk to Warren's brother, so I could find him."

"So the other day, you were telling me the truth?"

"I may keep some things to myself, but I've only lied to you twice. I lied about my birthmarks, they're actually scars caused by my daddy. He shot me last summer. I was embarrassed and humiliated...The second time was when you assumed I ran away because my uncle was hitting me. It's true, he did beat me, but he was making me do something that made him a lot of money. I couldn't keep doing it, so I ran."

"What was he making you do?"

"I don't want you to know."

Hallie waited anxiously for him to press, but he was silent. "My uncle means business. He won't stop until he has me back."

Lex lifted her chin to look into her eyes. "I believe you...so the sudden romantic trip you sent Matty and April on was not so much about romance, but more about protecting them?"

"I needed to get them out of the house and make sure they weren't followed. Charles thought you were safe at the condo, said he'd keep an eye out for you."

"That explains a lot."

"I needed to leave right away as well. If my uncle saw me with you, you'd be in serious danger. It was the only way to keep you safe. But I was unsuccessful, wasn't I? Because even though Zac gave my uncle's picture to all your bouncers, you were mugged right outside of Miaotsie. I have no doubt it was my uncle sending me a message. He left his calling card on your beautiful face, a reminder he's serious."

Lex was silent for a while. Hallie wondered what he was

264

thinking, but was too afraid to ask. Did he hate her for putting him in danger? His perfect, wonderful life that had never seen violence before she arrived; was now blemished because of her. She was a street kid with a dangerous past; and he lived a sheltered, privileged life. Being around her was causing his shelter to fall; it wasn't fair for her to throw the harsh realities of life at him, to knock down his walls.

Fact number one: She put him in danger that day last fall when she took him to Riverside to deliver gift cards to her homeless friends. Tyler had saved them. Fact number two: She put him in danger when she ran away to Riverside. Matty had gotten beaten; Lex could have been as well. Fact number three: And now, he was in danger again. If he stood in the way of her uncle, he would be dead. Fact number four: the anger she felt toward her uncle was unleashed on Lex. He definitely didn't deserve it. Conclusion: She was no good for him. She racked her mind for an analogy that would fit - a festering sore, a poison in his blood, a fungus...

He kissed the top of her head. "Thank you. No one has ever gone to such lengths to protect me. I appreciate it."

The love in his voice made her new conclusion much harder to swallow; it confused her. She hesitantly asked. "You don't hate me for putting you in danger?"

"Hate you? Hallie, don't be ridiculous." He tightened his hug for a moment and kissed the top of her head again. He laid his head down on top of hers, apparently content.

"Listen, right now I have to stay with Warren. Street fighting's second nature to him. He can protect me the way you can't. In addition to that, Samantha has temporary custody of me. I've hired her as my attorney, so Scott can become my legal guardian.

"I'm really sorry I yelled at you earlier. I guess I get frustrated sometimes, because you don't understand where I'm

265

coming from. You've lead a perfect life. You've always gotten whatever you wanted. But not me. The only thing I've ever wanted was for Scott and me to have a new life, to not sleep on the streets or wonder when we're gonna eat again. Now that dream's about to come true, and I'm scared. What if after everything we've been through, it doesn't happen? You have no idea what it's like to want something so badly and for so long."

"You're right, I don't. But, I do know the power of money, I can promise your dreams are going to come true. Scott will be home in three days, I guarantee you'll never live on the streets again. I'd never let that happen."

Hallie pulled away to look at his face. "I really appreciate the gesture, but Scott doesn't take handouts. He has too much pride to let you take care of us."

Lex pulled her back into his arms. "That's not a problem. You're employed by the band. As the G.M., I pay *you*, and as long as you're singing with us, I'll continue to pay you. In addition to the band, Scott can always get a job from me. I'll hire him as your personal bodyguard."

Hallie thought about how incredibly wonderful it would be to always have Scott with her.

"Think, Hal, your dreams are coming true. Now, show me that beautiful smile," He started to tickle her around the waist. "Come on, I know it's in there."

She laughed. He knew exactly where she was ticklish. "Thanks, Lex, for everything."

He hugged her again. "You're welcome. Now, come on, let's go to the bar, so I can get a drink, and we'll watch the boat pull into the harbor. Once we're on shore, I've made plans for us to do something crazy that I know you'll love."

266

Lex instructed the limo to take them to Safeway. Hallie was curious. This was an odd place for him to go.

"We're going to do something I once saw on TV. But first, stay here, while I go and verify all the arrangements have been made," Lex smiled. She knew he loved surprises.

He returned a few minutes later and told them to come inside. "Today, you're going to participate in a *Supermarket Sweep*. You'll have ten minutes to fill as many shopping carts as you can with anything in the store. You'll each get two employees to provide you with new carts and to take away your filled ones. All the items you grab today are going to the local homeless shelter to restock their shelves with food and essential items. Do you have any questions?"

Hallie looked at him amazed. "You arranged all of this?"

"Of course, we couldn't come to Hawaii without supporting your favorite charity of helping the less fortunate," He was grinning. "Besides, it's great PR for the band and The Hallie McKinley Foundation. Sweetheart, I'm going to make you a star; we're all going to be famous.

"Now, the manager's going to make an announcement, so the regular customers will move aside as you run through the store. He'll announce the start and finish of the race. Warren, Tom, Hallie, you don't look ready. You don't have a shopping cart in your hands."

Hallie laughed as they each ran over to grab one. Lex loved to have fun.

"On your mark, get set, go!"

Hallie ran wildly through the store grabbing as many items as she could - diapers, toothbrushes, large cans of food. It was a lot of fun; she couldn't help but laugh the entire time. At one point, she turned a corner and slammed into Warren's cart. He was laughing as much as she was. She saw Tom knock over a display and then try to fix it as quickly as he could. She spotted Lex over in the meat section picking out the best steaks; even helping out a homeless shelter, he kept to his high standards.

The manager's whistle blew all too soon. Hallie pushed her cart to the checkout, still laughing and panting. Lex paid for all the items; and the store employees helped load them onto a truck.

They rode over to Family Promise to unload. The local news was waiting to interview them. At one point, Hallie heard Lex tell the cameras. "This is all part of Hallie McKinley's dream, and The Foundation's mission to help the less fortunate. Twenty percent of our album sales go directly into The Foundation, to make events like the one today, possible. So remember, when you purchase a 5th Asterix album, you're also helping those who need it most. Also, anyone who brings a bag of food to one of our concerts will be entered into a drawing to win backstage passes to meet us. All the food collected will be donated to the local shelter. So, pick up a few extra cans of food the next time you're at the store, and together we'll lend a helping hand."

Hallie couldn't help but smile knowing her singing was allowing her to help others. *If I become a big star like Lex says, then imagine how many more people I can help.* She climbed down off the truck and gave Lex a big hug which prompted her interview.

(Warren)

Warren was impressed with Lex. Despite the showy way he acted all day, he was very generous. Warren also knew how much Lex's actions touched Ann's heart.

They headed to dinner and then for a walk along the streets. Lex spotted a club playing music. He turned to Ann. "Would you like to dance?"

"Sure," Her eyes lit up with excitement.

Lex waited for her to insert her ear plugs. He took her hand and led her to the dance floor. Warren and Tom stood off to the side to watch them.

"Wow! I've never seen anyone dance like *that* before. Whoa! That's quite seductive. It's like they're having sex right there on the dance floor. Are there any parts of her body where he hasn't run his hands?"

"I don't think so," Warren didn't hide his distaste.

"You don't like him dancing with her like that, do you? Am I detecting a bit of jealousy?"

Warren gave Tom an annoyed look. "Ann's a friend. I just think what he's doing is inappropriate. She's seven years younger than him. She's a kid, he's an adult. I don't want him taking advantage of her vulnerability and innocence."

"The way she's dancing, I don't think she's innocent. I think I'm actually getting turned on while watching them. Oh, ho, ho…whoa! That was really hot."

Warren turned away. He couldn't watch her dance like *that* with Lex. He realized he did find her to be sexy. He couldn't desire her like that, not now, not when she needed him to be her friend.

A few songs later, Ann came over to join them. "Where's Lex?" Warren was surprised he wasn't attached to her hip.

"He went to get another beer."

"He sure does drink a lot," Warren gave Ann a serious look.

269

"He's a harmless drunk."

"There's no such thing, and you know it."

"Would either of you like to dance?" She smiled looking out at the dance floor.

"Where'd you learn to dance like that?"

"Lex taught me. It's a lot of fun. You wanna try?"

"I don't dance," Warren smiled not wanting to hurt her feelings, but he knew he couldn't be like *that* with *her*. Touching her that way, having her body move against his that way, Warren might lose control, give in to his desires.

"What about you, Tom? Would you like to learn?"

Tom looked at Warren to make sure he wouldn't be upset. Warren nodded his head it would be alright. "Sure, it looks like fun."

Ann grabbed Tom by the hand. Warren didn't watch; he couldn't. He needed to bury his desires to kiss her and touch her. She was his best friend; and she was counting on him to be her safe harbor until Scott returned. Warren couldn't let his libido change their relationship.

After the nightclub, they headed back to California. A limo was waiting at the airport. It was four-thirty in the morning; Ann fell asleep with her head against Warren's shoulder.

When they arrived at the house, Lex turned to Warren. "Don't bother trying to wake her. I'll carry her, I'm used to it. When I come home late, she's always asleep on the sofa with the TV on." He smiled. "I used to leave her, but she'd have these terrible nightmares. I don't know why she doesn't just watch the TV in her room, fall asleep on her bed."

Warren thought about Lex's comment while he showed him

where Ann slept. "You *do* know she doesn't like to be alone?"

"No, I didn't."

"I'd be willing to bet she tries to wait up for you and falls asleep."

Lex's eyebrows scrunched together. When they got to Ann's bed, he gently laid her down. Lovingly, he took off her shoes and jewelry before he pulled the sheet up over her. He leaned over and kissed her on the cheek. "Good night, sweetheart. Sleep well," He whispered.

Once out in the hallway, Lex turned to Warren. "Can I ask you something?"

"Sure."

"How much danger is she in?" He was concerned.

"It's hard to tell. Her uncle getting her cell phone number's not a surprise, I know some people in Riverside have it. But the other morning, she swore she saw him here in Laguna Beach. I went looking, but couldn't find anyone.

"When she's frightened, it's not uncommon for her to hallucinate. She believes he's stalking her, and considering what he used to do to her, she has every right to be terrified of the guy. I just can't figure out how he'd be able to find her that fast."

"Do you think I need to hire some bodyguards?"

"No, she's safe. However, going to Oahu for the day was a good idea. It helped her relax, she knew he wouldn't be there. Ann also knows I'll mess up anyone who tries to hurt her. She feels safe with me, which is why she's here. So as far as bodyguards go, she already has one. I'm not gonna let anyone lay a hand on her."

Lex gave him a skeptical look.

271

"I know, I don't look like I'm from Riverside any more than she does. Until I came here, I didn't know people could live without fighting. Being in fist fights was part of daily life. I didn't go looking for them, but it seemed like I was always punching someone. Life was hard, people were bitter, they'd take out their frustration on anyone who looked like an easy target. You couldn't have an easier target than Ann...

"She was the first person who was ever kind to me, the gentlest soul I've ever met. I could rationalize why most things were the way they were, but I could never understand why an angel had been condemned to live in hell. Despite my rule to stay out of other people's business, because it always meant getting into more fights; I had to protect her. She didn't deserve the life we had."

Warren's eyes narrowed, his voice turned fierce. "No one's getting through me. I'll beat the shit out of anyone who tries to harm her." He clinched his fist, an automatic response to the anger suddenly swelling inside.

For a few minutes, he forgot Lex was next to him. Warren was remembering the faces of those who'd hurt her. Adrenaline pumped through his veins. He'd spent the past year learning how to control his anger, a stipulation of living at the Harris'. Now, he wanted nothing more than to punch someone, anyone.

I Promise You

Lex shifted uneasily next to him, moving away.

Warren realized he must have an intense, hostile look on his face. He brought his fists to his forehead, closed his eyes, and breathed deeply, trying to calm down. A few more minutes passed; Warren knew he was under control again. He opened his eyes, looking directly at Lex. "Anyway, I just thought you should know."

Lex looked wary, but relaxed a little nodding in agreement. "She made a comment earlier today; 'Scott will take care of our uncle'. What did she mean by that?"

"Scott's gonna kill the guy."

"What? Why?"

"He hurt Ann, so Scott's gonna make him pay."

"With murder? That doesn't make any sense."

"You're from a different world than we are. It's how justice is served in Riverside."

"But ... I can't believe she'd just sit back and allow someone to be murdered."

"First off, he deserves it after what he did to her. Second, Scott has been taking care of her, her entire life. She doesn't question him. Whatever he says is law. She accepts it and whatever consequences that follow. That's just the way it is."

"Is worry over Scott committing murder part of the reason she's so upset her dream won't come true?"

273

"Yes; she doesn't want him taken from her again. However, there's no guarantee he'll get caught. Scott will make it look like another random act of violence."

"I still can't believe this. I've never met Scott, but I've always gotten the impression he's a good guy."

"He is, but when it comes to someone hurting Ann; he has a terrible temper. No one is allowed to harm her. He will do whatever it takes to protect her. You see, in Scott's eyes, murder is his way of guaranteeing their uncle will never harm her again. Going to jail would be worth it."

"And he knows I'll care of her while he's away."

"You got it. You've given her a new life. She's safe."

Lex sighed and shook his head in disbelief. "Thank you for helping her. If she needs anything, please call me." Lex shook Warren's hand, wished him a good rest of the day since it was already morning, and walked back to the limo that was waiting.

Warren was tired. It had been a very long day and night; all he wanted to do was curl up in bed and wrap his arms around Ann. She was his, for now.

They slept until early afternoon. Warren woke up first. He lay in bed with his arms wrapped around Ann enjoying a few more minutes alone with her. Once she woke up, they decided to spend the rest of the day taking it easy at the house. They swam in the pool and played video games. Warren could tell she was relaxed and happy, the way he wanted her to feel.

The following morning, Warren, Tom, and Ann were sitting out by the pool having breakfast when Ann's cell phone rang. She gave it a scared look. "Let me answer it." Warren suggested taking the phone from her. "This is Warren." He harshly said.

"Warren Harv?" A cheerful, male voice asked on the other end.

"Yeah."

"Hey, Warren, it's Scott."

Warren smiled. "Hey, how are you doing?"

"Great! Hey, Warren, do you remember Fluffy?"

Warren chuckled. How could he forget? It spent many nights in his bed sleeping with them. "Of course I do."

"Well, Ann lost him, and I would really like to replace him for her birthday. I'm not gonna have a chance to go shopping. Would you mind getting her another one for me? I'll reimburse you when I see you."

"I'd be happy to." Warren grinned know how much it would mean to Ann. "Here, let me pass the phone to her; she's giving me a very curious look." Warren happily handed the phone to Ann. "It's Scott."

While Ann talked to her brother, Warren enlisted Tom's help as a distraction.

After breakfast, Warren told them he left some homework in his bedroom; he would meet them at the car. Once alone, he picked up his phone and called Danielle. "Hey, I was wondering if you could help me out? Since you're the shopping queen, I was hoping you could point me in the direction of where to find a brown teddy bear."

"Oh, you looking for a little company?" She jokingly answered.

"Ha, ha, it's not for me; it's for Ann. You see, Ann had this teddy bear named Fluffy that Scott gave to her. Fluffy went everywhere with Ann. He kept her from feeling lonely when Scott was away. When Ann was shot, I took Fluffy to the hospital to be with her. Somehow he disappeared just like I did; and she was left all alone."

"Oh, Warren, that's so sad." He could hear the sympathy in her voice. "So, now you want to replace him?"

"Yes, well actually, Scott does. Tom has talked Ann into going out on the motorboat after school. Her birthday is tomorrow, so I don't have a lot of time and was hoping you could point me in the right direction."

"I'll do even better than that; I'll go with you." She sounded thrilled to help.

(Hallie)

Early that evening, Hallie arrived on the roof of Lex's condo with Warren and Tom. Lex called saying he needed her to sign some paperwork right away and sent the helicopter to pick her up so she couldn't be followed. She wondered why he didn't just sent her a fax, but she remembered Lex did things his own, unique way. He reassured her the condo was completely safe; he had hired a security officer for the building. Warren insisted on coming with her; he thought this all seemed suspicious. Tom wanted to ride in a helicopter, so they both came.

As she walked into the condo, she called out. "R2, I'm home."

She noticed the foyer wall was all ripped apart. That was

strange.

A moment later, R2 came around the corner to greet them. Tom commented. "Oh, my gosh; you have a life-sized R2D2 unit?"

"Yeah, he's pretty cool isn't he? Lex found out I was a big Star Wars fan and the next thing I knew, R2 was running around the house." She smiled at her toy and patted him on the top of the head. "He's programmed to do several tricks. I like to call him when I walk in the door. It's nice to be greeted by someone, even if he's just a large piece of metal."

Warren was very intuitive. "He makes you feel like you're not alone."

Hallie nodded her head in agreement. Warren understood her loneliness.

However, Tom was puzzled. "While R2 is really cool, did you ever consider getting something cuddlier, like a dog?"

Hallie gave him a horrified look and tried to banish the image of a dog that had suddenly popped into her head.

Warren quickly commented. "Ann's terrified of dogs." He put his arm around her shoulder. "You alright?"

"Yeah." She told him despite the fact her breathing was accelerating. She needed to clear her mind. There was no dog in the room. "Um, come on, I'll show you around while we wait for Lex. I wonder where he is."

Hallie walked into the family room; Lex lunged toward her tossing her a toy lightsaber. "Defend yourself, young padawan!" He demanded.

Now she knew why he hadn't sent a fax. Hallie kicked off her shoes and grabbed the toy determined to beat him this time. The duel began. They moved back and forth around the family

277

room swinging and clanging their light sabers against each other. Lex was good, really good, but Hallie had devised a strategy. She jumped onto the sofa and then over the back of it. He wasn't expecting that move. She made him think he was gaining the advantage; that she was on the defensive. They dueled for a few more minutes before she attacked, and was able to knock Lex's light saber out of his hand.

"Hey, you beat me!" Lex called out surprised.

Hallie gave him a playful grin. "I told you I would." She tossed her lightsaber to him.

Warren looked baffled. "How did you learn to do that?"

"Lex took fencing in high school and taught me. We've had many battles in the family room. It's a lot of fun; I'll have to teach you some time."

Hallie turned to Lex. "What's up with the construction project in the foyer?"

Lex jubilantly replied. "You liked the snorkeling trip so much I decided to put in a saltwater tank, so you could look at tropical fish all the time. I think it will make a nice entrance into the place now that you've gotten rid of the sculpture that used to be there."

"Wow, you didn't waste any time getting started. That's really cool." She smiled at him, pleased with his choice of decoration. "So what was so urgent I had to fly over here?"

"Well, seeing that your birthday is tomorrow, and we're going to be very busy welcoming your brother home and celebrating your sensational seventeenth, I needed you to sign some contracts for the band. It's just legal stuff I need to have in order for the tour." He casually replied.

"Alright, what do you need me to sign?"

She followed Lex into the kitchen where there were a stack of documents on the table. Hallie was surprised there were so many forms. She signed her name where he pointed.

"Great." He commented when she was done. "I also thought I'd give you your present today. But before I do, can I have a dollar?"

"A dollar? You want *me* to give *you* a dollar?" Lex could be so eccentric at times. This was downright silly. He probably had several hundred dollars in his wallet.

"Yes, would you please give me a dollar; and you can't have it back." His eyes sparkled with excitement; she wondered what he was up to.

"Sure. You can have all the cash in my purse if you'd like."

"No, I just want a dollar."

Hallie looked in her purse and pulled out a dollar bill. She handed it to him.

"Thanks, Hal." He took the money and put it in his pocket.

She paused, waiting for him to say something, but he just beamed as he picked up the documents and put them into his briefcase. She then remembered what was coming after the dollar. "Lex, I don't want a birthday present. You have been beyond generous this past year; I can't allow you to give me a present on top of everything else. Please, I really don't want anything from you."

"Okay, I promise I won't give you a present." He smiled mischievously at her and kissed her on the cheek. "Oh, and by the way, congratulations on being a homeowner." He whispered in her ear.

"What?"

"When you handed me the dollar, you bought this condo from me."

Hallie couldn't believe what she was hearing. "What are you talking about?"

"The condo is yours. I told you that you would never live on the streets again; I meant it." Lex continued grinning at her. She now noticed it was a bit smug. "Having you pick out new furniture and putting in the salt water tank - all the changes have been for *your* new home. You just purchased the property. My real estate attorney drew up the contracts you signed. There's no mortgage, only utility bills to pay. This is Scott and your new home."

"But Lex, where will you live?"

"I bought another condo not too far from here. Where do you think all the old furniture went?"

She was stunned. "I don't know what to say. I can't believe you did all this."

"Believe it, sweetheart; it's all yours."

Tears of joy started to stream down her cheeks.

"And here come the waterworks." Lex laughed and gave her a big, long hug.

There was no electricity when he held her this time, but she was filled with something so much better - his love.

The next morning, the Harris house was filled with activity. Mike suggested they have the party at their house to make sure Hallie stayed safe. Crews arrived early to start setting up for the concert Hallie wanted to do for Scott. She woke up to the banging of hammers and knew they were building the stage over the swimming pool. Hallie rolled over in bed and shook Warren awake. She was so excited. "Wake up, wake up; it's morning!" Hallie leapt out of bed and quickly got dressed.

Warren laughed.

At lunch time, Matty, Lex, Paul, and Henry arrived. Hallie was thrilled to see Matty again and gave him a big hug. They spent a few minutes catching up before they were called over to review their plans for the performance. "I want to play *Homecoming* for the last song; I think it will be a great way to end the show." Hallie told them referring to an Asterix song they used to play. "Lex can be the lead singer. I want to play the dueling lead guitar part with Matty."

"Are you sure you can keep up?" Lex teased her.

"Of course I can. Hand me that guitar, I'll show you." Hallie joyfully challenged him, excitement and energy surrounded her.

"I didn't know someone could actually bounce off the walls, but Hallie, you're so hyper; I bet you could do it." Henry joked.

Lex suddenly grabbed her picking her up in his arms. He spun her around several times really fast and put her down. They all laughed as she dizzily tried to walk.

When she started to fall over, Warren caught her in his arms. Hallie laughed at the joke, but Warren didn't find it to be funny.

"You alright?" He was concerned.

"I'm fine." She laughed at him trying to get her balance. "Lex, I'm going to get you back." She playfully threatened.

"Just you try, sweetheart." He returned the tease.

Warren pulled her into the hallway. "He doesn't know about you, does he?"

"No, and he's not gonna find out."

"Ann, you know how dangerous that is.". He warned.

"Look, Scott comes home in a few hours. It's not gonna be a problem anymore. You're being overprotective."

"You came here for my protection."

"Yeah, from my uncle, not from Lex."

Matty walked into the hallway. "There you are. Is everything alright?"

"Yeah, Warren thought I was flashing, but I was just dizzy."

After a while, Matty offered to take her for a walk. She happily bounced down the street with him; Warren followed a few yards back. Matty was as excited as she was. They cheerfully talked about what life was going to be like having their brothers home.

When they returned, Hallie noticed more people had arrived for the party. Tyler and Domino were there along with Domino's cousin, which she thought was odd until she was told he was their designated driver. Hallie happily hugged Matty's parents and April. Danielle and Carmen showed up shortly afterwards; Warren told her Tom and Carmen had started dating. Hallie was so excited; she thought she could actually pop.

A camera crew was hired for the occasion. While they were out, the cameras were set up around the patio. Lex planned to have video and still pictures taken all night long.

Lex sat her and Matty down to talk to them; the video camera was rolling. "I know once your brothers arrive, I won't get a chance to speak to either of you the rest of the evening, so I wanted to take the opportunity to talk with you now. So tell me, how long has it been since you've seen your brothers? Matty?"

282

"I haven't seen Ron in seventeen months - since he shipped out to Iraq. I remember going down to his graduation from boot camp."

"There was a graduation?" Hallie was surprised.

"Yes, it was on a Friday. Right after the graduation ceremony, Ron got his orders that he was shipping to Iraq the following Monday. I remember there were a ton of things he needed to get done before he left, so we spent the weekend helping him get ready. It was a very short family reunion."

Hallie was suddenly deep in thought. Scott wouldn't have told her about the graduation, because he knew she wouldn't have been able to get to San Diego. He must have been planning to come home that weekend, but his plans changed.

"And Hallie?" Lex interrupted her thoughts.

She looked back at Lex and the camera. "I haven't seen Scott in twenty-one months." She whispered. "Now I understand how he left so fast. He couldn't reach me over the weekend; he needed to wait until Monday to contact me at the school."

She was feeling stunned, yet she realized how hard it must have been on Scott knowing he was leaving and didn't have time to get to her; his sudden departure was extremely painful.

Lex glanced at his watch. "I just spoke with Charles; they're about ten minutes away."

Her sullen mood instantly changed. "I can't believe he's almost here." She was excited again.

Lex was grinning. "I was wondering if you both wouldn't mind doing me a quick little favor before they arrive?"

"Sure. What do you want us to do?" Matty happily inquired.

283

"Please turn around?"

Hallie spun her head around and saw her brother standing on the other side of the patio. "Scott!" She screamed as she was suddenly on her feet, sprinting across. Her body couldn't move fast enough toward his smiling face. Hallie leapt into his arms, embracing him as tightly as her arms could hold, tears were pouring down both of their cheeks. The whole world stood still, nothing else mattered. Scott was back.

So many nights, she dreamed of this moment. She feared it would never come true. Now, here he was. The dream was a reality. Was it possible for her body to explode from happiness? If it was, she didn't care. If she died that second, she would die the happiest anyone had ever been in the history of the world.

Neither one of them spoke. They didn't need to. The love and happiness they felt was radiating through their bodies. They embraced for a long time. Scott's arms didn't seem to tire even though he was holding her almost a foot off the ground. Hallie never wanted to let go.

At some point, she heard Henry start to play the drums; Matty whispered in her ear. "Remember, you wanted to give Scott a concert? We can only play until ten; there's a noise ordinance."

"I'd love to see you perform." Scott released his grip, grinning at her.

"Alright, I'll go get ready." She wiped the tears off her cheeks with her hand.

A short little while later, Hallie happily took the stage. It was the best performance she'd ever done, full of sexual dancing and playful interaction with Lex. When the set was over, she bounced off the stage to go see her brother. The evening couldn't get more perfect than this.

To her surprise, Lex took the microphone. "We have one more song we'd like to perform tonight. Hallie, it was a year ago today you entered our lives. I remember sitting in the hospital anxiously waiting to find out the status of your condition. You touched my heart in a way I never knew could be touched. While we waited, Matty and I started playing around with a song idea. We stayed up all night writing this song for you. We've been waiting for the right moment to share it; we can't think of a better time than right now."

The music started to play and Lex started to sing:

"Alone in a phone booth sick and dyin,'
When I laid my eyes on you, my heart started cryin'.
You were so young, a life just begun.
A kid your age should've been out having fun.
Yet here you were, a cruel fate you'd been dealt.
On my knees beside you is where I knelt."

A warm, fuzzy feeling engulfed Hallie. She watched as Lex started to walk off the stage toward her.

"I promise you, I vow to you.
A new life,
A new beginning,
Your young life isn't ending.
I promise you,
It will come true."

He bent down in front of where she was sitting with Scott.

"I picked you up in my arms, carried you against my chest.
Unconscious, unknowing, you did rest.
I had to save you; there was no choice, no doubt.
Your life, I couldn't live without.

I promise you, I vow to you.
A new life,
A new beginning,
Your young life isn't ending."

Lex took Hallie's hand in his and pointed to her heart.

"I promise you,
It will come true.

Never again will you go hungry,
Never again will you be homeless.
I will make sure you are blessed.
I will shower you with riches.
All your dreams that once were wishes,
Will come true.
I promise you, I promise you."

Lex gently wiped the tears running down her cheeks. Hallie hadn't even noticed she was crying. She was too mesmerized by the song. He kissed her on the cheek while Matty played the guitar solo. Lex walked back up onto the stage and stood right next to Matty.

"You've made me feel things I've never felt before.
You've unlocked my heart and opened the door
To a world I never knew,
One that was all too true to you."

Matty sung the chorus with Lex.

"Never again will you go hungry,
Never again will you be homeless.
I will make sure you are blessed.
I will shower you with riches.
All your dreams that once were wishes,
Will come true.
I promise you, I promise you.

I will always be there for you.
I will protect you.
I will love you.
When your days are cloudy blue,
I'll be your friend I promise you.
I promise you, I promise you."

286

Matty was grinning a smile as wide as she was when he said. "We are so happy Scott is back home, but we want you to know you have four guys on this stage who also consider themselves to be your older brothers. We love you very much and will always be there for you."

Hallie was overwhelmed with joy. She sprinted up onto the stage and gave Matty and Lex a big, group hug. Paul and Henry walked over and joined in. They all kissed her on the cheek as the tears streamed from her eyes. In that moment, Hallie felt more love than she'd ever felt in her entire life.

The evening continued with people talking and enjoying the party. At one point, they sang Happy Birthday to Hallie. There was a birthday cake for her which was covered in pink frosting and a welcome home cake for Scott and Ron. Hallie didn't leave Scott's side the entire time.

(Lex)

Charles handed Lex a beer. "Hallie sure looks happy." He commented.

"Yes, I didn't know it was possible to be as happy as she is; Matty too. Bringing the brothers home was the best million I've ever spent." Lex was very pleased with himself; helping Hallie made him feel fulfilled, an aura he didn't have before he met her. In addition to that, he enjoyed Hallie's smile all day long. It made him feel things he didn't know his body was capable of feeling. She was amazing.

Lex sighed. "The only problem is that I didn't spend the money, so Scott could leave her again. I have to talk him out of committing murder."

"I don't think that's on his mind tonight. He looks too happy. Maybe after seeing his sister, he'll change his mind. I would think he would at least wait until the end of their time together."

"I agree, so I'm not going to mention it tonight; but I am going to try to talk to him tomorrow."

"I know it's not my place to say this, but I'm going to say it anyway. You did a really good thing with Hallie. Everything you've done to help her - I'm proud of you."

Lex looked at Charles, stunned. In all the years he'd known him, Charles had never said anything like that. As a matter of fact, no one had ever said they were proud of him. Lex wasn't sure how to respond, so he humbly answered. "Thanks, that means a lot."

From the corner of his eye, Lex noticed something move by the back gate. He turned his head to focus on the image. Nothing was there. He took another sip of his beer and chuckled under his breath. *Now, who was paranoid and imagining things?*

Hallie was safe, she had Scott, and the whole uncle scare was absolutely nothing, in her head as Warren said, just her nerves.

Everything worked out. Hallie was off the streets, Scott made it safely home, and today they started the life they always dreamed of. Actually, it was better than their dream, because they never imagined Hallie as a rock star. The fame and fortune had already started coming their way. It was two incredible dreams coming true. Lex believed no one deserved it more than Hallie.

(Hallie)

On the other side of the patio, Scott and Hallie were talking to Samantha.

She told them. "So, first thing tomorrow morning, the three

288

of us will go down to Child Services. I have everything arranged and my contact there said all we need to do is to have Scott sign some paperwork for the guardianship to become official. Once that is done, we will go to the police station and officially file child abuse charges against your uncle."

"Thank you for all your help, Mrs. Harris." Scott was appreciative. "To be honest, I was ready to come home and kill the guy, but Ron convinced me that sending him to jail was a better thing to do. And after seeing Ann today, there's no way I can leave her for another extended period of time. I want our uncle to pay dearly for what he's done. I can't think of a better way than to have him locked up for the rest of his life."

Later in the evening, Hallie was finally left alone to talk with her brother. They were sitting on a bench on the patio. Everyone else was in the house, out on the driveway loading equipment, or had gone home.

"That was an incredible concert. I want to know how the fireworks went off and you didn't even flinch." Scott asked her.

Hallie laughed. "For starters, I knew exactly when they were going off. Matty helps me map out the entire routine, so I know when there're gonna be any loud noises, so I'm not surprised. Secondly, I wear special ear plugs which mute the noise. I have a special register I put in my ear, and I put the earplugs on top of it. Our audio guy adjusts the volume of the music so I can hear everything that's going on, but I hear it at a quieter level than how it's being projected. It's a really cool adaptation which allows me to be around the loud speakers without setting off my brain. Our audio guy also alerts me to when pyrotechnics or anything else is about to go off, so I'm always prepared."

"I can't believe all of this. With your medical condition, I was planning on taking care of you for the rest of our lives. I didn't think it would be possible for you to live a normal life, and you've done it all on your own. I'm so proud of you. You look fantastic; and I never would have imagined you singing and dancing in front of a crowd of people. The intensity you and Lex add to the show is unbelievable. The way you look at each other; it's like you're connected in some special way and the audience is being allowed in on your secret. This is definitely the life you were meant to have. The happiness radiates from you when you're up on stage."

She beamed. "I do love it. I can't describe the feeling I have when I'm performing, but I know it's where I'm meant to be. It's like what true happiness is supposed to be like. The only thing that can top the feeling is having your brother return from Iraq." She hugged him, still amazed he was with her.

Hallie was beside herself with happiness. First, and most importantly, her brother was back, safe and sound. He would be able to spend the next four weeks with her before he needed to report to his next assignment. It was going to be hard to say goodbye to him, but he had a four-year commitment to the Marines; and she was going on tour with the band. While it wasn't ideal, it was still better than him being in Iraq. At least they could talk everyday; and Scott could come and visit whenever he got leave. It was a big improvement to the way things had been.

Second, she was going on tour. Hallie couldn't believe they were actually going on the road to perform in over fifty cities. She was looking forward to seeing some of the country while doing what she loved.

Third, Warren was back in her life. Amazingly, they were brought back together. He was alive and doing well. This time she wasn't going to lose touch with her best friend.

Fourth, she had gained a wonderful extended family. The

McKinleys loved her as a real member. Even Ron, who she'd just met, treated her like a sister. Lex and Charles were great friends who she could always count on. It was going to be a blast traveling with Paul and Henry; they always kept her laughing. Her extended family was awesome; she loved them all.

Fifth, tomorrow Scott was going to become her legal guardian. The nightmare was finally going to be over. They would start their new life and never look back - let the past just fade away.

She was happy; truly happy. There was just one thing interfering with her bliss. Why was her uncle standing across the yard from them?

About the Author:

Shawn Settle was born in 1973 and spent most of her childhood in the coastal town of Wilmington, NC. She has been writing since she was in the third grade; and is currently an elementary teacher in San Antonio, TX, teaching underprivileged children. She is an avid traveler and cross-stitcher. Her summers are spent traveling around the U.S. with her family with a goal of visiting all 50 states, which she will accomplish in 2017. It's not uncommon for places she has visited to show up in her stories.